SEVEN SOULS

Harrow: Book One

Kate Newburg

Bad Star Press

ATLANTA, GEORGIA

Kate Newburg / Bad Star Press
www.katenewburg.com

Publisher's Note: This book was previously published under the
pseudonym Elissa Stark.

Publisher's Note: This is a work of fiction. Names, characters,
places, and incidents are a product of the author's imagination.
Locales and public names are sometimes used for atmospheric
purposes. Any resemblance to actual people, living or dead, or to
businesses, companies, events, institutions, or locales is completely coincidental.

Book Layout © 2014 BookDesignTemplates.com
Illustration by Jeremy Aaron Moore / JeremyAaronMoore.com
Cover Design by Bad Star Media / BadStarMedia.com
Editing by The Dirty Editor / TheDirtyEditor.com

Seven Souls / Kate Newburg. – Second Print Edition.
ISBN 978-0-9903151-3-1

For Sally

*Rummaging in our souls, we often dig up
something that ought to have lain there
unnoticed.*
—LEO TOLSTOY

"You won't die tonight," the six-year-old girl hissed, before dragging me across the room.

In the classroom at Mossgrove Elementary School, my partner Detective Charlie Robichaux and I had finished a presentation on safety and what to do in case someone — a stranger, a friend, or even a family member — threatened or hurt them or someone they know.

After the presentation, the first-grader with her mousy brown hair and lost, dark eyes stood at the edge of her classmates. She stared at us like she had seen a ghost. Charlie should have been the one to approach the girl. Kids loved Charlie. But he was otherwise preoccupied. His eldest daughter Jasmine was a student in the class and she and her friends descended upon him as soon as they could. So that left me to the task, despite my inclination of giving most children a wide berth.

When I had gone over to the girl, she grabbed my hand and pulled. I let her lead me to the far side of the classroom where the students stored their belongings in cubbyholes. Her hand was small in mine and a strange jolt shot up my arm.

Before I could determine the precise emotion, she dropped my hand and my connection with her broke. That's when the smell overwhelmed me – stale graham crackers, spilled juice, and construction paper. No doubt residual in any classroom in the school. The girl pulled out her pink book bag, with a blue and yellow tiger screen printed on the front, and searched through its contents. Her demeanor was off in a way that struck too close to home, but I didn't want to jump to conclusions.

As she dug around her bag, I tried to process her little revelation. I crouched down next to her, rubbing my hands together as the statement turned around in my head.

Nope, her words still weren't making sense. I must have misheard her. "What?"

"You're going to be in an accident." Her voice remained quiet and her eyes wild. She glanced over to her classmates. They weren't paying attention to us. A luxury to us both. She looked back to me as she pulled out a piece of paper. "But don't worry, you're not going to die."

She handed me a crayon drawing that had been scrawled on handwriting paper. Turning it around in my hand, I saw two stick figures — both with a tangle of dandelion hair and triangle skirts. The one on the right had big black eyes and her skin was colored blue. The one on the left wasn't colored in but had a sad face. Orange and yellow squiggles and lines surrounded the two stick figures. Fire, maybe? An explosion?

"Did you draw this?" I asked.

She nodded.

Then I pointed to the non-blue figure. "Is this supposed to be me?"

She nodded again.

"I wish my hair had that sort of volume," I muttered. Not even a giggle from the girl. She was too young to get my bad joke. "Why do I have a sad face?"

"The accident," she said.

"Who's this?" I asked, pointing to the blue figure on the right.

She shrugged. "I saw it and I colored as fast as I could. And now you're here. So I gave it to you."

Her expression was sincere and uncensored. I studied the drawing in my hand for a moment. An old fear empathized with her and tightened around my throat. The odd girl out, with the strange look in her eye and indecipherable words. How old was I when I was the same way? Nine? Ten? Seeing things that I couldn't explain?

I shook the thought out of my head. No, I wasn't going down that path because a kid said some strange shit and handed me a crude drawing.

"What's your name?" I asked, stretching my legs to stand, towering over her.

"Tabitha."

"Hi, Tabitha. I'm Detective Harris."

"Phoebe," she said.

I raised an eyebrow. During our introduction, Charlie and I had steered away from first names. We figured that similar to addressing their teacher, the students could call us by our last names. Then I remembered — I looked down at the visitor name tag adhered to my chest. It had my first and last name scrawled in permanent marker.

Maybe I was overreacting. Maybe she wasn't special at all. Maybe she drew this picture and waited for the first blonde woman she saw. Maybe she was perceptive in a totally normal, non-special way.

Feeling a mix of foolish and hopeful, I nodded. "That's right."

"I like your name," Tabitha said. She shifted her weight from one foot to the other.

"Thank you. And thanks for letting me know about the not-dying thing."

"You're welcome. You'll remember who you are soon."

The honesty in her voice wrenched something

deep. Right. She's not special, I repeated to myself. If she's not special, I didn't have to get involved.

"Great. I look forward to it," I said and held up the drawing. "Can I keep this?"

A toothy grin broke out across her face. "Yes. I drew it for you."

Before I could respond, Tabitha ditched me to run over to some of her classmates. Left alone, I returned my attention to the drawing. I folded the paper once, twice, three times before I pocketed it. I couldn't do a reading here in public. When I was back at the precinct, I could see what memories or feelings the drawing had waiting for me.

Ms. Jennings approached me, a polite smile plastered on her face. I braced myself for small talk.

"Thank you so much for coming by today. I'm sure the kids really appreciated it," the teacher said.

"No problem. It was a pleasure." My knee-jerk response was the appropriate thing to say. But before Ms. Jennings could excuse herself, I nodded toward Tabitha, playing like nothing was wrong. "That girl — Tabitha. She came up to me after the presentation and I couldn't make sense of what she was trying to tell me."

Recognition dawned on the teacher's face. "Tabitha Gregory. She's a sweet girl. She sometimes says things that are a little out there, but she has a wild imagination."

Yeah, I hope it was only imagination. But if she

had any abilities like mine...

No, it wasn't my place to get involved.

"She said I wasn't going to die. I'm sure it's nothing. I wanted to let you know in case you notice any alarming behavior," I said.

The teacher's gaze settled on Tabitha. "Thanks. I'll mention it to her father next time I see him. But hey, at least it wasn't that you were going to die...?" She tried to spin the statement's creepiness on its head, punctuated with an awkward laugh.

On some level, I could appreciate her attempt. On another, my expression told her that was the wrong thing to say.

After Ms. Jennings left me to tend to her students, I watched Tabitha Gregory for a few moments. Retreating into my mind, I recalled my early school years and how my parents reacted to my abilities. I knew what it was like to grow up a little different. If this girl had the same experience, her parents had to know.

"Hey," Charlie said, sneaking up next to me in a way that was not actual sneaking. I snapped out of my thoughts and masked my surprise as he continued. "I was thinking of heading down to the teacher's lounge for a Coke before our next stop. Wanna come?"

"Sure," I said, thankful for an exit.

Once we were in the hallway and out of earshot of the students, I glanced over at him. My partner was taller than me, and though he was a few years older than me, he had a family – a wife, who had been his college sweetheart, and two young girls. "If your girls were anything like me growing up, what would you do?" I asked.

"Lock 'em up because like hell I'm dealing with that," he answered.

"No, I'm being serious. I mean… like *me*," I said, inferring what he knew about my abilities. I planted my feet in the hallway and he took a couple more steps before he noticed.

Confusion knit through his features. He smoothed out the tie against his chest a few times as he stepped closer to me. He kept his voice low. "Why do you ask? What's wrong?"

"Nothing's wrong. This girl in there… She reminded me of what it was like when I was in school. She told me told me I was going to be in an accident but it's okay because I'm not going to die. And then she handed me this drawing," I said, pulling the drawing out of my back pocket and passing it to him. Charlie unfolded the picture as I continued. "She said she drew it specifically for me. I don't think I believe her. But it… it made me wonder," I continued.

After a moment, he folded up the drawing and returned it to me. "You got the sight - did you see anything when you touched it?"

I shook my head. Nothing immediately came to me when I touched the drawing. I thought about elaborating but circled back around to my question.

"Seriously, though — if your daughters were like me, what would you do? Would you know? Would you want to know?"

Charlie touched my elbow to bring me back down to Earth. "Let's stop this serious talk. This isn't the place. We've got three more classes to visit before we can call it a day. Then we can talk about it all you want until I gotta go home."

He was right. The school hallway wasn't the place to talk about my powers. Tabitha had shaken me more than I realized and I needed to check my discretion. He ushered me down the hallway.

We entered the lounge, passing some of the teachers already on their early lunch break. There was a man and two women who each gave us varying degrees of attention. I assumed it was because we didn't look like we belonged there. Correction — that I didn't belong there.

Black and handsome, Charlie Robichaux would be comfortable in a classroom or leading Sunday school in his pressed khakis and light blue button-up shirt. He was from New Orleans with a healthy dose of Haitian Creole in his blood and a hint of Louisiana French on his tongue. You could put him in rags and you wouldn't be able to hide the charisma behind his flashing smile. I bet he won over hearts at all the PTA meetings. In fact, one of the female teachers snuck a second glance toward my partner. My favorite part was when Charlie didn't even notice the attention he got. His wife Julia was one lucky woman.

Meanwhile, my dark clothes and chronic bitch face were out of place in the cheerful, sunny lounge. I didn't have the welcoming presence required for most elementary school teachers. Sure, I was young and pretty. I recently turned twenty-nine and was all blonde hair, blue eyes and fair skin. I'd probably be prettier if I woke up fifteen minutes earlier every day. I didn't care about clothes. Most of the time, I opted for stuff I could pull out of my closet blind and get on my way. A classic t-shirt or blouse I probably bought in bulk, dark pants, and boots. Otherwise, people would be able to guess that I dressed in the dark. But an elementary school was different from the police station. Being confronted with all the pastel cardigans, I felt like the awkward duckling. Might as well be my life story.

We approached the vending machine in the corner as my partner pulled his wallet from the back pocket of his khakis. I leaned against the side of the machine and surveyed the room.

Charlie glanced up at me between counting change. "I don't know, *cher*. I don't know what I'd do if my Jasmine or Tess were anything like you, with the sight. I'd like to think I could be understanding and strong, but I can't be sure," he said, answering my question in the space between us. His sincerity was reassuring, even if he didn't know the answer to my hypothetical question. He dropped the coins into the machine. "You don't believe the girl or nothing, do you? That you're going to have an accident?" he asked.

It was my turn to laugh. Only when I did, it was in disbelief. "Yeah, right. You know me. I'm a walking disaster waiting to happen."

He grinned, punching the number of his drink selection. "Not going to disagree with that."

TWO

The Harrow-Creek Police Department's central precinct was located in historic Harrow, right smack dab in the middle of tourist territory. A few steps outside our doors, ghost tours and horse carriages were in precession. The visitors filtered from nearby counties or cities, trying to make the most of every summer night.

Our little city of Harrow, on the banks of the Eleusis River, once catered to shipyard workers and their families before it decayed during the early twentieth century. The city's historic center had been revitalized in the 1990s when the old money coughed up the funds for restoration of many of the city's public squares and historic buildings, like the old warehouse that was outfitted for the police department.

Even though summers could be muggy and hot, loyal tourists already flocked to Harrow for a chance to encounter some urban legend — the city gained a reputation for possible sightings of abnormal sea creatures down by the docks and more bizarre animals out on St. Matthews Island. But the real fun wouldn't start until autumn and Halloween season descended upon us. The sheer number of calls we got during the height of tourist season was both hilarious and exhausting.

The second week in July wasn't too bad. Schools were back in session for their year-round calendars. And the humidity kept most residents indoors in the air conditioning. In every corner of the room, fans oscillated to spread what little coolness they could throughout the large, open space of the work floor. I watched the fan shake its head no, counting the swipes it took before focusing my attention on piles of paperwork on my desk. The sun sank down behind the town skyline.

A few officers and personnel hovered around their desks after the day shift had gone home and the night shift came on. I meant to use this time to clear my head and get through my outstanding case paperwork. The monotony of filing my notes grounded me. But my thoughts kept going back to Tabitha Gregory.

Across the room, Charlie messed around in the kitchen as he cleaned up his dishes from the week — coffee mugs, a couple plates, some silverware. He mentioned heading home soon, and I wouldn't keep him late.

While I had some privacy, I pulled out Tabitha's crayon drawing again. My hand spread across it, pressing the waxy finish of the crayon. The familiar pang in my fingers shot up my arm as I tried to draw out the memories or emotions that went into the drawing. This was my fourth attempt to extract information from it since we returned to the office with no flash or vision, even if it felt like I should get one. My mind couldn't extract whatever information the drawing had, which troubled me more.

Granted, my power — psychometry, the ability to read the memory or emotion off what I touch — needed strong emotions or memory for me to pull it from the object's surface. I had to concentrate before any secrets would be given up. In a way, I was grateful for that limitation. I couldn't imagine what it would be like to feel everything.

Frowning, I shoved the paper into one of my desk drawers. It wasn't going to tell me shit. Maybe Tabitha didn't feel strong enough when she colored it. For all I knew, Tabitha's revelation could have been an indication of distress in her home life. I usually let the psychiatrist on call make those assessments. I didn't have much success with reading children. Most of their emotions were already on the surface, etched on their faces. I didn't need to go digging for them. Still, I wanted something from the drawing.

Another thought had plagued me since I'd glued myself to my chair — Tabitha's parents and whether or not they knew. I waffled between reaching out to them and keeping my nose in my own business. If they didn't know, would it make it easier for Tabitha if they did? My own parents were instrumental in helping me come to grips with my powers. I pulled my phone out of my desk, scrolled to find my mom's number in my contacts and pressed call.

The phone rang a few times before my mom Justine Harris picked up. From the background noise on the other end of the line, I could tell she was at her bookshop. My mom lived up in Atlanta still. The bookshop kept her busy after I moved away.

"Was I creepy as a kid?" I asked.

Mom laughed, saying something to a customer before returning to the line. "Hello to you, too, Phee."

"Hey," I backtracked. "So was I a creeper?"

"How do you mean?" my mom asked.

"Were there any instances where I saw something, told someone, and thus creeped them out?"

She chuckled again, softer this time. "A few times," my mom admitted. "Your father was always able to distract them or convince them you were only curious."

Bringing up my dad, especially when we were talking about my powers, dug a shard of glass deeper into a wound in my heart that had never quite healed. Oliver Harris passed away eight years ago, shortly before I dropped out of college and applied for the police academy in Atlanta. He had always been my biggest supporter and cheerleader, even if we didn't seem much like father and daughter. He was odd, but not in a way that he had abilities. He was a strange, kooky literature professor who talked to himself more than my mom or me. Even now, I sometimes wondered what drew him and my mom together in the first place.

"Do you ever wish you guys had anyone to turn to?" I asked, my words dancing around the real reason I called. Nothing but silence. "Mom?"

"I don't know, Phoebe. Your father and I didn't have anyone to turn to so we did what we could on our own. He did as much research into the issue as he could," she said, her voice tense. "Would it have been easier if we had someone to ask? Sure. But I think we did a fine enough job without it."

My mom hated the implication that she couldn't do something herself. We were a lot alike in that regard.

"How's the store?" I asked, changing the subject.

"Oh, it's going well. We had an author signing tonight," she said, grabbing onto the change of subject and running with it. She rambled about it for a little bit before she had to go and ring up a customer. We said our goodbyes.

By the time I hung up, Charlie was back at his desk opposite of mine. "You sticking around here much longer?"

"Maybe, maybe not. I keep thinking about that girl from earlier. I might reach out to her parents."

He hesitated as he pulled on his suit jacket, mulling over my words. "You're going to contact her parents?" he asked.

I nodded. "Yeah, I think so. I'm not quite sure what I'll say, but I want to help."

"You sure that's a good idea?"

"No, but I remember what it was like to have my parents help me. Maybe I can help them," I said.

Charlie sighed, his chin dropping and his eyes cast downward. I couldn't make out his expression. After a moment, he raised his head. "I'm not going to tell you what to do because I can only imagine what it's like to be in your situation. But as a parent, I can tell you that you better be careful. Nobody likes a stranger coming in and telling them how to raise their babies. My girls are normal, though. So whatever you do, make sure you're doing it for the girl," he said. "Not to feel like some hero. And who knows — hopefully she has a good family, but you don't know that. Could make things ugly for her."

That possibility had occurred to me but it was different hearing it come from my partner's mouth. "Yeah. If it's going to make things worse for Tabitha... I'll back off," I agreed.

He nodded as he gathered his things, shoving some files into his bag. "Let me know how that goes and be careful," he said as he shouldered the bag's strap. "I'm getting out of here. Don't cause too much trouble, no?"

"I'll behave as best as I can," I said, batting my

eyelashes. "Say hey to your ladies for me."

Charlie grinned. "Have a good night," he said as he headed toward the exit.

My gaze fell back onto the landscape of my desk. This paperwork could be finished tomorrow. Besides, I couldn't focus. All I could think now was contacting Tabitha's parents. I could search for them later to see what I could find on the Gregory family in Harrow. Even better, I could conduct my search over Chinese takeout. As soon as the thought of lo mien crossed my mind, I jumped out of my chair. Tugging at the chain, the lamp at my desk went dark and I gathered my bag and things.

My place was located about a mile outside the historic district, a clear shot from the main drag out of Harrow. The sun hadn't quite disappeared, but the stars were coming out. An earlier summer thunderstorm pulled much of the humidity out of the air. On the edge of town, the road between businesses could stretch miles. I hopped on the state route headed west, a straight shot to one of the only decent ethnic food places in the Harrow area. With the top down on my Jeep Wrangler, I steadily accelerated past the speed limit. I reached the last intersection before the final turn.

The traffic light switched to green. I had the right of way. But in the intersection, headlights coming from my left seized my attention.

It happened in an instant. I didn't have time to react or brace myself. A large grill collided with my door. Glass shattered. Shards flew. Air bags exploded. My head snapped forward and back, striking the headrest. Pain shot throughout my body. Metal crunched and tires squealed.

You won't die tonight.

The impact thrust my Jeep across the intersection toward the entry ramp. The Jeep's roll bar and the frame of the windshield smashed against the guardrail. My weight slumped against the seat belt.

As the air bags deflated, I pushed them down out of my face. My head jerked right to look down at the ground underneath the passenger side. Liquid seeped onto the asphalt – fluid from underneath the damaged hood of the Jeep. It wasn't gasoline, I told myself. Maybe washer fluid or antifreeze or something, but not fucking gasoline. My hands shook as I fought with my seat belt.

You won't die tonight.

I braced against either the guardrail or roll bar, whatever was over my head and in my reach at this point so I could leverage my weight to unbuckle my seat belt and crawl out. Never mind that I could've hurt my neck or spine. There was no use waiting for some damn ambulance if the engine could go up in flames in the meantime.

You'll remember who you are soon.

Something in a reflection caught my eye and I froze. The rearview mirror was crooked but still adhered to the cracked windshield. In the reflection sat a figure with blonde hair styled like mine. Skin, glowing blue. Coal for eyes, burning dark and black. Her eyes were sideways, blinking with vertical lids.

I stared at her through the reflection and she held my gaze.

I won't hurt you. Stay still and I will help.

You won't die tonight.

She smiled, wisps of flame escaping from the corners of her eyes and lips.

I'll never let you.

THREE

Two Weeks Later

"Ms. Harris, sorry to keep you waiting," the neurologist began as he moved behind his desk. Wherever he had been — going over my results, flirting with nurses, sneaking a smoke break — he had taken his sweet time returning while I waited impatiently in his office. The path from his door to his chair was the longest trip in my life. He dropped my file onto his desk.

"Let me guess. I can't go back to work yet."

He hesitated, forming his delicate words around my fears. "The MRI scans are inconclusive. Traumatic injuries to the brain can produce very different results. Since we are unable to determine how the injury will continue to affect you, I cannot say whether or not you're fit to return to work —"

"Except 'not saying' is definitely saying I'm not cleared to go back," my voice raised. Steeling my jaw, I focused on anything else in the room. The threat of tears burned in my eyes. Expecting the news is one thing. Actually hearing it was entirely another.

He leaned back in his seat and watched me for a long moment. His voice softened with a sincerity I hated. "This isn't the first traumatic accident you've experienced, Ms. Harris. Your medical records say you were nine when you suffered--"

I stopped listening. Suffered. Yeah, right. I couldn't remember it. There was no suffering, only an erased chapter of my childhood. It usually didn't bother me. How many people have clear memories of being that young anyway? I pushed my hands through my messy hair, lodging my fingers into blonde locks.

He continued. "This trauma may have compounded latent issues from the earlier accident, Ms. Harris. I'm sorry — I can't give you the clearance you need to return to work."

"Don't you get it? I've already been out of work for two weeks! There's cases to solve and Charlie needs me—" I shouted, snapping my mouth shut because otherwise I would definitely start crying. And I didn't want to be that person reduced to tears in the neurologist's office. Sure, no one else would know. But I would.

He waited to see if I had anything to add. I didn't. He opened my file and changed the topic. "Have you been taking your medication?"

"Yeah."

"Side effects?"

"Drowsiness, dryness of the mouth, inability to operate machinery…"

"That you're experiencing, Miss Harris."

He said my name in a personal way that cut through my nonsense. I let out a heavy breath, relenting. "Dizziness. Headaches mostly. Nothing out of the ordinary, I guess."

Then I heard her again. No, wait. Not hearing. More like feeling. I felt her presence again. The ominous hum in the back of my skull that arrived the night of the accident a couple weeks ago. Her voice was becoming familiar in my head, quietly egging me on as I tried to focus on who or what was in front of me. Like the time I saw her in the rearview mirror, she always seemed to be following me.

Why stop there? Tell him why you can't take any more pills. Tell him that no matter how many you take, you can't rid yourself of me.

The neurologist documented my confessed symptoms in my file. "All right. Try to limit potentially dangerous activity, continue to take the medication as directed, and let me know if anything changes before our next appointment."

"No BASE jumping or riding my bicycle without a helmet." I gave him the least enthusiastic thumbs up I could muster. "Got it."

The neurologist dismissed me. As I left his office, I wondered how long it would take him to recognize that I wasn't taking the medication. Maybe paranoia and dissatisfaction were side effects of not taking the drugs. Maybe it was the voice squatting in the back of my head.

Either way, I had to believe there was something that the doctor couldn't tell me. The way he recounted my accident and symptoms — seizures and all — was not how I remembered my accident a couple weeks ago. Granted, this could all be accounted for the supposed head injury but label me a skeptic.

Something tugged at me. I couldn't let this go and take my pills as directed. Tabitha Gregory said I'd survive the accident and that I'd remember who I was. The only thing I could have forgotten was everything before the age of nine, when I had been in my first car accident. Though, there's a chance I wouldn't remember forgetting something, so maybe that point was moot.

I had a lot of unresolved emotions now and I didn't know where to direct them. I couldn't return to a job I loved. And more annoyingly, the words of a young girl haunted me as I tried to reconcile the unfairness I felt.

The facts weren't adding up. I needed to revisit them to draw my own conclusion beyond police reports and medical paperwork. If I couldn't find anything, I would relent. Take my two pills and call my doctor in the morning. But if my gut instinct was right, that something wasn't adding up...

Your survival is key to mine.

Reaching my rental car, I pressed my hand against the side of my head. I waited for the throbbing to subside before climbing behind the steering wheel. Operating a motor vehicle was another activity I had been advised to avoid — what could I say? When I ignore doctor's orders, I throw caution out the window.

After fastening my seat belt, I glanced at my clock on the console. Twenty-five minutes until two.

When did Mossgrove Elementary let out?

* * *

The neighborhood of Mossgrove was far enough from the heart of historic Harrow to escape the attention of tourists with the added benefit of being close to the city. Mostly renovated bungalows from the 1920s, young families cropped up like rabbits in this area. Idyllic and lush, words which real estate agents would use to lure happy families to the area. It reminded me a lot of the neighborhood where I grew up in Atlanta, except Mossgrove had larger plots of land and far more shade from the sun. True to its name, moss overwhelmed the abundant trees that lined streets of colorful homes.

At the heart of the suburb sat the school —

Mossgrove Elementary, site of my encounter with Tabitha Gregory. The neighborhood's largest trees stood tall amid playgrounds. Yellow buses lined up on the street, ready to shuttle kids who lived outside the immediate neighborhood. Parents congregated on the front lawn to collect their brood.

My stakeout this afternoon was off to a dull start. I sat across the street in my rental car, with the driver's side window rolled down. Propping an elbow up on the door, I scrolled through the contacts in my phone to find my mom. She picked up during the first ring.

"Hey, honey, how'd the appointment go?" she asked, lowering her voice.

"Fine," I said.

These conversations we had about doctor visits followed a particular pattern and sure enough, my mom's next question was par for the script. "Did he ask too many questions? Did he seem suspicious?"

My parents raised me with the mentality that I had to avoid medical attention. They didn't want doctors to find out about me. Their fear was justified, I guess. Charlie didn't freak out too bad when he found out, but he wasn't a doctor. "No, he told me I can't go back to work yet because he can't figure out what's wrong with me. I'm getting really tired of sitting on my ass," I admitted, tracing circles on the car door.

"Maybe you can find another project or look for another job."

Whatever expression was on my face dropped. I

frowned and my eyes squeezed shut. "It's disability leave, Mom. My job is waiting for me and it's a job I like," I said, keeping my voice calm.

"This might be a good time to examine what you're doing in Harrow—"

"I gotta go," I said, tiring of her conversation. "I'll talk to you later."

I hung up before she could persuade me otherwise, leaning my head against the steering wheel. After a moment, I noticed a missed call from a friend. I called her back, hoping to wash away the crap feeling left over from my conversation with my mom.

Sarah Kim was always ridiculous and I adored her for it, even if her schemes were exhausting. When the call connected, people chattered and phones rang in the background. She was at her office — the Harrow Tribune, a small newspaper.

"You rang?" I said.

"What are you doing Friday?" Sarah launched right into her reason for calling, her voice chipper as usual.

"Probably nothing," I said, lifting my head. My eyes locked onto the school.

"My brother is flying back Friday morning. You two can finally meet and fall in love and have babies."

I bit my tongue. Sarah made it a game to try to set me up with eligible men she thought could fulfill me on whatever level. Her latest target was her twin brother, David. She had spent the last few months talking him up and showing me pictures. All I knew about her brother was that he spent the last five months in Ghana conducting research. He probably had a thousand interesting stories and from the pictures she had shared with me, he was certainly a cute guy in a dorky sort of way. But I wasn't interested.

"I'm not sure how much he's going to like a welcome party, Sarah. You told me your brother was more into the library than clubbing," I reasoned with her, leaving out the love and babies bit.

"Yeah, but it's his first night in town," she said, exuding her pout over the phone.

I held the phone to my ear, somewhat contributing to the conversation against my will. "His first night in town after flying back to the United States. He'll probably want to sleep."

"He can sleep all he wants the rest of the weekend. He doesn't even have to get up before noon."

"All I'm saying is, after a transatlantic flight, I wouldn't want to do shit for at least forty-eight hours."

"You're being no fun about this. Do your affirmative grunt noises and go along with whatever I say," she whined.

She talks too much.

I laughed. Maybe my reluctance to humor her had less to do with consideration for her brother and more to do with the fact that I wasn't looking forward to meeting him, given my current troubles. Not that I ever went along with her dreams of matchmaking. My powers made it a gamble to touch someone for extended periods of time. And unlike Charlie, Sarah didn't know about my powers. Charlie found out because of a case. I was unsure why I never told her. Probably out of habit.

If Sarah continued, I didn't hear her. Something — correction, someone — caught my eye.

At first glance, nothing special jumped out about the man but my eyes were drawn to him anyway. The longer I watched him, the more interesting I found him to be. He hovered near the edge of the parents, focused on something in his hand — his phone, most likely. My eyes wandered as I took in the facts. Dark blond hair. Defined shoulders and arms from this distance. Strong jaw line. Looked like he spent a good amount of time out in the sun. Black t-shirt and frayed jeans that hinted at a nice body underneath. Confident posture but not exactly welcoming. There was something off-putting about how he carried himself. The back of my head started humming.

"Phee! Are you listening to me?"

"Huh? No," I admitted. I tried to pin down what was bothering me. He wasn't like the other parents.

"What are you doing?"

"Nothing."

Sarah grew quiet for a second. "Phoebe, are you at that school?"

Of course, I had told Sarah about the stuff with Tabitha Gregory. I might have also tried too hard to prove I wasn't obsessed and landed squarely in crazy territory. Since my post-hospital outburst, I kept further speculation from Sarah since I had raised that red flag.

I grasped for an explanation to make it seem not as bad as it sounded. I couldn't think of anything. "…Yeah?"

"Oh my god, I cannot believe you. What are you doing there? Are you there to find that girl? Phoebe, that is so creepy." The words couldn't fly out of Sarah's mouth fast enough.

"Hey! I know there's something going on that my doctor is not telling me and I need some more answers." Beat. "For closure."

"It was a freaky coincidence! You can't possibly walk up to her and what? Start a conversation? That's crazy! Which is exactly how you're acting!"

I dismissed her accusations. "You're the queen of freaky coincidences. You try to find meaning in your tarot lady's readings. You're telling me you're not the least bit interested in hearing if she might have more to tell me?"

"There's a difference between paying women to tell me I'm going to find Mr. Right and purposefully seeking out a creepy little girl because she predicted that you'd survive a car crash. Which, by the way, is not that much of a mystery." She took a deep breath.

"You are inviting something bad by not letting this go, Phee. Please. Let it go."

There was movement from the corner of my eye. The kids were spilling out of the school and into the front lawn. I considered Sarah's advice but it took me one second to discount it. I was never good at being left in the dark.

"I'll catch up with you later. Let me know what you plan for Friday night."

After I hung up, I climbed out of the car. I waited for another car to pass before jogging across the street to the school lawn. Scanning the faces of the children, I wasn't sure what I'd even do when I found Tabitha. Children ran past me to their parents as teachers guarded the huddle of unclaimed children. There was no immediate sign of her.

"Phoebe?" someone said behind me.

I froze. The voice didn't sound familiar and I slowly turned to find the guy I spied at the edge of the crowd. Now, he was standing a few feet away from me… and he knew my name.

He carefully removed his sunglasses and didn't shy away from eye contact with me. His mouth was set in a firm line as if he waited to see how I would react. My eyes stayed locked on his. That sinking feeling in my stomach spread through my veins as I considered the possibility that I knew him.

He can't keep you.

We stared at each other in a sea of children. Ignoring the voice, I shook off the weird feeling and mustered a smile. His attention was drawn elsewhere before I had to say anything, thank god. But then he met up with a girl — Tabitha Gregory.

Tabitha walked with the man, happily bouncing beside him. He had to be her father, guardian, or something. They headed toward one of the streets that branched off from the side of the school. I followed after them, growing more uncertain about what I would even say to Tabitha much less her father.

The girl must have sensed me or my nerves because she stopped after hopping off the sidewalk and spun to face me. She stared at me with saucer-sized eyes. My heart was beating fast and my palms sweated. I watched as she sought her father's hand, as he turned to see me.

I mustered a smile for the girl. "Hi Tabitha. How are you?"

"I'm good." She partially hid behind her father's leg. "I'm glad you're okay. I was worried."

Her father didn't appear to hold the same interest in me that he did earlier. I must have failed some test when I didn't respond or recognize him. He looked between his daughter and me before extending his free hand toward me. "Jack Gregory."

"Phoebe Harris." I wiped my hands on my thigh before I gave him a short handshake, releasing his hand before he let go of mine. I refrained from adding that he already knew my name. For all I knew, Tabitha told him all about the encounter and he made an educated guess. Actually, that could make a lot of sense. Maybe he wasn't so dark and mysterious after all.

"Tabitha's teacher may have mentioned," I continued, gesturing toward the school behind me. "But I wanted to see if I could talk to you and Tabitha about what she said to me the other day."

If he considered my request, he didn't show it. "Yeah, I wanted to apologize for that. My daughter has a very active imagination. It's something I encourage... but I understand she told you one of these stories. I apologize if it upset you."

He's lying. He's not sorry.

I ran a hand through my hair and stumbled over my defense. "Your daughter told me I'd live after an accident. I was in an accident that same day. And I walked away as your daughter predicted. Doesn't sound like imagination to me."

Tabitha's face lit up, coming out from behind the shield of her father. "Have you remembered who you are yet?"

"Tabitha," her father interrupted, placing a hand on her shoulder. He met my eyes. "I'm sorry, Ms. Harris. I'm sorry about your accident. I'm sorry about whatever my daughter told you. But you should forget it."

Her head jerked up to look at him. "Daddy!"

Jack's eyes closed as Tabitha tugged at him. He

stood like that for a minute as he seemingly collected himself. Momentarily, I forgot about Tabitha and focused on him. What he was saying didn't match what I wanted to hear. He was either restraining himself in front of his daughter or trying to rein her in. Either way, it was a punch to the gut.

"Please, I wanted to ask you and your daughter some questions. I think we might have a lot in common," I said. Like the ability to see things we shouldn't. "I just need a little bit of your time."

When he lifted his chin and spoke up, his eyes and voice were distant. He looked past me. "I need to get Tabitha home. Sorry for any strangeness this may have caused."

He pulled Tabitha away. She struggled to keep up with his pace, looking over her shoulder at me. I raised my hand in a wave as I watched them disappear into the neighborhood.

Left in the middle of the street, I'd reached a dead end if Jack Gregory wouldn't talk to me. The doctor couldn't feasibly explain the voice in the back of my head. Hell, I don't even think the voice could tell me anything. And even if I told my doctor, he'd find some other treatment to prescribe. I couldn't think of anyone else to approach. That was it. No more leads.

I guess I didn't consider not being able to talk to Tabitha. The idea of having to rely on a medical professional was more upsetting than I expected.

The throbbing in my head morphed and spread.

The voice in my head pushed me to seek out answers. I wasn't sure where my thoughts ended and her sass began.

Looks like it's you and me, girly. I am all you need.

FOUR

Later that night, I found myself at Lethe, a brewery popular with Harrow locals and Amadeus College students. Classic rock poured out of the sound system and mingled with the patrons. Dark-stained wood and framed autographed guitars emphasized the music and its atmosphere.

More importantly, it wasn't a cop bar and had some of the cheapest pitchers of beer in the city.

The place was empty for a Thursday night. I sat in a rear booth and ordered a pitcher of blonde ale to nurse my bad feelings. Alcohol also kept the voice quiet. The beer helped me retreat into my mind in order to solve this puzzle before my self-imposed deadline. The more I drank, the more I wished for any last ditch connection.

Then the door from the street swung open. The

sound drew my attention up from my glass and I chuckled. Jack Gregory. He smirked when he met my eyes and I shook my head in disbelief.

"I wanted to apologize for earlier," he said once he reached my table.

After assessing him, I gaze dropped back to my beer. "Do you always apologize this much when you first meet someone?"

"Not usually…" Jack tapped his knuckle on the table as he moved beside my booth. Tucked under his arm was a thick manila envelope. He didn't say anything as he studied me.

I could only imagine the look I shot him — somewhere between confused and unimpressed. Maybe a little bleary-eyed. I was halfway through my pitcher.

"Sorry, I—"

"Instead of apologies, I'll accept answers," I interrupted with a suggestion.

Amusement flickered across his face. "Fair enough." He scanned the bar before gesturing toward the seat across from me. I nodded. He slid into the booth and I focused on my beer.

"About earlier…" he trailed off. His eyes were fixed past me and I turned to see what caught his attention. The waitress was approaching my — now our — table.

"Hi, Jack," she smiled brightly, sauntering up to us.

I recognized her from earlier when she brought me

my beer. Next to the blue Lethe logo across her chest, her name tag indicated that she was Patricia. She was maybe a little older than the college students in this town which told me either one of two things: she was a born-and-bred local or she loved her experience at Amadeus so much she decided to settle for a Harrow lifestyle. Either way, she ignored me in favor of my new guest. Her eyes ate him up.

"Can I get you something? Or a cold glass?" She gestured toward my pitcher without acknowledging me. I fought the instinct to draw it to myself protectively.

He waved off her offer. "Nah, Trish. Water's fine tonight."

She didn't leave right away to fetch his drink. Instead, she tucked her notepad into her apron and her posture changed, cocking her hip to the side as she sought some way to prolong the conversation. She fiddled with her pen in hand.

"You know, we hardly see you around here these days. Gonna start taking it personally if this keeps up," she said.

He laughed. I recognized that type of laugh, all throaty and flirty. Rolling my eyes, I turned my attention toward the knick-knacks on the wall and refused to witness the touching reunion of Jack and Trish.

"I've been busy. Nothing against you, I swear."

"Busy? Busy with what?"

"Oh, you know. This and that. Work stuff mostly."

"Boo," she pouted, tapping her pen against the edge of our table. "Tell you what… if you start showing up, I can probably get you some food or beer on the house. You know the owner still owes you for that favor you pulled." She gave him a significant look.

Finally, Jack relented to Trish's efforts and asked the magic question. "You gonna tell me when you're on duty these days?"

"Mostly Thursdays and Sundays, in the evening." A grin broke out across Trish's face.

"I can't promise anything, but I'll keep that in mind."

"Guess I'll have to take what I can get. Let me go get you that water."

As she headed back to the bar, Jack leaned over in order to get a better view of her departure.

"Charming," I said, once she was out of earshot.

"She's a nice girl."

"You were laying it on a bit thick there."

He waved his hand dismissively. "That was all her. Besides, no harm in being friendly."

"So while you're here with me and apparently flirting with the wait staff, who's at home with your daughter? Your wife?"

Jack's face changed in an instant. He glared at me hard before he averted his eyes. But before I could feel smug about pegging him, he surprised me.

"Not that it's any of your business but… Tabitha's mother passed about five years ago."

His expression shamed me. My face grew hot and I looked down at my glass. It was my turn to apologize. "I am such a jerk."

"You didn't know."

Picking up my beer, I considered finishing it off but I pushed it away. "Still. Doesn't mean I should make assumptions about you or your situation, especially when you could have kept on walking."

He lifted his eyes toward me, sizing up either me or my sincerity. After a moment, he cleared his throat. "A friend of mine is looking after Tabitha. I wanted to try and find you so I could offer some sort of explanation."

I must have assumed that he was here for a drink or that pretty little waitress Trish because when I responded, I barely recognized my own dumbfounded voice. "You came looking for me? How'd you even know where to find me?"

"There's only so many places in town." He put our conversation on hold when the waitress returned with his water. He strained a smile at her before she picked up on the fact that this was a private conversation. Trish shot me a look before she turned away and let us be.

Once she was out of earshot, he continued. "You need to understand — I've been trying to teach Tabitha that she can't tell perfect strangers what she knows. She's a bright girl, but she doesn't realize that one day she might tell the wrong person something and they'll try to take advantage of her or take her away. So when you approached us today, I wasn't prepared. I guess I was hoping you didn't actually believe what she said and wouldn't come asking questions."

"If it's any consolation, I was more concerned about the fact that she had something to tell me and if I should approach you," I said, being as vague since we were in public.

He ran a finger down the condensation of his water glass. He lowered his voice. "Tell me, do you believe that sometimes shit happens that you can't explain?"

I snorted. "You don't even know the half of it."

He didn't smile. He leaned in. "Then I guess it'll come as no surprise to you that, yeah, Tabitha's a special girl with special abilities. She's always been able to see to the truth of a thing... person, place, or situation. She was born with this gift. She's still too young to know how to filter out what she knows from what's actually going on around her. Sometimes she says the wrong thing and it can cause trouble."

Listening to his every word, I mulled over the implications without revealing why it fascinated me — I can't think of anyone I ever met who also had confirmed powers. Hearing the words from Jack's lips was almost too good to be true. "Why are you telling me any of this?"

He raised his eyebrows. "Asks the woman who showed up unannounced at my child's elementary school, looking for answers about a first grader's drawing."

"Hey, it was a good drawing," I said. I still had it. Somewhere. Probably at home. "Besides, there's a difference between my somewhat questionable behavior and disclosing information about your daughter's unique... sight." My volume dropped toward the end of my defense.

"It's all interconnected. The accident. Tabitha. Even me and you," He drew a sharp, impatient breath. "She also said you'd remember who you are."

"Yeah?"

"I should probably be there when you do."

I narrowed my eyes, regarding him suspiciously. "And why's that?"

"I'll be able to explain what's happening. Maybe even why it's happening," he answered before glancing away. "And because I need your help."

If anything, I needed his help. Now he was saying he needed something from me? Something did not compute. "I don't understand."

"In exchange for information on what's happening to you, I need your expertise on a case I've been investigating."

His words sunk in and it took a moment for my brain to untangle them. "You're a private investigator," I said, already growing annoyed. The meaning of his gesture soured.

"Sort of." He rubbed his jaw. "Most of my caseload is verifying the existence of a haunting or auditing an exorcism. However, sometimes I get individuals interested in my work. I'm currently working on a case for a young lady who believes her family is cursed. I've been digging into the past to determine who and what is targeting her family."

I was neither sober nor drunk enough for this conversation. A private investigator who hunted ghosts and the boogeyman? He couldn't be serious. And he wanted my help. The absurdity of the situation had me laughing.

Ignoring my laughter, Jack leafed through the contents of the envelope he brought in with him, plucking a photograph out of it. He slid it across the table toward me as I took a moment to catch my breath.

He watched me with his own amused expression until I calmed down. He tapped the photograph. "I think you'll recognize her."

Yeah, sure, I'd entertain this conversation a little longer. Picking up the picture, I inhaled deeply as I regained my composure. The first thing I noticed was the red hair and dark eyes. When my eyes focused on her face, my blood ran cold and my grin faded.

My eyes darted to his. "Emily Banner."

He nodded and I returned my gaze to the picture.

It felt like the breath had been knocked out my lungs. The photograph in my hand was a color copy of her school identification from the University of Georgia. The Banner case came rushing back to me. I hadn't seen Emily since her cousin confessed to the murder of his brother.

Did I know the case? Yeah, a bit. A few years ago, the Banner murder had been my first case with the Harrow-Creek Police Department and Charlie was my new partner. At the crime scene, he tried to keep me from seeing the gore. Meanwhile, I didn't want to be shielded from it because Charlie felt like being a gentleman. I could see things he couldn't, but only once I could get my hands on the evidence.

My palms sweated and I wiped them on my jeans. I couldn't properly describe it even after memorizing the forensics report. White and gray matter smeared everywhere in intricate patterns. Sprawled in the middle of the floor was Travis Banner, leftover tissue spilling out the back of his demolished skull. The mere thought of it turned my stomach to this day.

The younger brother Kyle confessed to the crime. It should have been an open and shut case. We had the crime and the credible confession. But the facts didn't add up. The prosecution couldn't connect the dots between his confession and the gap in the evidence that placed him at the scene. Not that it mattered. The case never went before judge and jury. Kyle was found unfit for trial.

I cleared my throat and pushed the picture back toward Jack. "If you've done your research, then you probably know I was one of the detectives assigned to the case."

He didn't deny it. "Emily Banner came to me concerned about her aunt Karen. Said the woman started seeing things around the house, creatures that resemble Travis or Kyle. Stuff that would have been upsetting on its own but slowly started driving her aunt mad. Karen became obsessed. She apparently sought out other sources in order to communicate with her dead son. Then she went missing."

Unease settled deep in my bones. Part of me could understand the danger lurking in shadows. But I couldn't see Karen Banner, a grieving mother after the death of Travis, giving into such paranoia.

"Why didn't they go to the police?"

"Logan Banner's wishes," he said, mentioning the patriarch of the Banner family. "He managed to convince himself that his wife is off trying to find peace with what happened with her sons."

Being in that house without either of her children, after what had allegedly transpired between them... I couldn't fathom what that woman was going through. And if I honestly believed someone could put me in contact with my dead child, what wouldn't I do? But aside from the troubles that fell on Karen, the fact that Emily Banner sought out someone like Jack Gregory did not sit well in my stomach.

Jack continued. "I believe whatever is tormenting Karen Banner will continue to target her family. The same way it targeted her sons." He held my gaze for a moment. "I don't know if anyone has asked you this before but... did you think Kyle Banner committed that crime against his brother?"

I took a deep breath and deflected. "It doesn't really matter what I think. The Banner case is closed."

"Legally," he pinned on the end of my rebuke. "Whatever has tormented the Banner sons, whatever is tormenting Karen Banner... my sources are all pointing something darker and I can say that it will kill again, all for a ritual it never got to complete."

"What ritual?"

"That's what I'm trying to figure out," he said.

I scoffed, shaking my head. "Then you can't call it a ritual."

"Remember when I asked if you believed in things that weren't normal? This is one of those cases," he urged quietly.

The fact that his daughter had special powers was easy to accept because I myself had special powers. Asking me to go along with the assertion that the Banner case had to do with some prowling dark entity... that was beyond my grasp. I didn't want to think about something like that being true, much less when I was on the ass end of a pitcher of cheap beer.

But Jack Gregory puzzled me as much as the case he made. He seemed so composed about the whole thing, not deterred or fazed by my skepticism. I felt like I was getting dangerously close to a line I shouldn't cross.

Taking a deep breath, I relented. I leaned forward.

"All right. Say I believe you. Disbelief suspended. Why go back to the Banners at all? If whoever is seeking out new victims to complete this ritual, as you say, why would he go back?"

"That's what I'm trying to figure out. It might be to finish the job. It might be punishing the Banners for throwing a wrench in their plans. Either way, it has to point us in the right direction to stopping this thing."

Us. I laughed sadly. He was already talking about it like he already knew I would go along with him. This whole thing was too ludicrous for me to follow, which made it more concerning to me when I found myself actually considering what he proposed.

My eyes fell on the upside-down photo of Emily. Knowing the next words out of my mouth pushed me one step closer to getting mixed up in Jack's investigation. "If anyone's family was cursed, I'd bet on them."

He leaned back against his side of the booth. "If we were able to find out who's targeting the Banners…"

"We'll be able to prove Kyle's innocence," I said, running with his logic.

He nodded. "While hopefully preventing any additional murders."

"And keeping whoever from accomplishing whatever ritual they set out to do in the first place," I filled in the final blanks.

"Exactly."

That was when I caught a glimpse of that smile of his. Sure, he smiled at Trish earlier but this smile was for me. A faint scar divided his right eyebrow, I noticed. He had a good, strong nose. I was even a fan of the stubble. His hair, medium length, was brushed back. I shook my head. Beer was clouding my judgment. I pushed any stray, objectifying thoughts far from my mind.

Jack dug in back pocket for his wallet. He pulled out a card and handed it to me. I flipped the business card over in my hand. On one side, his name was printed plainly in raised navy ink. On the other, an address and a phone number. No company name. No job title. No description of his business. A plain calling card.

"If you decide you want in, swing on by and I'll fill you in on what I've found."

I held up his card before tapping it against the table. "So, if you investigate the supernatural around Harrow, you don't really advertise, huh?"

He laughed, getting out of his seat. "Nah. People who need me know how or where to find me."

Was that true? Didn't I, on some level, know how to find the man who could give me answers?

FIVE

The next morning, I woke up on my couch. My mouth felt like sandpaper and a dull headache cushioned my consciousness. One of the beauties of living alone was crashing wherever when I came in a little too drunk. I wiped my mouth. A vague recollection of a cab ride home and my rental abandoned downtown dawned on me. I could only put off waking up for so long. Once I stirred, forcing myself back to sleep was impossible.

I fished around the couch cushions for the remote. I had to get up eventually, and the broadcast would either annoy me or move me to put my feet to the ground.

The remote was lodged in the crook of the couch arm and shoving a button lit up the screen. A reporter from the WHRW news team was at a crime scene this morning. That was one thing I didn't miss about the job — the constant badgering from the local reporters. When you worked for a small-town police department, knowing the victim or suspect was an inherent risk. Half the time, either Charlie or I knew the people involved. It was worse when the victim was a local celebrity. That's when WHRW or the Harrow Tribune sent a few guys to tail us. I was never good with reporters, but for different reasons than my aptitude with children.

The fact that the news station was already all over this suburban scene must have been causing some officer a headache this morning. The grogginess from my sleep dissolved and the anchor's words sank in.

Wait a second — springing up, I narrowed my eyes at the screen.

"Blair Henderson, eighteen, was a few short weeks from starting his first semester at the University of Georgia on a football scholarship. However, the young man was found brutally murdered in his Ivy Heights residence after his mother returned home from running errands," Nina Marquez, the anchor, explained. The broadcast streamed the live footage of the neighborhood. "Police have the victim's older brother, Aaron Henderson, in custody with no other suspects at this time."

Searching for the time, I saw it was after nine in the morning. My attention returned to the screen, watching replays of the same content and statements given by neighbors. Everyone was shocked something like this could happen in Ivy Heights. The Hendersons were such good people. The boys were close as brothers could be and Aaron, the suspect, was really excited to see his brother start playing for the Bulldogs that fall. The mother, who was cooperating fully with the investigation, had received numerous phone calls from her younger son before the attack.

Sure, it was a broad range of information but what I saw paralleled the Banners case.

The camera zoomed out to show the pretty reporter on the scene as she spouted an update. In the background, the investigation scene came into view, including police tape, several uniformed officers securing the perimeter, and a familiar detective.

I dug my phone out and scrolled to find Charlie's number, pressing call.

"Pick up, pick up, pick up," I muttered, keeping my eyes glued to the screen.

He began searching his pockets. He dug out his phone and answered.

"Charlie, it's me."

His face was concealed from the camera so I couldn't read it. "You got spooky timing, Harris," he said, his voice hushed.

"Is it true what the reports are saying? That the brother's already been taken into custody? Has he confessed to anything?" I spit the words out, scanning the broadcast for any new information.

"Yeah, he's down at the precinct. Same with his mom."

"Were the markings there?" I asked, my words deliberate and my voice dropping low.

Charlie grew silent. I watched as he tensed, his shoulders shrugging as he ran a hand over his smooth head. A familiar gesture I had seen countless times. Now, a knife twisted in my chest.

"No, nothing like that. But the victim… yeah, it was just like that," he said.

Other officers hovered near him. That, or professionalism forces him to keep his words vague. He knew exactly what I was asking, the same images brought to my mind the night before when Jack took out Emily Banner's photograph at the bar. Charlie wouldn't openly acknowledge the old case if others were listening, but I could.

"Like the Banner murder?" I asked. "Head cracked open and all?"

"Yeah," he said, his voice heavy. "Yeah."

My shoulders deflated and I dropped back against the couch. "Shit, Charlie," I said.

Silence filled the line for a moment. "How did you even think to call?" he asked.

"Look left. Your other left. You got company."

He turned his body toward his left until he spotted the WHRW camera team that had their lenses trained on them. He sharply looked away, swearing under his breath.

"Nice shirt... it does wonders for your complexion. You got a face for television," I teased, trying to bring some levity to the conversation. It didn't reach my voice. "You should smile more."

He shook his head. "I should go. We got lots of work to do, Phee."

"Wait," I blurted before he could hang up. The idea that the crimes could start up again plagued me since Jack brought it up. If this was something darker, like Jack promised, I couldn't be around to watch my partner's back. "Charlie, be careful."

"I will, Harris. Take care of yourself. Get some more rest," he urged. "We could use you back."

I nodded, though he couldn't see me. We disconnected.

I jumped up from my couch and dug through my bag from last night. Finally, I found that navy blue business car with Jack Gregory's number on it. I dialed it as fast as my thumb could fly.

He picked up on the third or fourth ring. "This is Jack."

"Hey, it's Phoebe Harris," I said, squeezing my eyes shut. I paced around my living room. "From yesterday."

"Phoebe," he said, his voice hard to discern.

"Yeah, so... Emily Banner. When were you going to meet with her next?"

"She's coming by the office later today," he said. "Does this mean you made up your mind?"

My mind wasn't what changed. The situation had. I glanced at my television. Before catching the news this morning, I already knew I would call Jack Gregory and this development solidified my position. The Harrow Tribune and WHRW would be crawling over Ivy Heights for any information from investigators. Broadcast time would be dedicated to the Hendersons and their tragedy. The community would become obsessed with the details.

Could I really go along with helping Jack? If I agreed to assist him, I would be opening that whole can of worms again. The Banner case defined me, defined the beginning of my career as a detective. I couldn't *not* react emotionally to the possibility of setting things right. But if Jack Gregory meant to crack the mystery of Kyle Banner using his unorthodox approach, I wanted to be there.

Besides, didn't I tell my mom I was tired of sitting around?

"Yeah," I answered him. "I am. Hope your offer is still good?"

"It is," he said.

"Have you seen the news?"

"Not this morning."

"You better turn it on. You'll want to see what's happening in Ivy Heights before you meet up with Emily."

Later that morning, before I got called away to Jack's case, a knock came to my door. Coffee in hand

and blonde hair not brushed, I answered it, finding Sarah Kim on the other side.

"Are you still annoyed with me?"

It took me a moment to comprehend her question. In reply, I held the door open wide enough for her to sweep into my Misty Rivers apartment and immediately I felt underdressed in my own home. The Harrow-Creek PD shirt and running shorts I had changed into after my shower did not compare to her pressed powder blue blouse, gray pencil skirt, and heels. Even her hair looked professional, straight and black and perfectly parted on the side. Bah. Honestly, it was too early this morning to entertain visitors, much less tiny, well-dressed ones who needed some form of validation.

I sighed. "I don't know. Are you still annoyed with me?" I wasn't annoyed with her. Only too exhausted and conflicted to stomach her judgment. I felt better today.

After I flipped the deadbolt on the front door, Sarah followed me to the kitchen. She took her usual spot at the bar counter. She unloaded her arm, plopping her leather briefcase and khaki trench coat in front of her. The concern in her voice lessened. "I don't know. Are you done being crazy?"

I pressed my lips together and tilted my head to the side. I would neither confirm nor deny that.

She laughed before launching into what brought her to my door. "David's flight's been delayed. I took off the entire morning to drive to Savannah to pick him up but now it looks like I might have to take off the entire day."

"Aw, poor you," I said before sipping on my coffee.

Sarah wrote and edited obituaries for the Harrow Tribune. From what I understood, the pay and perks weren't great. Not that salary was a concern for Sarah. The sole daughter of one of the wealthiest families in Harrow since her grandparents came over from South Korea, she took the job because she wanted to know all the nosy details of someone's death, and because she needed to entertain herself. How else was she going to fill her days? Stopping by my place all the time? I had been out of work for a few weeks and I felt like I was going stir-crazy.

"What do you have going on today?" She perked up. "Do you want to go to the airport with me?"

"No."

I did not want to spend an hour in the car to Savannah... nor did I want to be stuck in a moving vehicle with Sarah in case I said anything to further incriminate myself.

Her face twisted and she looked at me with her disbelieving eye so I offered up an excuse. "Not that you're not wonderful, but I'm meeting someone after lunch."

"That so? Would it happen to be your doctor? You never did tell me if he was cute."

"It doesn't matter if he is cute. And anyway, it's not him." I could see her disapproval in her face so I threw her a bone. "But it is a guy I am meeting and he's all right."

She narrowed her eyes at me, sliding off her stool and entering the kitchen. "*All right* as in he's hot but you're not going to admit to it because in Phoebe-land, you'd rather die than say anything like that?"

"No, *all right* as in he's good-looking, just not my type," I stated.

She went through a cabinet above the microwave, pulling out a plate and helping herself to some toaster pastries on the counter. "So is this a date? Because a post-lunch, non-dinner date does not sound like he's trying very hard. In case you were wondering."

"It's not a date. I've been asked to work as a consultant on a case. Since… he's a private investigator." The volume of my voice dropped and I hid behind my coffee mug. My eyes stayed on Sarah as she stood in front of the cabinets, placing her food into the toaster and pushing the lever down.

She turned to me, her expression shifted from skeptical to concerned. "You're working? Are you supposed to be doing that?"

"The fact that I can't work is killing me, Sarah. I have to do something with myself or I'm going to go mad."

She took a deep breath and offered up her best listening face. "Sorry. Fine. Tell me about your private investigator."

"Not sure if you get to hear now. You lost your chance."

"Phee!"

"It's nothing like that," I insisted. Besides, I wanted to be professional. Well, as professional as I could consider Jack Gregory's business in exorcisms and haunting verification to be. Presented with the opportunity to link him to yesterday's confrontation at the elementary school, I decided to let it slide. Sarah wouldn't have liked to hear that. "He was hired by someone who's connected to an old case I investigated. He asked if I'd help out and offer any insight."

The toaster popped and Sarah plucked the pastries out and tossed them on the plate. She leaned against the counter as she broke off a frosted corner. "You know this is how it starts, don't you?"

"What's that?" I asked.

Sarah usually invented some flaw in my social graces that sounded feasible, and I was too curious to know what she figured out. She sucked the crumbs off the tip of her thumb before continuing.

"It's all business now. But then you'll justify spending more time with him because you're working toward a common goal. Then there'll be some late night and he'll suggest you order Chinese, you'll be sitting close on the couch of a dimly lit room…"

Sarah's imagination got away from her again and I didn't want to file her version of events to my library of bad ideas. I set my coffee mug behind me on the counter. "Hey, I can maintain boundaries."

"With your fellow cops. How about the lawyer?"

"That wasn't anything serious," I dismissed her point.

"Yeah. And then he was appointed county attorney. Bad timing on your part."

Her lighthearted assertion startled a laugh out of me. When I ended that fling, I let her reconcile the break-up however she saw fit. Truth was, after a while, I got sick from touching him. Too much information and none of it good. He may be county attorney now, but he wasn't a good guy.

Sarah stayed for another thirty minutes as she finished her toaster pastry. She filled me in on the details of some drama at her office. Finally, it was time for her to go pick up her brother. As she put her plate in the sink and collected her belongings before her departure, she made sure to bring up the festivities later tonight. "You'll be there, right?"

"Unless the earth opens up and swallows me whole," I assured her one last time.

I waited in the doorway and watched Sarah descend the stairs. My coffee had gone cold but I sipped it anyway. My eyes did not stray from her vehicle until she pulled out from the parking lot. I shoved the door shut and twisted the dead bolt. I hurried back to the kitchen and shelved my mug. Dropping down, I crouched to swing open the cabinet beneath the counter. Earlier, I had stashed a manila envelope there when I realized I had company, sure that whoever was at the door wouldn't want to go through my pots and pans. The file was unmarked, but I knew its contents well.

Before Sarah showed up, I had spent my morning showering and getting ready for my meeting with Jack. But more importantly, I had pulled the file from the fireproof safe in the corner of my living room. I kept important items in the safe — birth certificate, passport, information about my final wishes should something go wrong in the line of duty. I also kept this packet — a duplicate of the Banner investigation file. I never admitted such to Charlie, but once the case had been resolved and Kyle Banner institutionalized, I kept the duplicate copy locked up. A morbid keepsake of my first case in Harrow.

It's a relic of your own history. Never apologize.

I extracted the file from behind the wok my mother gave me for Christmas one year. Gripping the edge of the counter, I pulled myself up. I rationed my breaths as I unraveled the closure of the envelope and pulled out the folder inside. The paper felt electric underneath my hands. Low-level vibrations hummed from pages. The energy washed through me, like I was stretching old muscles that longed to be used.

If the file had a story to tell, its history extended past the case inside. It could tell you about the long hours Charlie and I spent going through details with a fine-toothed comb, about how his wife invited me and expected me over for dinner on Sunday nights, about the lost feeling after Kyle Banner was committed. The presence of the folder took me back to late nights I spent poring over the Banner case, getting to know the particulars of one of Harrow's suburban families as well as getting to know Charlie. We had camped out in my apartment, duplicates of the photographs and evidence reports spread out over my coffee table and taped to a nearby wall.

I opened my eyes after the thoughts of Charlie. I was a bad friend. Charlie had called numerous times after the accident but I didn't call him back until this morning. He was a much better friend than me. He even dropped in on me with a Tupperware full of food so I wouldn't have to worry about feeding myself. He was so proud about the food he swore he made himself without Julia's help. I didn't even have the heart to tell him he burned the chili.

My mind wandered to Charlie's partner on the Henderson case. Was it someone I liked? Was it someone who would get Charlie like I did? Would Julia be so willing to invite them over for dinner? A wave of panic washed over me and my breath stalled in my lungs. I had avoided this feeling by focusing on other things like running, catching up on daytime television shows and chasing answers to my strange questions. The fear that I'd never return to the Harrow-Creek police seized me for a long, agonizing moment. The longer I spent away from the station, the more likely I was to convince myself that I wouldn't be able to return.

A ridiculous fear — once I passed both my psych evaluation and firearm qualification, I'd be back on the force.

We have a better way to occupy our time.

As much as I hated to think of the voice as reasonable, it had a point. I couldn't focus on useless speculation right now. Thoughts like these did no good. Working again would feel good, even with a guy who claimed to normally handle hauntings and exorcisms.

I spent some time going through the Banner file, refreshing my memory and reliving the details until the time came for me to head to Jack's office. I locked the file back in the safe and in the back of my head. Then I went and got presentable, ready to take on Jack and his case.

SIX

Another day of gorgeous weather beamed down on Harrow. After I retrieved the damn rental car, I pulled my hair back into a ponytail and drove with the windows down. The experience was no substitute for the Jeep with the top down, but I made do. One good thing about leaving the car downtown was the short distance to drive to Jack's office.

On this summer afternoon, hordes of people traveled along the main drag. Friday nights usually meant campy walking tours or carriages with loud, flamboyant tour guides. I made a mental note to drive back a different way when I was done meeting with Jack Gregory.

Past the area where vacationers flocked, I followed the one-way traffic around the squares with their broad tree canopies. I counted the potential points I could rack up for all the jaywalkers. Just because I could be more patient than some drivers about breathing obstacles in the road didn't mean tourists who stepped before they looked weren't idiots.

A small residential stretch separated the tourists from offices that may have been homes a century ago. Dentists, therapists, law firms, a bar or two. I held Jack's business card in my line of sight as I steered toward the approximate address. The businesses here were in unremarkable buildings that revealed their mundane purpose. The properties weren't well maintained like the privately owned residences a couple blocks back, nor did the city's tourism board clean them up. These businesses served Harrow residents only.

Jack's office was located next to a small African Methodist Episcopal chapel. Less foot traffic meant my foot weighed heavier on the gas pedal as I hunted for a parking space. I circled the block a couple times before I decided on a spot, quickly turning the steering wheel one way then another to maneuver the sedan into the parallel space.

Climbing out, I stared up at the side of the building — I had the right street address. I whistled low, not sure what the owner was thinking painting it sky blue. The paint was peeling back in spots to reveal that the building had been the color of terra cotta at one time.

I rounded the corner toward the entrance and took the stairs up to the front door. The inside of the building looked nicer than the outside, complete with hardwood floors, white crown molding, and a staircase that must lead to additional office space. A tax accountant occupied the first office to the right, according to the listing on the wall. Down the hallway, a sign was tacked to the outside of the far door, indicating the office was open for business. Other than that, the only indication I was at the right place was the suite number on the doorframe – Suite B.

As I approached the door, two silhouettes cast shadows across the frosted glass. I stalled in the hallway as the door opened. Jack appeared first, holding it open for his client. My stomach flipped. Anxiety, which was dulled by alcohol last night, was in full force today. What on earth was I doing revisiting this case? I wasn't ready. I needed more time.

It was one thing to go through the case file yet another to reintroduce myself to the family. As I squared my shoulders and prepared to retreat, the redheaded Emily Banner saw me. "Detective Harris?"

It had been two years since I saw her and the emotional toll on her family matured her prematurely. Deep frown lines accentuated her tired expression. The dark circles under her eyes indicated what little sleep she was getting or how poorly she was eating these days.

"Hi, Emily." I pressed my lips together into a polite smile. I couldn't say it was good to see her under the circumstances.

Jack glanced between us, stepping next to Emily. "Detective Harris has agreed to consult on the case and help me recover your aunt, but only if that's all right with you, Emily."

A series of emotions flashed across her weary face. Surprise, uncertainty and finally relief. She gave a small nod. "Yes, of course. That'll be great. I'm sorry, I have to go."

She pushed past me, her gaze on the ground as she pulled the door open and slammed it after her. I stared after her, trying to decipher her sudden departure.

"Sorry I missed the meeting," I said, gesturing to the door behind me as I moved closer to Jack's office.

He shook his head. "She got a call and had to cut our meeting short. Apparently Kyle is no longer in custody."

That, mixed with the news about the Hendersons this morning, churned in my stomach. "Checked out?"

"She doesn't think so. She's on her way to her uncle's house right now to find out more information."

"What do you think?" I asked.

He sighed and leaned against the doorjamb. "I imagine the same person or entity that's behind Karen Banner's disappearance is also responsible for Kyle's. Or maybe even Karen has him."

Had Charlie or the police been notified? Or had Logan Banner even reported the disappearance? He didn't call when his wife went missing but her disappearance could have been construed as voluntary. Could Kyle somehow have checked himself out? Unless he figured out a way to escape or was taken —

A strong hand clamped down on my shoulder and broke the stream of questions.

"Did you catch the news like I told you?"

"Bossy, aren't you?" he teased. The humor in his voice disappeared as the seriousness settled between us. "Yeah, I saw it. Doesn't look good. But we can talk about that more inside. Come on. I want to show you something." Jack nodded toward the office, herding me inside.

The space was small and cozy. Light filtered in through aged blinds, positioned over cabinets that bore the towering stacks of files. Three rooms branched off from the waiting area — a small kitchen, his office, and a closed door to who knows where. The lounge area itself had a couch and a secretary's desk, though it didn't look like he employed a secretary. He gestured toward his office for me to take a seat while he disappeared into the kitchen. I stepped into the other room and sat across from his desk, spinning my keys as I scanned the office.

His office was sparse. Across from the window, a whiteboard was mounted between the door and a huge, in-wall safe, like one of those you'd find in a bank. Maybe this building used to be a bank or the office of some financial advisor. Jack's desk was clean and neat, not something I expected from a private investigator. On the side of his desk, a block of an old computer sat silent. It was possible it wasn't operational. But it was the only sign of a computer in here.

A moment later, he joined me and handed me a bottle of water.

He moved around my chair but didn't sit behind his desk. Instead, he ducked into an old bank safe. When he didn't come out right away, I jumped out of my seat and went over to the safe's threshold. He stood under a bare light bulb, flipping through some journal. Upon seeing me, he snapped it shut and began wrapping it in the leather strap.

"Is that what you wanted to show me?"

"Yeah," he said, not looking at me for a minute. He cleared his throat. "Just making sure this was the right one. It really helped me when I first came to Harrow to understand a lot of what you'll see." He ran a thumb over the cover of the journal before extending it out to me.

As I took it, first I noticed the weight. The book was hefty with ragged paper and brown, aged leather. The leather was embossed with something akin to Celtic symbols without the complicated knots. I ran a hand over the leather and along the loops, feeling the steady hum vibrate up my arms. The journal had to be older than the case file I held earlier and I was fascinated by the different frequency it was radiating.

Be careful what you read. Be careful what you

wish for.

Unsure of how long I stared at the symbol of four entwined circles, I snapped back into reality. Jack watched me, his hazel eyes dark. I tucked the journal under my arm and acted like nothing happened. "I'm not really into homework. How about you give me the Cliffs notes for now?"

His serious facade broke, a half-grin now on his face. "Heaven and hell and all that's in between? Can't really summarize that."

I narrowed my eyes at him. "If it's got something to do with the Banner case, then you should give me the highlights until I get a chance to dive into the material, professor," I teased.

Jack exited the safe, brushing past me. My eyes scanned the shelves and tried to catalogue what I saw back there. The energy in the air back here was so different. Mellow radiation. That's it. Strangely relaxing. Mostly books, some boxes, other items in jars or pinned underneath glass — and that's what I could catch in a glance.

Jack cleared his throat then gestured for me to exit the safe, beckoning with two fingers. I was tempted to ignore him and go back to scouring his shelves. What other information did he have back here? Curiosity outweighed the skepticism I held for his line of work. Figuring it would be rude to snoop through his stuff right now while he stood there, I stepped back into the office.

"The content of that book relates to more than the Banner case. I think you'll find it also can give you context about what's happening in Harrow... and to you, with your abilities," Jack said, sliding his hands into the front pockets of his jeans.

So maybe homework wouldn't be so bad. I pulled the journal out from under my arm and held it, tempted to break it open right there. "If this thing can tell me all of that information, why do I need to work with you at all? Maybe I should run away with the book and we can go about our separate ways."

"One, you wouldn't have the journal if it weren't for me. I'd like to think you wouldn't resort to abandoning me yet. Two, something tells me you like to ask questions. You'll probably have more after reading," he explained.

"I like asking questions as much as I like finding answers," I said.

"Three," he continued. "You agreed to help me with the Banner case and I don't think you're a woman who goes back on her word when it comes to finding the truth. Is that a fair assessment?"

"Yeah, well, you said I could get answers if I help. Seemed like a fair trade after I slept on it."

Jack laughed, taking a seat behind his desk. He moved some files around before pulling out one and flipping it open. "If you're not doing anything tonight, I have a lead I thought we could investigate."

There were worse ways to spend my Friday

night... like being forced to meet Sarah's brother when he'll most likely be tired and cranky. I should tell Jack about my questionable availability but I could meet up with Sarah later. "I'm free for a little while."

"The Banners were targeted long before any murder took place. So if Aaron Henderson was tortured before he killed his brother, it would have taken place before he moved back home."

The news had reported that Aaron Henderson moved back after losing his job. "Okay, following so far. What's that got to do with us?" I asked.

"He lived at Magnolia Plains, over in Dundee."

Dundee was the next town over, but what caught my attention was the name of the property. Magnolia Plains was notorious in Creek County, thanks to its high crime. "Those apartments were condemned and scheduled to be demolished."

"But they haven't been yet," he said. He handed me a piece of paper — a survey of the property. "He was in unit 1657."

The connection smacked me in the face. The markings had been present at the Banner scene, but Charlie told me there was no sign of them at the Hendersons. If Aaron had lived away from home before the crime, the markings could very well be at Dundee. "Shit."

Jack had the gall to grin at me like a damn Cheshire cat. "So... that sounds to me like you're in."

My mind went to the Harrow-Creek Police. If Jack and I found anything, how could I report it without seeming suspicious myself?

They wouldn't be able to understand. You can see so much more than them.

I couldn't pass up the opportunity to tie the Banner case to the Hendersons. If I needed to call Charlie or get them involved, I'd figure it out when I got there.

"You wouldn't be able to shake me if you tried."

SEVEN

Jack had to pick up his daughter from school and get her settled in with a babysitter. He met me back downtown later that evening and I left my car at his office. We headed west to Dundee, a forty-five minute drive from Harrow.

Being a passenger in his white Ford Ranger offered me the chance to learn more about Jack. I scanned the cab, discreetly looking for any evidence that would give away his business. The middle console was stuffed with receipts and other trinkets, giving an indication of his time spent on the road. But it all seemed too mundane. No rosaries, chalk, scrolls, or other eclectic pieces of crap that paranormal investigators were supposed to carry around.

Before I could be disappointed, my eyes landed on a tackle box wedged behind the driver's seat. My gaze turned back to the windshield as I ruminated over the possibility. I bet that box was it — his secret stash of tools against the otherworldly. It would be very practical. He could drag the tackle to a site and he was open for business. What other kind of items would he need? How strange could his business get? I inclined my head to look back at the tackle box, imagining its contents. Harrow did have a reputation for the supernatural. What if, beyond the tourist season, the reputation wasn't speculation?

You haven't scratched the surface. So much deeper you could go.

The truck braked hard and I lurched forward, bracing myself on the dashboard. I squeezed my eyes shut as my heart pounded hard in my chest. We were at a stop sign — not an almost accident. We probably weren't going fast, but the sudden stop mixed with the voice reminded me of that night three weeks ago. Melting back into the seat, I adjusted the seat belt against my chest. The truck sat still for what seemed like an eternity. When I opened my eyes, Jack was watching me. I looked away.

"Something the matter?"

"I'm good," I lied, staring straight ahead as I hoped he couldn't read the embarrassment on my face.

He waited for a moment before turning right onto the intersecting street, lined with fast food restaurants and a thrift store.

"You said something about Heaven and Hell earlier when we were in your office. Care to elaborate, given that it might have something to do with the Banner case?"

Jack considered my question for a long moment. "Harrow is very special. It's always been positioned at the intersection of a few different realms, so to speak. Because of this, sometimes things will happen in Harrow that you might not experience in other places."

"Like so-called monster sightings?" I asked.

He chuckled. "Everything stems from marketing these days. If you can repackage some supernatural occurrence…"

"Might as well make a dime from it," I finished his sentence. Strangely, that part made sense to me possibly because I could see Harrow turning it into a profit.

"The four rings on the book I gave you," he started. "They correspond to the realms that intersect in Harrow. For example, we're on Earth—"

"No shit," I muttered.

"—where humans and animals are rooted. But there are others that occasionally overlap with our geographical locations." He took a deep breath. "The Aether and Netherworld are your main ones."

"Aether and Netherworld?"

"Essentially heaven and hell but what the locals call it."

One of my eyebrows cocked. "The locals?" I

asked.

"Angels and demons," he said casually.

Uh huh. I watched him for a long moment to see if he'd contradict himself or reveal the punch line of the joke. When he didn't, I sighed. Angels and demons. Why not? I had powers, his daughter had powers, and monsters were tourist traps. Why not angels and demons?

"Is that the same reason Tabitha has powers?"

Jack tensed, his hand squeezing the steering wheel as he stared through the windshield. "How do you mean?"

"Being born here in Harrow around the locals," I added, already distracted by the thought and what it could mean for my powers. I'd have to do some digging into that book he gave me later to see if there was anything about that.

"In a way, yes," he answered, easing his grip on the wheel.

Outside of Harrow, Jack drove slowly. I watched the passing scenery, morphing from bricks to green, from green to concrete. The town was overdeveloped without enough business to sustain so much real estate. As such, many of the shopping centers were vacated or foreclosed. Because our jurisdiction expanded past Harrow city limits and into Creek County itself, every police officer had experienced Dundee firsthand. Crime had ballooned in recent years.

Magnolia Plains Apartments had been vacant for

nearly three months since the city bought it. Dundee officials evicted the property's residents as part of a redevelopment deal. The plan was to raze the buildings to the ground and sell the land to developers — good luck on that. Prior to the city purchasing the property, the degradation of the living conditions of the apartments had been hard to witness. A brand new shopping center or condominiums in place of Magnolia Plains would not necessarily improve life in Dundee.

We arrived at the abandoned apartment complex, circling twice before Jack parked the truck on the street behind the property. The sun hung low in the sky as we climbed down from his pick-up truck. The city had put up a chain-link fence around the property, the first time it had ever been considered gated. I scanned the perimeter while Jack rounded the side to unlatch the tailgate. He searched underneath a tarp for something.

I paced next to the truck, with my arms folded tightly across my chest. I had a bad feeling about this. Pinpointing the bad, however, was more difficult. There was something buzzing in the air, pushing against me like humidity. It was growing. I turned back to Jack as he dug around his truck bed. My eyes fell on his broad shoulders, the worn fabric of his shirt giving away the shape of his muscular back as he leaned forward. My gaze drifted further south. It wasn't the denim or cut that made his jeans nice. As soon as I realized what I was doing, I shifted my attention to the asphalt underneath my feet and cleared my throat.

He stood straight and gave me a strange look. "What?"

"We're trespassing." It was the second thing that came to mind, but still a plausible reason for why I felt uneasy.

"Looking around," he reworded.

"Trespassing," I stated, more confident this time. I glanced back at the fence. "Not really looking to explain this to my peers, Jack."

"Then don't." Even though he turned back to the truck, I could hear the grin in his voice. He pulled out the bolt cutters from the bed of his truck, hoisting them up onto his shoulder. He lifted the tailgate and slammed it upright. Then he faced me. "Tell me — if it bothers you so much, why'd you agree to come?"

I wasn't dumb. When we left Harrow, the possibility of us illegally searching private property was one hundred percent certain and I tagged along anyway. Narrowing my eyes at him, I replied, "To make sure you don't cause trouble."

"I don't buy it," he said, shaking his head. He patted down his jeans before he wandered back to the driver's side, grabbing a camera from the door. He shoved it in his back pocket. Then he locked the truck and moved past me, heading in the direction of the apartments. "I think you're as curious as me. Maybe more."

I followed after him. "That so?"

"Uh huh. Either that, or you needed an excuse to spend more time with me."

"You're the one who got a babysitter so you could run around breaking and entering," I said, wanting to mask whatever truth might be in his statement.

"Who says this isn't a regular thing? Maybe I always have a babysitter for Friday night."

"Because you're always breaking and entering?"

"Among other things." He grinned.

"Oh, okay." I rolled my eyes and failed to keep the corner of my mouth from twitching upward. There was something infectious about his teasing and our little quest. It gave me the same sort of rush I would get when I skipped class. Besides, there was something about the way he worked. Less procedure, more gut feeling. I could get behind that.

The ordinary, non-supernatural lock and chain on the gate were no match for Jack's bolt cutters. He caught the metal before it hit the ground, tossing it over to the grass. The metal gate scraped against the asphalt as he pulled the fence open enough for us to slip through. We crossed the parking lot toward the cluster of buildings. The vibrations pulsed from one particular corner of the complex. I knew the location of whatever was calling to me but I let Jack lead us.

We climbed the stairs to the top floor of the right building. If the Harrow-Creek PD were going to investigate Aaron's last residence for any evidence, I doubted that they would have made it here yet. They had their hands full within Harrow city limits. What would Charlie think about me working on this private case? I couldn't think about that — if I started obsessing, I'd persuade myself to go back home. If I didn't assist Jack, I couldn't tell if he would be so forthcoming about what was happening to me. Besides, the Banners needed help. This visit was only going to tell us if the cases could be connected.

The apartment looked untouched. Compared to the other apartments and buildings we passed, this would have stuck out if it weren't for the strange energy. No one wanted to go near it, but here we were. With a swift crack from the butt of the bolt cutters and a few thuds of his shoulder, Jack broke the latch away from the doorframe. I cringed, standing behind him. If the police came out here at some point, several conclusions could be drawn from a broken door and whatever else we would find inside. Jack disappeared into the unit, leaving the door open for me.

If there were a time to turn back from this, it would be now. I stared at the door and the splintered frame, swallowing back the growing anxiety of being so close to the source of the vibrations. I went over the facts in my head while crossing the threshold. Karen Banner was gone. Now, so was Kyle. As far as we could tell, Karen's husband and Kyle's father, Logan, had reported neither disappearance. If whatever came back for the Banners also had a hand in the Henderson murder, we needed to find that out.

Man made laws. All are fallible. Seek what you came to find.

The musty, rotten smell of the vacated apartment distracted me from the buzz. I scanned the scene. Remnants of the last occupant, presumably Aaron Henderson, were strewn throughout the space. Discarded cereal boxes and crumpled food wrappers littered the floor and bar counter. Matted dog hair and dirty shoe prints disguised what used to be carpet. There were too many negative vibrations ringing through the air, like we reached ground zero in Magnolia Plains for anything evil. It radiated from all corners of the room.

It was absolutely nauseating.

Trying to distance myself from the worst of the energy, I wandered into the kitchen. Keeping my hands mostly to myself, I scanned the room. The kitchen was a mess like the rest of the apartment. Unknown food substances and I don't know what was spilled all over the counters. The rotting smell that permeated the main area turned out to be the garbage disposal. It hadn't been cleared before the unit was evicted, leaving old food in the once-damp drain.

Still, a nasty sink was preferable to the energy in the other room.

For all the damage, no insects or rodents infested the place. Maybe they had been driven away by the same energy that kept this apartment from being vandalized prior to demolition.

"So what was he doing living here? Can't say I know many who choose to move from Harrow to Dundee," I said.

Jack reappeared from wherever he was taking pictures. "Something about a girlfriend. He moved out here for her, found a job at a restaurant where she worked. They lived together, apparently against his parents' wishes. But then he lost his job, so I guess he decided to move back home."

The girlfriend. She was on the news report I saw that morning. Her name was Cindy or maybe Cynthia. So Harrow-Creek PD did have their sights on Dundee in some respect. I exited the kitchen, hands on my hips. "Or maybe something happened between the two of them. We can track the girlfriend down. See if she can give us more information."

Jack nodded, going through the pictures on his camera. He glanced up at me. "Once we can get her name, let's run into her. Just to chat."

"Her name was on the television. You said she worked at the same restaurant here in Dundee? Do you remember which one? If you can be hungry later, we might as well check her out while we're here. Can't be too many Cindys or Cynthias."

"Breaking and entering and dinner. This is shaping up to be a nice date."

"The fact that the restaurant is in Dundee tells me

it ain't going to be a high-class place."

He cracked a smile. "Doesn't need to be."

"I was right," I said. "You need a chaperone... or maybe a muzzle."

He laughed. The warmth in the sound melted some of my apprehension. However, my smile disappeared as soon he ducked into another room.

Seek what you came to find.

I didn't want to go in there. The energy that came from that room was more than I could handle, and I hadn't even touched anything yet. But I didn't come this far to not see if the markings were here. Part of me, maybe the voice, knew what I'd find. I took a deep breath and followed the well-worn path from the living room toward the epicenter, the source of the mounting vibrations.

Once, the room had been a bedroom. As I slowly pushed the door open with my foot, the darkness swelled and poured over my arm. Somewhere behind me, Jack came into the room and turned on the lights. A bare bulb pushed back the dark and I stepped further into the room. Some debris accumulated against the baseboards and the state of the carpet matched the condition of the rest of the apartment.

But my eyes were drawn to the literal writing on the wall.

We've seen this before.

The voice whispered what I was too scared to think. My eyes ran up and over the graffiti, unease creeping in the back of my throat. The familiar swoops and angles took up every inch of the far wall, from floor to ceiling, from corner to corner. The carpet at the foot of the drawing was wet, waterlogged. Soft cursing and the click of a camera drew me back to reality. Jack stood next to me. He was examining the wall, taking more snapshots.

"It's the same markings," I said, my voice strange and calm, unlike whatever rattled in my head. "It's the same markings that were in the Banners..." The same markings that were written with Travis Banner's brain matter.

I don't know if it was what I said or the crack in my voice, but Jack temporarily abandoned his photographing. He squeezed my shoulder, but the gesture didn't help me feel better. The vibrations in the room were reaching a boiling point. My hands trembled against my will and I scanned the wall past Jack, desperate to somehow make sense of the writing. Attempting to steady my breaths, I concentrated on the strength of his hand gripping my shoulder, trying to cast anchor in the sea of growing panic.

When I glanced over at him, his attention was back on the wall. He was mouthing something quietly to himself. I squinted at his lips, trying to focus on what he was saying. Then it occurred to me — he was reading the words to himself.

He could read it? Actually understand it?

My pulse pounded in my ears. Where was Jack

when Charlie and I were investigating the Banner murder? During the original police investigation, we were unable to decipher the message. The sheriff determined that the message was a moot point after Kyle confessed to killing Travis. He figured it was the ravings of a mad man, if it was anything significant at all

Still, the fact that Jack could read it was both helpful and troubling. Jack could know about the translation by other means, even being involved himself. I mentally shelved the possibilities to review when I could get away and clear my head.

He muttered to himself before he tilted his head. After a moment, I did the same as if that would unlock the translation. The black substance told me nothing. I hoped it wasn't written in brains this time.

"You can read it?" I asked.

He nodded.

"How?"

"My daughter is clairvoyant. I'm... good with languages."

"You expect me to believe that you can read whatever this is? We couldn't even identify if it was a language!"

"You wouldn't have been able to look hard enough. It's not human."

My expression soured. "Not human," I repeated.

"No."

"So that must mean... angels or demons?"

"Yes."

"And you can read it." Disbelief dripped from my words.

"Yes," he said, drawing out his affirmation.

"One day soon, you will have to explain to me how. But for now, what the fuck does it say?"

He inhaled, scanning the wall one last time before he answered me. "It's a gateway. The writing summons a connection between the realms — in this case, between the human world and the Netherworlds. And it looks to be signed, but I can't make out the signature. If Aaron Henderson was a victim, his tormentor would have to be able to get here without anyone important noticing."

My eyes settled on the wall before us. "So you thought it might be coming through the wall?"

"Yes... but this isn't an entrance," he continued. He stepped back to take in the entire wall, scanning from right to left, floor to ceiling. "It is a door. But they weren't coming. They were going. Whoever or whatever it was, they made a jump back."

My mind went to that day at the Banners, when I arrived to meet my new partner and survey the crime scene. If this was an exit, someone used Travis as the ink to make a similar departure. I never thought for a minute that Kyle Banner could have drawn those symbols. Even though Jack talked about angels and demons, it sounded more like mythology. But I entertained the idea that maybe this language was demonic, that Kyle was a victim of diabolical influence, and that this may be the case for the Henderson murder too. Whoever was responsible for the crimes, even if humans physically carried them out, hadn't been caught.

"Okay, they left. Where'd they go? How can we find them?" I asked.

His eyes cut through me as dread gathered in my stomach. I don't know if it was the dread, the voice, or even the expression Jack was giving me but I knew finding them wouldn't be so easy.

"There's only one direction this door could go."

"One way ticket to the Netherworlds?"

"Yeah — the symbols, they're demonic in origin."

"It's not... gross, is it?" I asked.

"Gross?"

"The last time I saw writing like this, it was written in brains."

Jack shook his head. "No, its coal."

Coal. I could handle coal. The wall tugged at my senses, reeling me closer. The overwhelming vibrations that flooded became more focused, almost sentient, calling out to me. It had a story. It wanted to explain to me what happened in this room.

My hands tingled. Curling and uncurling my fingers as my arms hung at my sides, I had to decide how much I cared if Jack witnessed what was about to happen. The sane part of my brain knew I shouldn't touch it but I needed to know. However, the tug was similar to the Banner case file. Only it was stronger. And unlike the case file, I wasn't sure what the wall would share with me.

As I approached the wall, Jack's presence was no longer a concern. Each footstep squished against the soggy carpet. I wanted to listen to what the wall had to tell me. "If this is how they leave..." my voice trailed off as I twisted the rest of that idea around in my head.

Jack stood behind me and watched. His eyes felt heavy on my back. "Are you all right?"

"If this is how they leave, how do they get here? Where are they coming from? Where are they going?" My voice grew quiet and eerie, not addressing Jack's concern. I was whispering back to whatever happened in this room.

My fingers grazed the black on the wall, smudging the coal. Then my palm flattened against its surface. The energy snaked up my arm, tightening around my bones until it reached the base of my skull. Bright lights crowded my periphery and I could sense Jack at my side. Darkness replaced the lights and invaded my vision.

Fight to breathe, fight to breathe, don't let them take that from you.

The sharp spike in the back of my head took away my sense of gravity. Gasping, I lost my balance as the ground fell out from beneath me.

EIGHT

A chill trickled down my spine and my eyes blinked open. I didn't recognize the pillowcase or nightstand within my line of sight. I closed one eye, then the other. Nope, still nothing. The change in perspective offered no solid identification. Groaning, I squeezed my eyes shut and listened to the shower running on the other side of the wall. My brain sifted through what bits and pieces I could dredge up from the night before. Any memory of a bar and a man and drinks to put the night within some context. Anything for me to retrace my steps.

Dundee. Magnolia Plains.

Jack.

I shot up from the mattress and pain seared through my skull. Shit. Easing back down, I buried my face into the bedding and ran through what I could remember.

Last night, I went to Dundee with Jack, out to the condemned Magnolia Plains complex. Jack said the wall in the apartment was a gate. The gate called out to me and I was the dumb ass who reached back.

My senses flooded. The putrid smell. The heavy air. Fire, strange and familiar, twisting and turning, growing brighter and pushing back the dark in the cavern where I landed. The flame took off like a dart and leading me through a maze, further into the darkness.

More memories from the night returned, becoming sharper in my mind. The flame had led me to the center of the network of tunnels. In the main cavern was a woman but her body was in many pieces — shattered glass, segments of her porcelain skin suspended in air. A beacon radiated from somewhere behind the shard of her chest. Ribbons of deep red hair flowing as if she were submerged underwater. Her floating expression was locked into a vacant stare, an eerie smile on her face.

I circled the broken woman as her pieces orbited the central light, casting strange shadows along the walls. Underneath her feet was a white serpent. Always moving, never ending. My eyes searched its flank for its head or tail. The powerful muscles under the scales moved in tandem with the rotation of the woman above.

The rhythm mesmerized me and the footsteps behind me went unheard.

Tat, tat, tat.

The man stood tall, his back and shoulders straight. Dark, rich fabric draped across his shoulders and cascaded down to the rocky floor. A hood hung over the top half of his face, casting its shadow across his expression. In his right hand, he held a cane taller than himself. He beat it against the floor in a rhythm, in time to the flame-haired woman and the serpent.

Tat, tat, tat.

He paced, reciting words I didn't understand until he started speaking English. What did the man say before he lunged at me? He said something important, but I couldn't remember it now. I grasped for words but caught nothing. That was the last thing I remembered before I woke up here.

I stayed in bed as I combed my memory for more clues, anything else I could have picked up in the periphery but didn't process.

Was it a vision, or had I gone through the gate? And if it was real, how the hell did I get out? If I saw the other side of the gate and woke up somewhere else without a scratch, whose bed was I in?

The spray of the shower in the bathroom nearly lulled me into another bout of sleep, before I could fully consider the implications of last night. Extracting my phone and car keys from the pocket of my jeans, I relieved myself of the objects that had spent the night digging into my side. I tossed them on the quilt. The phone lit up, showing a string of missed notifications. I twisted the phone around, unlocking the screen. Numerous missed calls from Sarah, including a couple text messages and one voicemail. All from last night. Shit.

I pushed myself to sit up and waited for the throbbing in my head to subside before I glanced around the room. Blinds shut and curtains drawn. Laundry basket with folded laundry, next to a chest of drawers. Books haphazardly piled on any flat surface of the room. As I squinted at the spines of the books, the subjects ranged from ghosts to magic, mutants to shamanism, chaos to a bunch of names I didn't recognize. All the things I would expect Jack to read.

I had a hunch on who was in the shower now.

The house had to have another bathroom. Throwing my legs over the side of the bed, I got up. I focused on the hardwood floor, steadying myself before entering the hallway. Two doors down on the opposite side was a bathroom with blue tile. I stumbled in. Standing in front of the sink, I opened the medicine cabinet. Nothing. As in, it was completely bare. Huh. I closed the mirror once before opening it again, to make sure my eyes weren't playing tricks on me. What kind of person doesn't keep aspirin in their medicine cabinet? My eyes fell on the pink toothbrush in the cup, next to a tube of toothpaste with a cheerful cartoon character on its label.

I splashed cold water on my face, leaning on my

forearms over the porcelain for a few long moments. If I stayed still long enough, the pain retreated. But I couldn't stay hunched over a sink all day, especially in Jack's house.

Gripping the side of the sink, I lifted my head to look in the mirror. The color was drained from my face and my eyes were puffy and red. The cold sweat killed my hair's volume while I was unconscious. I pushed back blonde strands off my forehead and then I dug around in my pocket for the inevitable hair tie. Hitting the faucet, I wet my fingers and ran them through my hair a few times before twisting it into a bun and securing it. Next, I stared the cartoon character down. Snatching the bubblegum toothpaste, I squeezed a small pink, sparkly bit onto my index finger before rubbing my finger against my teeth. Grimacing at the flavor, I rinsed my mouth out and spat into the basin. And rinsed again.

I patted down my face with a hand towel. The grogginess clouding my mind cleared the more I moved around. When I returned to the hallway, a certain six-year-old with bare feet and messy hair was waiting for me. Tabitha's face broke out into a toothy smile.

"You were asleep when you came over last night so I didn't get to say hi. And today my dad said, 'Tabitha, make sure you are nice to Phoebe'," she launched into her explanation. "But he didn't have to say that. I would've been nice to you anyway."

How charming…

"Thanks." I flashed her a pained smile and exited the bathroom.

She frowned and trailed after me. "Are you sick?"

Are you?

The voice either became Tabitha's co-conspirator or maybe she was questioning Tabitha. I wasn't exactly sure.

Wincing, I shook my head. "My head hurts. Does your dad have any aspirin?"

Tabitha shrugged.

"Okay," I said, inhaling deeply. "Does your dad take anything when he's not feeling well?"

She glanced around the room until she looked in the direction of the kitchen. An idea lit up her face and she spun back toward me. "He likes to drink coffee…?" she said, dangling the answer to see if that's what I needed.

Bless that man. I could kiss him. "That might make me feel a little more human."

The voice's laugh was hollow and tinny, jingling around in my skull. Tabitha was already en route to the kitchen. I trailed after her once the laughter faded. She pulled a chair out to reach the higher cabinet and began climbing up on it. I could see it now — her losing her balance and smacking her forehead on the counter and I would have to explain that to the hospital and Jack.

"I think I can get it from here," I intervened.

Tabitha's shoulders slumped and she climbed down from the chair, dragging it back against the linoleum. She pointed toward the top of the cabinet. "Daddy keeps it up there." She retreated to the kitchen table. She must have spent most of her time there. Picture books, coloring books, crayons, and several pieces of paper covered most of the surface.

After the coffee percolated, I poured myself a cup and joined Tabitha at the table.

"We're almost the same," she announced.

"Oh yeah? How's that?"

"We both have special powers because of our dads."

Jack told me about his fluency with non-human languages as if it explained why Tabitha has such abilities. Maybe such gifts were hereditary. I proceeded with caution, pushing down the lump forming in my throat. "I don't think my dad could do anything special like yours. My dad was a teacher."

"No, he wasn't."

"Yeah, he was. I think he even taught at Amadeus for some time. You know, that college in town."

"No, I mean, the teacher wasn't your dad."

Leaning back in my chair, I stared at her — really studied her. She sipped her juice and flipped through her book. My mind turned around her words. "Tabitha, how do you know that?" She didn't look up from her book. I tried again. "You mentioned special powers. Why don't you tell me about yours?"

Tabitha took a deep breath and then deflated. She pushed her book away, folding her hands on the table. She rested her chin on her knuckles. "My dad says I shouldn't explain it because people wouldn't understand it."

"I can try." I pressed my lips into a thin smile. "I think I'd understand a lot more than you realize."

"You're not ready. But don't worry. We'll be spending lots of time together."

If it was anything like this, I needed more time with Tabitha like I needed another hole in my head.

The voice laughed again.

"Phoebe!" Jack yelled out from down the hall. Instinct pulled me out of my chair and on my feet that second, passing underneath the archway and into the living room.

From his door down the hall, Jack emerged as he was pulling a t-shirt on. His head popped through the collar and he caught sight of me. His body and pace relaxed, no longer in a rush to throw on his shirt. He tugged it down, covering his abdomen. His hair was still soaked. Water seeped into the fabric around his shirt collar. After a quick survey of him, I averted my eyes.

He came down the hallway, putting his hands on his hips. "You're awake."

"Yeah," I said.

He realized something else he forgot in his hurry, glancing down at himself. He zipped and buttoned his jeans. He cleared his throat. "Figures you would get up as soon as I got in the shower."

"It's usually how these things happen."

He nodded but I got the impression he didn't really hear my comeback. His eyes were focused on the room past me — the kitchen. He moved around me. With the small bit of privacy, I rolled my eyes at myself. I rubbed my face and turned to follow him back into the kitchen.

"Tabitha, can you go to your room for a bit?" Jack asked.

"But —"

"Phoebe and I have to talk," he said, his voice authoritative.

Someone's in trouble.

Tabitha pulled her book off the table and grabbed a handful of writing instruments. She sulked during her exit, followed a few seconds later by a door slam.

Jack took a seat at the table, leaning back in his chair. He gestured to the seat next to him, where my coffee waited for me. "So... how are you? Feeling any better?"

"Define better." I hovered near the table.

"Apparently better enough to be sassy."

"That wasn't sass."

"I've lived in the South long enough," he said.

Years and years and years...

Closing my eyes for a few seconds, I tried to chase away the voice as best as I could. I had enough to deal with right now and I needed some silence.

I sat down next to Jack, cradling my coffee for a moment. How do I even start this conversation? I tapped my fingers against the mug. "So you brought me back to your place…"

"You were out cold. Didn't have your address and didn't feel like digging through your clothes for any keys."

Either Jack didn't want to talk about it or he was ignoring the elephant in the room that I needed to know more about: last night. I leaned close to the table, spreading my hands across the surface. I searched his face. His brown eyes had flecks of amber, I noticed now. Amber and gold. He was watching me closely and didn't shy away from my eye contact.

"What happened to me last night? Was that really —"

Jack held a finger to his lips, his expression turning hard and I stopped. He inclined his head slightly to the left. My eyes followed, looking past his shoulder. A pair of big eyes watched us. When neither of us said anything for up to fifteen seconds, she spoke up.

"Daddy, I'm out of paper."

He turned around in his chair to face his daughter. He pushed himself to stand. "Paper? You're supposed to be packing. Grandma's going to be here any minute..."

He escorted her out of the room and was gone for

a few minutes, leaving me alone with my coffee and thoughts until he returned.

"Sorry about that. My mother-in-law is going to watch her tonight —"

"Do you work a lot of nights?" The question fell out of my mouth.

He eyed me, gripping the back of his chair. "Sometimes. Depends on the case."

"Do her grandparents normally look after her?"

"Yeah. If not them, friends or sitters." He drummed his thumbs against the chair back. "Anyway — once they come by, we'll be able to talk a little more freely. Do you think you can drive?"

The idea of getting behind the wheel right now was nauseating. I shook my head.

"We can go to your place then. You can get your car later. It's still at my office."

Raising an eyebrow, I leaned back in my seat. "Inviting yourself over?"

"I figured you'd feel more comfortable talking about what happened to you in the privacy of your own home. And given your reaction to the Nethergate, we've lost the luxury of time."

Answers. It was all I wanted from him. Answers about everything — about me, about the Banner murders, and now about last night. But something else he said struck me, brought back to mind what I encountered. "Nethergate?"

"A gateway to the Netherworlds," he explained,

the corner of his mouth twitching upward. "I imagine whatever you saw was more than you can explain."

NINE

"Just because you have a fancy name for it, doesn't mean I went through it," I insisted as Jack pulled his truck into the lot of my complex.

Since we left his place, he had explained more about the gate and what lay beyond it. I had to admit, his description of the Netherworlds matched what I encountered — dark, cold, oppressive, rotten. The broken woman with red hair seemed straight out of tragic legend. My vision felt real and stayed with me longer than any dream. But I didn't want to think about actually going to a place that Jack painted as Hell.

"You didn't physically go anywhere," he said, impatience creeping into his voice. He parked in front of the building I indicated. He turned off the ignition. "Must have something to do with your powers. Maybe you projected yourself through the gate to the other side."

"But how could I have —"

"As soon as you touched the gate, you dropped. I had to carry you out of the apartment myself." He climbed out of the driver's seat. "Pretty sure I would've noticed you disappearing."

After he shut the door, I stared at him through the windshield before getting out of the truck myself. He locked the truck behind me and I led him down the sidewalk. We took the stairs up to my apartment. I was grateful Jack kept quiet as we moved past my neighbor's doors and I got out my keys.

Outside my door, something flashed across my mind. I stopped and glanced his way before turning toward him. "You know, all of this talk about heaven and hell or whatever made me think of something."

"Oh yeah? What's that?"

Folding my arms in front of me, my eyes darted toward the parking lot. "My mom used to tell me this story when I was younger about a mountain at the edge of the world. On top of the mountain was a gate to the heavens. And built around the gate was a city of angels that watched over everyone and made sure everyone was safe."

Jack didn't say anything for a long moment. When I looked at him, he was watching me with a strange expression. "Did your mom tell you anything else?"

I shrugged. "About the mountain? I don't know.

It's a story." But maybe it was more in line with what little he has told me about the Aether. His expression told me I struck close to something and I filed that information away. I unlocked my front door and left it open for Jack, I couldn't tell if it was the voice that felt smug or if it was me.

He stood out in the spillway while I made my first stop at the refrigerator. After a few minutes, he stepped in and closed the door behind him. Jack looked foreign in my apartment. Any company was rare, much less that of a man. The exceptions to that rule were Sarah and Charlie — they had earned their invitations. I watched him from behind the refrigerator door, across the bar. He surveyed my living room as if he was looking for something. I snatched a yogurt from the shelf.

"So Tabitha told me that her special powers are because you're her father, same as you implied when you could read the gate," I recounted, loud enough for him to hear me in the living room. The fridge door slammed. His eyes found me and I continued. "Does that mean abilities like that are hereditary?"

"In our case, yes." He approached the bar and leaned against it.

"Is that the same case for me?"

He rubbed his hands together. "It's possible. There are different ways people can acquire abilities. By birth, by learning, by instrument. Then there are the actual angels and demons themselves."

"That sounds like a non-answer."

"You wanted help, but you haven't told me what you think the problem is," he said carefully. "I need to know more if I'm going to be able to help you."

My mind went back to the appointment I had with the neurologist. I didn't want to be examined, but what Jack asked was fair. I dug around the drawer for my favorite spoon. "Yeah, okay."

"Why don't we start with your abilities? You touched the Nethergate last night. And you saw through to the other side."

The opportunity to explain my abilities to someone who was curious and nonjudgmental was new to me. When Charlie found out, it was an accident and I had to explain to keep him from freaking out. Jack, on the other hand, had experience with this. "Yeah. I've always sort of been able to read what's happened. Objects, people, places, they put off vibrations. I can't read all the time, but it's like the ability has been getting stronger since the accident."

"Read memories or visions?" he pressed.

"Mostly memories. Sometimes visions. It depends on what or who I touch. Whatever I see, it's usually all tied to a big emotional moment."

"But that's not why you approached us the other day."

"No. I thought maybe I'd reach out to you in case Tabitha was special and you didn't know, or needed help."

He smirked. "A bit misguided."

"I knew how much trouble it was for my parents to raise me with my abilities. I didn't want you to go through the same thing, if I could help," I clarified. "But no, that's not why I approached you two at the school. I wanted more answers because I started... it sounds crazy, but I don't.... There's..."

The words were on the tip of my tongue but it was like I couldn't spit them out. Not that I didn't want to, but something was censoring me.

"Been a development since the accident?" he offered.

I nodded.

"You've been experiencing these symptoms, for lack of a better word, for how long?" When I didn't look at him, he pressed further. "How frequently?"

I shook my head, slowly at first then a few definitive shakes. "It's gotten worse since the accident. Nearly every day —"

Shut up, shut up, shut up.

"And before that?" he asked.

A pang shot through my mind and I squeezed my eyes shut. Droning. No sound. Minutes passed. When I opened them, Jack was staring at me.

Before I could explain, he continued quietly. "Harrow is a weak spot between the fabric of the realms. Demons flock here, angels tread here. There are even creatures you couldn't fathom."

The voice's presence subsided. But then his words

registered. "Prove it."

His eyebrows shot up. "You want me to show you angels and demons and all sorts of things… as proof?"

"Yes," I said, setting the yogurt and spoon aside. "If they're real and Harrow is a special magical place, you should be able to introduce me."

"Is that what it's going to take to convince you?"

Less certain, I held my ground. "Yes."

He scratched the back of his head and folded his arms in front of his chest. "You should understand, it's not easy to discern most angels and demons from humans when they live among humans. They're not going to look any different."

"Uh huh. That sounds like an excuse to me," I said.

"You think I'm crazy. Even after what you saw last night?"

"Maybe I'm crazy, too."

A smile grew on his face. "I have a friend who works down at Oakview —"

"The funeral home?"

"Yes, the funeral home." He shot me a look. "I was going to meet her later tonight. She has some information on the Nethergate. If you're up for it, we can go down there together. You know, in case you need to hear it from someone other than me."

"I'll need a shower. And get something more substantial to eat." Considering the yogurt would've been the first thing I had eaten since last night and I couldn't even touch it, I needed a real meal if I was going to function.

"Go. Shower. I can wait."

Trusting Jack, much less anyone, for fifteen minutes unsupervised in my apartment was no easy task. I took the hottest, quickest shower I could and climbed out once the hot water felt like it had permanently seared my skin. Showers helped me clear my mind and this one was no different. It put distance between me and what I encountered, washing away whatever bleak residue clung to my senses after last night. After a rush job of moisturizing and combing my hair, I grabbed my short, yellow terry cloth robe and cinched the belt tightly around my waist.

When I exited the bathroom, Jack was watching the WHRW broadcast. I stopped, not making it to my bedroom for clothes. Jack stood in front of my couch and coffee table, arms tightly folded across his chest as he held onto my remote control. On the television was the local news. A serious expression was etched onto Jack's face. His eyes flickered over to me and briefly to my robe before he nodded in the direction of the screen.

"There's been another murder this morning," he explained.

Moving next to him, I watched for a few moments and read the text across the bottom of the screen. A news van was parked outside a house and the camera picked up grainy footage as law enforcement crawled over the scene.

We watched the broadcast, standing together in silence. The Lance family had no comment, but the neighbors couldn't shut up. Similar to the Henderson murder the day before, the reporter dug for comments and the neighbors offered up surprise, shock that this could happen in such a tight-knit community. I grew impatient with the broadcast, until it left the field reporter and returned to Nina Marquez back in the newsroom. She relayed the facts, for those just tuning in. The boys, Curtis and William, were seventeen and fifteen, respectively. Their parents wished for privacy during this trying time.

Jack shut off the television. I glanced up at him, his expression unreadable.

"Any arrests?" I asked, my voice feeling loud with the television off.

The muscles in his jaw tightened. He nodded. "They took the victim's brother into custody."

"Shit."

"You should get dressed."

TEN

"Of course, you brought an audience."

"Be nice," Jack warned.

Victoria's eyes scanned me. Then she scowled at Jack. "Nice would have been receiving a phone call prior to you showing up… with an audience."

The three of us stood behind the sprawling Oakview Memorial Home, underneath its dark green awning. Jack's friend Victoria stood guard at the rear door. She was not who I was expecting when Jack first mentioned a friend working at the funeral home. A mix between a porcelain doll and a pin-up model, I'd expect her to run a shop or something downtown — maybe a tattoo parlor or a cafe — but certainly not preparing the dead for their final resting place.

I stood one step below Jack. My hip rested against the painted railing and I glanced between them to determine who would win the staring contest. Jack had intense eyes but Victoria's resolve was impressive. As they fought it out silently, I scanned the parking lot. Years had passed since I was last out to Oakview. Ill feelings stirred in the pit of my stomach. At least if we were talking about the Nethergate like Jack and I came here to do, my mind wouldn't focus on what the funeral home itself meant to me.

"She has a point," I muttered and drummed my fingers against the railing. "So apologize so we can get on with it."

Jack shot me a look from over his shoulder. Victoria, however, raised an eyebrow in surprise at the support she received. Her shoulders relaxed and her expression turned smug. She shot Jack a look and cleared the doorway, sweeping her arm in a gesture for us to enter. I swallowed my misgivings and fell in step behind him.

We followed her through the back of the funeral home, past offices and the administrative area. We came out into the main lobby. My eyes were immediately drawn to the sitting area, with its neutral colors, upholstered couches and glossy pamphlets, such as *Selecting a Funeral Home* and *Preplanning Your Funeral at Oakview*. Past the lobby was a chapel and two viewing rooms, plus a smaller chapel in the back. Déjà vu swamped my thoughts and my eyes trained onto Jack's shoulders so I would keep moving.

The three of us took the elevator down into the

basement. Victoria walked fast but Jack moved as if he knew the way. I didn't want to know why. I stuck close to him, feeling my body relax the further we moved from the public floor. We passed through the set of metal double doors, complete with a sign warning Danger - Flammable Liquids - No Smoking. I braced myself for the chemical stench of formaldehyde and ethanol, but neither hit me in the face. The chemicals didn't cling to the air at all. Huh.

Jack and Victoria moved around the embalming table to her workstation set up on the counter. He pulled his digital camera out from his back pocket while she got settled on her stool and woke the desktop computer from its screensaver. He opened the memory card compartment and ejected the card, passing it off to Victoria. My eyes fell away from them and onto an exposed cadaver on the metal slab.

I've seen corpses. They got ugly even if they died of natural causes. But this one was damn near glowing. A flush warmed his face. His blood hadn't collected where gravity held him down. And Jack and Victoria acted as if the body wasn't even in the room.

My eyes returned to them, watching and waiting to see if they had any sort of delayed reaction. Nothing. "Not to alarm anyone," I interrupted their shoptalk. "But this guy seems… not dead."

They both looked at me and I pointed at the body, in case there was any confusion about whom I was referencing.

Victoria narrowed her eyes at Jack and her voice dripped saccharine. "You bring her here and she doesn't even know the ways of Harrow? Did you expect me to be the one to tell her about the facts of life and death?"

"I wasn't expecting you to keep someone out in the open."

"Again, it would have been nice to receive some notice. And if you educated your guests before they step foot in my business —"

"Again," I interjected. "This guy seems fresher than the rest of us."

Jack squeezed the bridge of his nose. After a moment, he stepped toward the embalming table. He stood across from me, pulling the sheet over the body. My eyes stayed fixed on the shrouded figure. Jack moved next to me. His voice was quiet and close. "Remember how I told you Harrow was a weak spot between the realms?" I nodded and he continued. "In Harrow and places like it, angels know they can make their final arrangements at one facility. That way, they're properly interred until they're released back to the Aether."

"Angels?"

"You said you wanted to proof."

I turned the information around in my head, seeking a conclusion, waiting for the voice to chime in. Blinking, I shook my head. "Doesn't count if the proof is dead," I spat. "Is he dead?"

"There are different classes of angels," he continued, ignoring my barb. "The Aether sends angels to take mortal form in order to complete assignments. Protection, care, prevention, whatever is deemed necessary. These angels act and age as any other human. Even if I knew who they were, I couldn't introduce you to them without their mission being compromised. Their nature should only be revealed after their human death."

A weight pressed against my heart. Jack had to be the crazy one. He had to be, because if he wasn't —

"What about the other kinds of angels?" I asked.

Jack opened his mouth but electricity spiked in the air. Light shattered throughout the room. My vision returned after a few seconds and I found that someone else was in the room with the three of us. An older woman with a curly mane of copper hair and dark skin, she was dressed in a suit of ivory. Light radiated from her and slowly dimmed into a steady glow — nearly the same shade as the cadaver.

With his jaw clenched, Jack's eyes flickered to mine and he answered my question. "They have an annoying habit of showing up uninvited."

My brain was racing to rationalize the woman's sudden appearance. Maybe she came in while I was looking at the cadaver. Maybe she slipped in quietly through another door. My eyes darted around the room, looking for another entrance or even a faulty light fixture. No lights but UV lights on the ceiling and track lighting mounted underneath the cabinets. No doors but the ones behind us.

Victoria pivoted on her stool to face us. She folded her arms tightly across her chest and craned her neck to glare at Jack from around the other woman. "Are we expecting anyone else, dear? Should we turn on an open sign?"

"Have you found the source of the Nethergates?" the woman asked Jack, her voice calm yet determined. Behind her, Victoria rolled her eyes and turned back to her computer.

"Not yet. Victoria hasn't had a chance to review the photographs."

"The pictures are loading, your highness," Victoria said dryly.

Realization dawned on the woman's face as if she understood there was one more person in the room. She pivoted on her heel to face Victoria. "Demon," she acknowledged.

This was a damn joke. Leaning closer to Jack, a retort sat on my tongue. But then with no forewarning, the woman was facing us again, startling me. Jack offered no explanation, only an introduction. "Phoebe, this is Beatrix."

When her eyes landed on me, electricity shot through my veins and my mouth went dry. Her eyes, now that I could see them, weren't brown or hazel as expected but dark orange. Those strange eyes ran from my head to the toe of my boots. "You're awake."

I glanced over at Jack. Nothing. All right. "Yeah," I said, feeling uncomfortable under gaze.

"You should be more careful, Phoebe Harris, and open doors to which you know what waits for you on the other side," the woman told me.

Dread with a dash of annoyance swept over me. "Not like there was a peep hole or anything," I said, through a tense jaw.

Victoria chortled. "Oh, Jack. I think I like this one. You can keep bringing her around."

"Enough," Beatrix said, inclining her head toward the so-called demon. She then turned her attention to Victoria's computer. I swear she had shoulder pads in her power suit.

When Jack spoke again, he kept his voice low for my ears only. "I believe you said an introduction would suffice as proof."

My eyes were going to bug out of my head if he kept saying things like that. I stared at him, waiting for some elaboration. When he said nothing, I pressed further. "And how does she know about me? You told her?"

His eyes met mine and he rose to his full height. I've dealt with larger men. I've arrested larger men. Size never intimidated me. But when those golden flecks in his eyes flashed as the only sign that he heard me, I swallowed.

"Because she found us last night after you blacked

out. This is her territory. She'll find out whatever goes on — the Nethergates, the fact that you connected with one, the fact you have abilities at all. Sometimes cooperation is your best bet."

"Why in hell would I cooperate?"

"Beatrix isn't who you should worry about. She's one of the good ones."

My eyes flickered over to the two women. Victoria was pulling up the photographs from Jack's memory card as Beatrix stood over her shoulder. The two women were opposites in many ways. Victoria was petite with her black hair slicked back into a tight bun, her sentences clipped and her expression blank. By contrast, Beatrix was maybe over six feet with a full head of shiny curls. A crown, really. Or even a — no, I wasn't going to think halo. Not at all.

This was ridiculous.

I folded my arms across my chest. "So what — are you going to tell me she is a guardian angel?"

"More like parole officer."

A laugh escaped me and Victoria shot us a dirty look. I pressed my lips together to keep from smiling and Jack winked at me.

Beatrix, however, seemed aloof to the whole exchange. She scrutinized the images on the screen and stood up straight. "I expect to be kept informed about any developments," she said to Jack.

And then Beatrix vanished. Exited the same way she entered in the room, the same way my brain fought to rationalize. Light cracked through the air and with a flash, the air was clear — of the light and of her. The difference with her departure, however, was that I had been looking right at her before she split. Her exit looked like lightning and seared itself into my vision. A familiar pain throbbed in the back of my head.

Do you believe in angels now?

I was going to be sick.

Jack caught me by the elbow before I felt my knees starting to buckle. He was talking to me but my ears couldn't process the words. My lungs couldn't get enough oxygen. A strong hand pressed against my back and he guided me back to my feet. He then escorted me out of the room, retracing our steps till we reached the back door.

Once outside, I made it so far down the steps before my legs gave out from under me.

You need to calm down.

How in the hell was I supposed to do that?

Focus on breathing.

I squeezed my eyes shut and pressed my forehead against the handrail.

One, two, three...

A strangled laugh escaped me, triggering something deep in my gut. I tried to focus on the voice's presence in my head, something with which I had become comfortable with since the accident. What was churning in my stomach, through my blood, was something strange and dangerous. Like something unlocked and I couldn't shake it off. It uncurled and unleashed itself.

Jack knelt down in front of me, watching me. I tried to hide my face. Torn between tears and laughter. Tears? Was I really crying? I laughed harder.

When the laughter died down and I could catch my breath, I asked, "Are they always like that?"

"Pretty much. I stay out of it."

I stared at him before realizing what he meant. "No, not Victoria and Beatrix — I mean, angels. They can be human, or appear out of nowhere, or... or..." I stammered, bringing myself to look at him.

He needed to tell me it was a big joke, that what I saw back in the embalming room was a trick of the light or something wrong with my vision, that there was a logical reason I was laughing like a mad woman. But he didn't say anything for an excruciating moment while my fears bubbled to the surface. Jack's eyes flickered between both of mine as if he were searching for something. He touched my hair and I jerked back.

"Everyone has a different reaction when they see their first true angel," he explained. He rubbed his hands together and sat down on the concrete step next to me. "I've seen people vomit like *The Exorcist* or want to throw themselves off buildings. Granted, you can't find a place taller than ten stories here in Harrow but it'd still do some damage. Either way, the core of it is disorientation —"

Realization. Revelation. Truth.

Shut up.

You've started listening.

I blocked out the voice and tuned back into Jack, missing whatever tangent he took. He was going on about the funeral home.

"Oakview is one of the few places in Harrow that caters exclusively to angels. The man on the table, for example," he explained, gesturing to the door behind us. "His funerary plans probably stipulated that he be sent to Oakview, so he wouldn't be cremated or otherwise artificially preserved. The family doesn't think to ask questions, probably because they think he was well preserved or that the funeral home did an outstanding job with the preparation. After the funeral, he's laid to rest at Rockhaven Cemetery. Then he waits to be released."

Jack's explanation unnerved me. My eyes searched his face and dread sat heavy on my chest. Angels and demons crawled all over Harrow since it was a weak spot. Angels made their final plans to be carried out here at Oakview. Angels can come and go as they please, in a flash of light, but angels can also appear human. A billion questions raced through my head but one bubbled to the surface.

"You said Oakview caters to angels?"

He nodded. "Victoria's been in the business a long time." I must have given him a strange look because then he clarified. "She owns Oakview."

I filed the information away. My brain couldn't process anything else right after Beatrix's blinding exit and something else that was bothering me. For now, I'd accept whatever he told me and would try to make sense of it later. Otherwise, I was pretty sure my head might explode.

Poor Phoebe. Not the night you were expecting, girly?

You know it's not.

There's still so much for you to learn.

My eyes squeezed shut. I didn't need to start having conversations with the voice in my head. It was one thing to accept its residence but quite another to engage it. I focused on my breathing, inhaling deeply and exhaling slowly. If I did as the voice earlier advised, it would stop talking to me, right?

Jack rubbed my shoulders and this time I didn't shake him off. "Hey, you don't have to be here. I can take you home."

"Sorry, I need a minute."

"You don't have to explain it to me. It's a bit much for anyone's first time. Frankly, I'd be a little more worried if you seemed okay —"

"You're okay with it."

"I've been around it for some time," he said, his voice distant. He pushed himself up, brushing off the back of his jeans. "I should get back inside and help Victoria look at those pictures. But I can take you home first, if that's what you want."

The concern in his voice fueled my pride. Perhaps it was the same issue that got me in trouble last night but I indignantly replied, "No, I'm fine. Let's do this."

He watched me for a moment before he held out a hand. I took it and grabbed onto the handrail at the same time, pulling myself to my feet. My knees were shaky but I could stand. I took those breaths the voice urged me to take.

Jack moved away from me toward the rear door, and my eyes followed him. As my thoughts cleared, the fact about angels admitting themselves to Oak-view remained. For the same reason, the memory of my own father's funeral service came to mind.

It had been held here eight years ago.

If what Jack was telling me was true, whatever Beatrix happened to be was the least of my concerns.

ELEVEN

After reviewing the photographs of the Nethergate with Victoria, Jack drove me back to his office so I could retrieve my rental car. We rode in silence, thank god. I needed the break.

The information Victoria gave us about the doorway raced through my head. She had identified certain markings of the gate, telling us that they were unique to whoever created it. Similar to handwriting analysis, the symbols that made up the gate could tell us who forged it.

She also told us that it was clear that the markings were made by one entity — person, demon, or creature. At least that was a step in the right direction to finding out whoever or whatever was behind the killings.

I rolled down the window and the Harrow night air

hit my face. My elbow propped in place of the window and I leaned my head against my hand. My brain or neurons or whatever were still on edge from seeing Beatrix disappear via lightning bolt. If I had heard about that mode of entrance or exit, I would've laughed it off before. But I saw it with my own eyes. The light was burned into my vision.

Angels.

Fuck.

The Banner case file waited for me back at my apartment and I could look at the crime scene photos with new eyes, thanks to Victoria's information. Hopefully, the markings would be the same.

Jack pulled his truck into the vacant parking spot next to that ugly rental sedan. I climbed down from the passenger side of his truck before he could cut the ignition. He got out of the cab as I dug around for my keys and met me by the driver's side door of the car.

"You wanted proof."

"Yeah, I know," I relented. "Still doesn't mean I can just switch gears and believe whatever you'll tell me. When you told me you were a private investigator, paranormal, whatever — I pictured white noise machines, doctored photos and séances."

"I pull that shit out when that's what the client wants."

"And other times you get mixed up with angels and demons," I said without any conviction. Something Beatrix said earlier came back to mind. "Beatrix called Victoria a demon."

"Yeah," Jack said, taking a deep breath. "She is."

"Does that make her one of the bad guys?" I asked.

He shook his head, glancing at his office building. "No. I've been working with her for a while. As I understand it, her departure from the Netherworld wasn't exactly her choice."

"She was kicked out?"

"Expelled."

"So because she was *expelled*, she's on the side of the angels?" I asked.

"Something like that," he said.

"What kind of work does she do for you?"

He laughed under his breath. "I was right about you and questions."

"Can't take me to the dragon's nest and not expect me to be curious. Besides, I'm naturally inquisitive."

"I'd hope so, or else you went into the wrong business," he said. He leaned against my car. "Victoria's a good contact for crisis management. She has a wide set of skills that can be useful. Like her reading of the photographs tonight."

"Yeah. I can't even fathom what skills someone must acquire after they've been kicked out of hell," I said, sarcasm creeping into my voice. "Do you even know who kicked her out? Please don't tell me Satan."

Jack shrugged. "Don't know. She doesn't want to

talk about it. Could've been any number of reasons."

"So you go to her when you need information, yet you don't think it's a little suspicious not knowing who kicked her out of the Netherworld? Do you even know why she got kicked out?" I pinched the bridge of my nose. "I mean, what can one even do to get kicked out of hell?"

"We all have our pasts. I'm not exactly a boy scout and I'm sure you aren't innocence personified," he said. "Victoria's been on Earth for at least a century. Any demonic loyalties she may have held aren't fresh. Her powers are fading. Every time she uses her abilities, she gets closer to becoming human—"

And then Jack stopped in the middle of his defense of Victoria. Realization sparked across his face and his eyes darted to meet mine. He stood up straight, away from my car.

"I need to go."

"What?" I spat out.

"I'll see you tomorrow morning. Me, you, and a visit to Logan Banner?" He pointed at me as he moved back to his truck.

"Wait, you can't drop all this info about angels and demons on me and leave. What is it?" I asked. What did he realize?

He waved my questions off. "Be here tomorrow by nine A.M. Do you remember where the Banners live?"

I nodded. They had moved after the murder a couple years ago, but I knew their new address.

Jack smiled at me but I could tell it was polite. His mind was elsewhere. "I'll even let you drive," he said.

"Jack," I pleaded and for a moment, he froze before he climbed into the cab of his truck.

I don't know if it was that I said his name or the way that I said it. Even I was shocked by how vulnerable I sounded. He stood across from me, his eyes locking with mine across the bed of his truck.

The last couple of days, since Jack Gregory had come into my life, had turned my world upside down. Gates to hell, angels, demons, and who knew what else. To be truthful, I didn't want to be by myself right now even if I had a lot of processing left to do. I'd rather ask Jack questions than be left to my own thoughts. And the voice.

The moment expanded between us as we stood, eyes locked. I wasn't ready for him to leave my side yet. Things were getting interesting. And if anything, he realized he could help shed light on what was happening to me. I wanted to be there when he found out the truth.

"Where are you going?" I asked.

His mouth opened and shut, a firm line in place of my answer. Before I could say anything else, he broke our gaze and climbed into his truck. I watched as he drove off, red lights disappearing as he turned off the street.

In the dark Harrow night, I slumped against my

rental car. The weight of the last twenty-four hours weighed against my joints and muscles. I would be sore tomorrow. I had seen an angel and met a demon. I remembered something that Jack had given me yesterday.

Unlocking the car and jerking the driver's side door open, I went for the glove compartment where I had stashed the book that Jack had given me before we headed out to Dundee. I fumbled to click on the dome light, illuminating the bleak interior of the rental.

The journal looked even more sinister and more promising in the dim light. Jack had said it helped him when he was first starting out. Maybe the journal could help me reconcile what I saw tonight with what I had known before I met Jack. The vibrations hummed up my arm, much more sophisticated than anything I felt regarding the Banner case. I unraveled the strap, careful with the worn leather as I peeled open the cover.

The handwriting was strangely familiar, written with a fountain pen in a hurry. The paper was aged and delicately preserved. I flipped to the first page. A note by the author greeted me.

'*Everything written here is true. Everything I have seen has taken place. If you're reading this, you need to be ready. And even then, you may not be ready for what it means. I'm sorry.*'

Pursing my lips, I read it over again. The wording

was strange, not what I would've expected in a book this old. Maybe it was added after the fact — a note left for Jack?

Who would have given him such a gift?

I frowned at the voice's question since it mirrored my own. *I don't know — Victoria?*

This journal is older than her time spent on the surface.

You can tell that?

You feel so much. But I feel more.

Paging through the journal, I skimmed passages — information that seemed way over my head for someone who was learning there was more to Harrow than some people with special powers. I knew I should wait until I was home rather than parked on the street, but curiosity got the best of me.

If you're ready to read this, are you finally ready to listen to me, Phoebe Harris?

Maybe. I'm not sure yet.

I've been waiting for you to listen.

I shut the journal and I couldn't take deep enough breaths. I was about to tell the voice that I knew she had been waiting for me. Did I know that? Had she been around longer than the couple weeks she's been present? I glanced at the rear view mirror, almost hoping to see her as I saw her the night of the accident. If I could see her, maybe I wouldn't feel so crazy about talking to her.

I knew I was on the verge of something I wasn't

sure I wanted to dive into just yet. My powers had been with me since I was a kid. I had known I've always been a little different. It's why I moved back to Harrow to find answers.

Maybe I wasn't ready to have them handed to me.

I tossed the journal into the passenger seat and rested my forehead against the steering wheel. I counted my breaths until I inserted the keys into the ignition. I'd have to make a stop by the store for some caffeine or maybe an energy drink.

I had a lot of homework to catch up on tonight.

TWELVE

I was exhausted when I met Jack at his office the next morning. A thermos of coffee in hand shielded me from having to say much, which was great, because I was still processing a lot of things — Beatrix, Victoria, the journal, and other things. Our drive over to the Banner residence was tense. We took my rental car and I steered, white-knuckled all the way to Ivy Heights.

Many of the neighbors were at church or still sleeping this Sunday morning. I parked the car down the block and still couldn't look at Jack. To his credit, he didn't say much to me either. I sipped at my coffee then got out of the car, leaving my thermos behind. He followed along as we headed to the Banner house.

"Do you have a game plan?" I asked.

"No," Jack said. "Thought we'd make it up as it

goes."

I shook my head as we walked up the Banner driveway and approached the front stoop. I made it to the front door first and Jack stood one step below me, scanning the neighbors for any sign of life. I knocked hard three times before Logan Banner came to the door. It had been years since I'd seen the man. And by the way he blinked at the daylight, it must've been days since he'd seen that, too. With the state of his facial hair and the stains on his shirt, I imagine he hadn't been outside in a while.

"Detective Harris?" he asked, confusion lacing his words and features.

"Logan," I said with a small smile, and then gestured behind me. "This is my associate, Jack Gregory. He wanted to come here this morning to ask you a few questions."

"I don't understand," he said, looking between the two of us before settling his gaze on me. "Is he police?"

"Private investigator," I said, trying to maintain a professional tone.

"Mr. Banner," Jack started, drawing Logan's attention back to him. "Your niece Emily hired me to look into your wife's disappearance. Detective Harris here has graciously offered to help since she's familiar with your family's past."

"He approached me to help," I corrected him.

"May we come in?" Jack asked Logan, ignoring

my snip.

Uncertainty flashed in Logan Banner's eyes, but he nodded, gesturing for us to come into his living room. I entered first, scanning the downstairs area. His living room was full of heavy furniture and looked like it had been overrun by dirty dishes and take out boxes. The blinds were closed, blocking out the sun as much as it could. The house was much bigger than their last house, where Travis was killed. As I moved along the perimeter of the room, Jack stayed by Logan's side in the entranceway.

Logan's voice was clipped and tinged with anxiety. He watched me like a hawk even as he addressed Jack. "Emily shouldn't have gone to you, Mr. Gregory. I'm sorry she bothered you."

"She's concerned about her aunt. Emily mentioned that she had taken some more peculiar habits. Do you know anything about that?"

"Karen… oh, I don't know. She always has her hobbies. She likes to keep busy. But I think she's just taking time away," he babbled. "She's still grieving the loss of our two sons, Mr. Gregory. Maybe Detective Harris told you that. My wife has never recovered — we've never recovered. I'm giving Karen all the space she needs to explore her grief. It's a shame Emily didn't recognize that. Karen always needed time away to reach closure."

Without missing a beat, I chimed in from the other side of the room. "What about your son's disappearance, Logan?"

Logan hesitated. Jack and I both studied his expression. He was slow with his words, shaken. "I'm sure the police are doing everything in their power to find Kyle."

"The police are busy investigating other murders around town, so they're stretched a little thin right now," I snapped. "And as far as I know, they aren't even looking into a missing person. Do you know if the home reported it?"

Logan's chin dropped and he shook his head.

"Did *you* report it?" I asked.

He was shutting down underneath my scrutiny. His hands were shaking.

I tried to show sympathy but anger coursed through me. Logan Banner was wasting away here and doing nothing to find his wife and son. My voice grew louder and more pointed but I didn't know what to do to stop it.

"Then how in the hell do you expect anyone to know where to find him? To even go looking for him? Unless you think your wife knows where he is. Isn't it a least bit odd to you that your son has gone missing right after your wife left you?"

"Phoebe," Jack said, his tone clearly warning me to back down.

I didn't look at Jack, focusing instead on this scared, cowering man. "Logan, we want to help you. Emily wants to help you. Maybe even Jack wants to help you. If something is going on, if something has happened to your wife or Kyle, you need to tell us. We can't help you otherwise. Please, let me help you. You've already been through too much."

Logan lifted his head slowly, pain etched across his face. He stared at me for the longest moment until I felt my expression relax. He gave a small nod, moving from the center of his living room to the desk off to the side. He scrawled something onto some stationary and tore it from the pad. He folded it.

Logan walked back to the front door, opening it wide as our cue to leave. Jack headed to the door and received a swift handshake.

"Thank you for visiting. I'm sorry my niece has wasted your time," Logan said in a very calculated voice and Jack said nothing in return.

When it was time for Logan to say goodbye to me, he gave me the note. I opened it and read quickly over Logan's words. He shifted and fidgeted, pushing his hair out of his face. My mouth pressed into a thin line as I read it a few more times before I refolded it and stuck it in my back pocket. Then I held my hand out for a shake. Logan took hold of my hand and I tightened my grip. An image flooded my mind — a hooded figure watching, waiting. I tried to get more information from my prolonged handshake with Logan, but he shuddered and jerked his hand away. He shook it out to lose whatever sensation had taken hold of him.

I exited the Banner home, pushing past Jack and down the front steps. Jack pulled out his wallet and handed a business care to Logan.

"If you change your mind — if you have any information about your wife or son, don't hesitate to reach out to us," Jack said.

Logan took the business card and stared at it as he shut the front door without one last look at us. I was halfway down the driveway, stalking in the direction of the car.

"Hey, wait up!" Jack shouted after me, chasing to catch up. "What was that back there?"

"He wasn't giving us answers. Thought I'd expedite the process."

"By pouring lemon juice on his wounds? He was shutting down."

"He was censoring himself," I spat, stopping in my tracks. I unfolded the note that Logan had given to me and recited Logan's words. "'Help us. If you find them, tell them I'm sorry. I love them. He's listening.'" I shoved the note at Jack and continued stalking to the car.

Jack turned the note around, reading over Logan's note before he jogged after me. "Hey—"

"He hasn't reported his wife or son missing because someone's watching him. He can't even ask for help. He's a prisoner in his own home by some fucker with some hold over him."

"We're lucky he even told us anything after you

confronted him in there. What's wrong, Phoebe? You haven't said a word to me all morning and then you're ready to rip into Logan Banner since he couldn't talk."

"What's wrong — what's *wrong*?" I shouted, spinning to get in Jack's face. "How about ever since you walked into that bar, I've had to tear open too many old wounds? I've had to learn about things that go bump in the night. I've seen angels and demons and portals to hell!"

"You said yourself that case didn't feel right to you. You knew Kyle couldn't be capable of killing his brother," he said, his voice calm.

"Yet, he confessed! He was locked away!" I shouted. "Sure, I don't think he did it, but I also didn't think demons were involved."

Jack glanced around the neighborhood, probably checking to see if anyone was overhearing our conversation. Not that I cared. Let the whole world know. He moved closer to me, not stopping until I took a few steps back and he had me backed up, pressed back against the car. "I've shown you a lot since you joined the case, Phoebe. I think I've been very patient with you. What else do you want? For me to make all the demons and angels go away?"

"Yes," I sneered, even though that wasn't a real answer.

He narrowed his eyes at me. "I can't do that. They're real and they're living in Harrow. And one of them is targeting the Banners and other families in the area for reasons I need your help finding. But if you can't accept what I'm telling you, you can read that journal I gave you the other day."

I leaned back so I could look right at him, fire in my eyes. "Oh, I read your fucking book. Read as much as I could until I couldn't keep my eyes open. Read all about angels, demons, heaven, hell. Yet I'm not any closer to figuring out what the hell is wrong with me."

"Nothing's wrong with you," he said.

My laugh was ugly and I broke our eye contact, looking down the street. Jack watched me and stood way too close.

He continued. "I mean that. I know it's a shock to learn all of this at the same time. But as far as I know, there's nothing wrong with you. And if there is, we'll figure it out."

"Maybe I don't want to talk about it. Maybe I don't want to be the topic of one of your investigations," I spat, looking back up at him. Tears burned in my eyes and I scowled deeper to keep from showing any vulnerability. I needed more space between us. Turning away, I unlocked the car and swung the driver's side door open, missing Jack. He closed the door for me once I was seated and then took his time to get into the passenger side. Thankfully, he gave me the breathing room I needed. I didn't want him to become the target of my frustrations, even if it would be so easy to rip into him. He climbed into the car and settled into the seat without saying a word. The engine was still off and we sat in silence for a long moment.

"You said he was being watched by someone. Are you saying you saw something when we were in the house?" he asked me in a low voice.

I stared out the windshield before answering him. "I read his energy when he shook my hand goodbye. Someone's watching his every move, listening to anything he says. And it's gotten worse since Emily interfered. She pissed whoever off. And now they're locked in on Logan and he's trying to appease them."

"You could tell that from one handshake?"

I nodded, glancing over at him. "Logan Banner is not some heartless man. He was devastated when Kyle killed Travis. I tried everything I could to prove with evidence that Kyle didn't do it. But Kyle confessed. The silver lining was that he didn't go through a trial. Did you see the fear in Logan's eyes just now? He was terrified. *Terrified*. Why else wouldn't a man go to the police to find his wife and child? Something's keeping him from coming forward because he's scared they'll do worse to his family."

"How much worse could it get than losing your wife and son?" he asked no one in particular.

"Forcing one of your sons to murder the other," I said, answering anyway.

Jack rolled down the window, remaining quiet for a long time. "What do you say about going back to

Dundee and finding Aaron's ex? Think she's working the Sunday brunch crowd?"

"Even if she's not, I'm still hungry."

THIRTEEN

The Dundee cafe where we found Sandy — so I remembered her name wrong, but close enough — opened before the church crowd got out. A bell jingled as Jack held the door open for me and I entered the small cafe. The dining area was decked out in polished chrome, accented by alternating blue and yellow tile. Natural daylight overwhelmed any fluorescents overhead. The cook behind the counter nodded toward us. A dark-haired waitress fought with the cash register. We sat ourselves.

Jack slid into the booth across from me. I leaned my head against the glass and closed my eyes. The after effects of the reading from Logan Banner were still coursing through my system. Like cobwebs caking my skin and rib cage. Despite these jitters, I ordered coffee when the dark-haired waitress came to our table. Her name tag read Sandy and the facts from the news report broke through the fog. Sandra Collins was Aaron Henderson's girlfriend when he lived in Dundee, in that apartment with the Nethergate. His parents didn't like her. I couldn't recall if they broke up or not.

I stopped listening when Jack began to sweet talk Sandy. Now that I had stopped moving, Logan Banner's energy was making me dizzy. My hand shot out and grabbed onto Jack's, needing something to replace the dark shadows that were clouding my brain.

That was probably a mistake.

Something in my head flinched as the smooth vibrations spread up my arms and through my chest. Whatever vibrations Jack projected weren't like anything I had seen when I touched someone before, nor were they accompanied by any sort of flash of images. It was more like pure emotional undercurrent. Raw and almost feral. If Logan Banner was a puddle, Jack's energy felt as deep as an ocean. It washed away the stale darkness that had clouded my mind.

Sandy looked at me with wide eyes — I can't imagine what I must've looked like going straight for Jack's hand so fiercely. She excused herself and scurried back behind the counter.

"Sorry," I muttered, letting go of Jack's hand. My thumb rubbed the back of my hand to erase the sensation but a residue lingered.

Jack's gaze went from my hands to meet my eyes.

He let out a small laugh, adjusting in his seat. He leaned against the wall and propped his arm against the back of the booth. "I don't have cooties."

That got a smile out of me, for a number of reasons. "You do have a daughter in grade school. Maybe she brought up something home from the playground."

"The moment anyone is giving my daughter cooties on a playground will be a day of reckoning," he said. He grew serious. "You looked a little pale a moment ago."

I shook out my hair, unsure of even how to explain it. Moving the salt and pepper shakers to the center of the table gave me something to focus on while the words percolated. "Logan left a bad impression. I needed to wipe my nerves clean and you put off a different vibe. That's all," I explained.

"Is that so?"

"Normally I don't get readings like that from people," I admitted. "And when I do, they're more specific. Like seeing what Logan Banner was going through. Glimpses of what's going. Though, honestly, that might've been from the note he passed to me if it was in the same room with him at the time he started being watched, if you know what I mean."

Jack watched me, the flecks in his eyes glinting. He didn't waver from direct eye contact and I was starting to believe that was his thing. Staring into your soul was an everyday thing for him. I wasn't feeling up for the challenge after this morning.

"What reading did you get from me?" he asked, his words deliberate.

I shrugged a shoulder. "I don't know. It's not so clear. Feelings that pulse. General state of your mind. It's like you're on a different wavelength from anyone I've ever read before."

The corner of his mouth tugged upward. "I'll take that as a compliment."

Lacking the desire to burst his bubble, I looked out the window and squinted at the sunlight. My own question came to the surface, something I never got to ask someone since I kept my abilities hidden. "Did you feel anything?"

"When you grabbed my hand?"

I narrowed my eyes at him. "Yes, when I grabbed your hand."

He didn't say anything for a moment. "Butter-flies," he said with a straight face. My breath got stuck in my lungs but then the corner of his mouth twitched.

"Shut up," I cut him off, tossing a sugar packet at him. "You know that's not what I meant."

Jack laughed as Sandy returned with our coffee. She set both mugs down at the same time. Her hands trembled and she wiped both her palms off on her apron once she'd set them down. She took a deep breath then launched into her spiel.

"Sorry it took so long. Had to brew a fresh pot

since the other one had been sittin' a little too long. Hope y'all don't mind." She fished for her order pad in her apron and held it, posed for our order. "Are y'all ready to order or do you need a few more minutes?"

I ordered a couple scrambled eggs with grits and toast and Jack ordered something with bacon. Sandy nodded to herself and mouthed the words as she scrawled our orders down. She then flashed an awkward smile. She was delicate and a little clumsy, polite and eager to please. I could see why Aaron would follow her out to Dundee. Sandy Collins was pretty and seemed caring and probably gave Aaron Henderson more attention than his younger brother received from the rest of his family.

Our waitress's vulnerability twisted something in my heart and I didn't want to interrogate her with the same force that I showed Logan. After she brought us our breakfast, she disappeared into the back for a little while. Jack and I ate our food in silence, which suited me fine. My mind was racing with how I would approach her without repeating the faux pas I made earlier against Logan Banner. I didn't want to scare her away before she could tell us anything.

When Sandy returned to clear our plates, I broached the topic with gentle but direct words. "Sandy, we have some questions for you," I said.

She stiffened and held her breath for a moment. "What kind of questions?"

"The kind that might upset you. I saw you on the news the other day, talking about Aaron Henderson—
"

One of the plates dropped from her hands and shattered against the linoleum, spewing left over bits of egg and grits at Sandy's feet. She stood frozen, her eyes dilated and chest heaving. The cook spun around, looking toward our table with a worried expression. "Sandy girl?" he said in a thick, country drawl.

"Sandy," I said, trying to coax her as I took the other plate from her hand and set it on the table. I held both of her hands in mine and a crash of sadness swept over me. The tears that stung her eyes welled in mine. "It's important we talk to you. I don't know if you saw the news but—"

"There's been another killing," she whispered. She blinked and a few tears spilled down her cheek. She looked away from me and out the window, but continued to hold onto my hands. "Like the one that happened with Aaron's family."

Jack stood up and guided Sandy around the broken glass to take what had been his seat across from me. She openly wept for a few good moments. Flashes of Aaron appeared in my mind, tied to so many emotions. The love she felt for him, even now. The heartbreak she endured when he left her. The devastation when she found out he had been arrested and accused of committing such a heinous act against his own brother. The emptiness she carried deep in her chest in order to get out of bed each day.

Her grief and longing blanketed my psyche.

I extracted my hands from her grip, sure to give her a squeeze before I breaking our connection. A breath whooshed out of me and I regained some of my own emotions, mixing with Sandy's grief. I focused on getting my breathing under control as she got some tears out of her system. Jack had gone to work cleaning up the shattered plate, taking the dustpan and broom away from the cook when he had approached our table.

When Sandy regained some composure, she raised her head and looked at me with a blank expression. I handed her some napkins from the dispenser on the table so she could clean her face. She held the paper in her hand, folding it and then unfolding it again.

"Sandy, my friend and I have been hired to investigate a crime that may be related to what is going on in Harrow," I said, skirting around accusations pointing at Aaron. Sure, he confessed. But if Kyle didn't kill his brother and was under some influence, I had to hope the same was true for Aaron and the latest killer, Curtis Lance. "Can we ask you some questions about Aaron's behavior before he moved back home to Harrow?"

She nodded and sniffled. Jack returned to the booth, sliding in next to me. From the corner of my eye, I saw his arm move to rest on the seat behind me.

His proximity to me was noted and ignored to the best of my ability.

"How long were you and Aaron Henderson together?"

"Almost two years. The first year was mostly on-and-off, because of the stuff with his parents. But then everything changed. He got real jealous and started coming around more often, being territorial. It was nice."

"Why didn't his parents like you?" Jack asked. I winced.

Sandy stared at Jack in disbelief. "I'm black. His family's white. His parents weren't mean to me and they never said anything to my face, but the couple times I met them, I could tell they were disappointed. Aaron told me that our relationship made them real uncomfortable. It didn't matter with our friends, and his brother liked me—" Her voice hitched when she mentioned the murdered brother, Blair.

I changed the subject to happier thoughts. "Aaron moved out here to be with you?"

She smiled. "Yeah. His parents didn't want him to. But I begged him to give us a try or else we had to stop seeing each other. He showed up one day with a duffel bag of his stuff and said he'd give it a week or two. He ended up staying out here for almost a year, living with me."

"Y'all were down in Magnolia Plains, right?"

She nodded. "Yes ma'am. Before it was condemned and we had to move out. Before he moved back home with his folks in Harrow."

"Do you know anything about Aaron or one of his friends vandalizing the apartment?" I asked.

Sandy's eyes widened. "No. I had heard something about other residents taking out some of their frustrations on their apartments before they left, but nothing about Aaron. The apartment was clear when I moved out."

So the Nethergate must have been after the complex was abandoned. I glanced over at Jack and he nodded.

"Before Aaron moved back home, did you notice any changes in him or his behavior?" I asked.

She hesitated. "A few weeks before we got our eviction notice, he started hanging out with this one guy a lot," Sandy admitted. "He told me they were trying to start a rock band and had to practice a lot. But then he started acting weird. Distant. Never called me if he was going to stay out late. He started skipping his work shifts here, too. He got fired and didn't seem to care. He was focused on this band thing. It was weird."

"How so?" Jack asked.

"Well… Aaron never played an instrument before." She fidgeted with the folded over napkin before tossing it aside. "At least, he never told me about it. Surely he would have. What guy wouldn't like to be that musician that gets the girl, right?"

"If he didn't play an instrument, what did you think he was doing?" I prompted.

She swallowed. "I suspected maybe he was getting involved with drugs," she said, her voice wavering. "I didn't know how to confront him. Max, our cook over there, he tried to help me out. Other waitresses offered me advice. I felt like Aaron wasn't my Aaron anymore. When we moved out, he went back to Harrow and he never called or texted me. And then I saw the news..." she trailed off.

"Can you tell us more about that man?" Jack asked. "Do you remember what he looked like?"

Sandy wiped a tear from underneath her eye and concentrated. "Not much. I saw him from far away. He looked sorta average. Taller than me, like every guy. Wait, a little taller than Aaron. Always wore button-up shirts and jeans. He was either bald or buzz cut. He drove this silver car, I think. He hardly came around if I was home. Well, I mean, Aaron wouldn't invite him in."

"Did Aaron ever tell you this guy's name, Sandy?" I asked.

She shook her head, pressing her lips together.

"Aaron must have been trying to protect you," Jack said.

Her lip trembled and her face contorted as a fresh batch of tears came. She covered her face and cried. I stole a glance over to Jack, feeling something well in my chest — fondness, maybe? He must've meant to comfort Sandy with his words and the effect they had on her turned something in me.

We didn't have much to go on from Sandy's description of Aaron's new friend. He could've been human or demon. But at least we had more than some sinister shadow or monster.

Jack left one of his business cards and he paid for both of us in cash, leaving Sandy a generous tip. When we stood up, she remained in the booth. Max the cook watched us leave, raising his hand in a goodbye gesture. I tried to shake off the melancholy from connecting and seeing Sandy cry.

After we exited the cafe, Jack held his palm out to me. "Need to cleanse your palate?"

"She was so sad," I said, my voice sounding distant.

He took my hand before I could step off the sidewalk. The sadness dissipated and warmth replaced the desolate feelings that had resonated in my heart. My eyes squeezed shut and a stray tear fell from my lashes. He laced his fingers with mine and took hold of my other hand as well. The clouds parted and sunshine shone down on my psyche.

"So we're friends, huh?" He smirked.

I stared at him for a moment before realization dawned — I had told Sandy that he was my friend. I dropped his hand and rubbed my sweaty palms against the denim of my jeans. But when he led me back to the rental car with his hand at the small of my back, I didn't move away.

Somewhere in Harrow right now, Sarah's spider senses must be tingling because she could predict when I found someone attractive. By first impression as I had told Sarah, Jack Gregory hadn't been my type. But he was getting under my skin.

I dug my keys out of my pocket and unlocked the car. "You're going to need a time out if you keep this up."

FOURTEEN

With as much time as I spent with Jack Gregory over the weekend, one would think I would relish a little down time. But it felt strange being alone in my own apartment during the day. I slouched on the sofa, popping Pringles into my mouth as I watched reality television on what was once considered an educational network. I couldn't explain why I liked watching shows about wedding dresses — I had never been so entrenched in a relationship that marriage was a threat, nor did I know much about fashion. But dammit, if I didn't like the cattiness of the women on these shows as they made the search for the prefect dress more important than their relationship.

It was mindless drivel, yes. But it helped clear my head from all the crazy that battered me recently. Angels, psh. Demons, yeah right. An A-Line skirt with that woman's hips? Blasphemous.

My phone buzzed next to me, as it had been on-and-off all afternoon. Since Thursday or Friday, I shut out most of the world. Too much information, too many revelations. I was still digesting a lot of it. However, when Sarah's name flashed on the screen, guilt twisted in my gut. After a long string of missed calls and unanswered texts, I didn't know if I could even muster up the right words to explain why I avoided her or what I dealt with this weekend. Maybe she would have understood, but I had to figure out how to say it.

The journal sat on the coffee table next to my foot. I had tried reading it several times, only to grow frustrated with the content. Whoever wrote it wasn't great at explaining things in a coherent order. If anything, the handwriting itself was rushed. The descriptions were unorganized. Some pages were water damaged. The author tried their best to use simple language to explain the extraordinary — the Aether, the hierarchy of angels, the royal families of the Netherworld, the numerous, damp, underground caves — but I felt like the journal was more of a dictionary. Not anything to help explain the order of the cosmos or make sense of the shit Jack shoved my way.

Giving me this journal to read was like giving me the instruction manual to a nuclear bomb. The content was way over my head, and I knew if I somehow misread it, disaster was imminent.

Nudging it aside with my foot, I returned my attention back to the screen. Three loud knocks echoed throughout my living room. The banging on my door could only be one person. I should've known that if I continued to ignore Sarah's texts and calls, it was a matter of time until she sought me out.

"Phee, I know you're in there! Your sorry excuse for a rental car is out in the parking lot!"

I froze in my spot, reaching for the remote to mute the television.

She knocked again for longer this time. "Come on! I heard your phone ring so I know you're not out with someone! And I'm pretty sure I hear *Wedding Story*, so you better let me in right this minute."

Furrowing my brow, I stared at the front door for a moment before shoving another chip into my mouth. I set the cardboard canister on the coffee table and went to let her in. As I opened the door wide, I wiped any crumbs from the corner of my mouth. "Hello."

"Hello?" Sarah shot back at me. "*Hello*!? Phoebe, I've been calling you since Friday. It's now *Sunday*. We had plans. I came by. You weren't here, which is a whole other question for later. And then you've not only ditched me on Friday, you disappeared for two days. You could've been dead!"

"Then I probably still wouldn't have been able to answer the phone," I reasoned.

Steam could have spurted out of her ears. Sarah narrowed her eyes at me and barged into my apartment. She dropped her purse on the floor next to the couch. She scooped my phone off the cushion, checking to find her most recent missed call.

"So your phone's not broken."

"I had a rough weekend. I needed to decompress," I defended myself, snatching the phone back from her. "Pretty sure there's missed calls from other people, too."

"You could've at least texted back that you were busy or some shit came up. Maybe you were getting laid. I don't know. Instead, I've been imagining the different ways people could find you dead — in an alley! In a dumpster. Maybe on a sidewalk. Or the park. I don't know."

"Surprised you didn't call the police," I said.

"I was going to," she said. "If I came by here and didn't see your car or couldn't find you today? You bet your ass I was going to call Charlie or the station. Seriously, girl. Where in the hell have you been?"

I chuckled at her choice of words, sitting back down on the couch. Some bride on the screen was twirling in a beaded number while her entourage tried to hide their disgust. Right now, I was a little disgusted with myself. Sarah had struck all the right chords to make me feel shitty.

"Been working, is all."

"No, this is different. You usually at least let me know you're alive when you're working. You've been off the grid."

"It's complicated. The case I'm working is intense." I raised my eyes to meet hers. "Really intense."

"You better be sleeping with the guy because that is the only excuse I will accept."

"I'm not sleeping with him," I said, annoyed. "Just working with him."

"Is that where you were Friday night when you said you'd hang out with me and my brother?"

"You're starting to sound like a jealous girlfriend, Sarah. I'm having conflicting emotions about that," I teased.

Sarah threw the closest accent pillow at me. "Shut up. You know what I meant."

I shrugged, deflecting the pillow. "If I shut up, how else am I supposed to answer your questions?"

"I swear to god, Phoebe Harris. If I wasn't so relieved that you're not dead, I would kill you myself."

I saw the opportunity to turn this interrogation away from me. "How's your brother?"

She rolled her eyes. "Not around. He's been hanging out with his old high school buddies. He has nothing in common with them, so I don't even know why he bothers."

"What a dick," I mimicked her tone and she cracked a smile.

"Shut up, I know how I sound right now. I've been so worried about you and then David hasn't been around so I get all worked up with these thoughts and you could've been dead and what if y'all never got a chance to meet and fall madly in love or whatever."

I responded by throwing the accent pillow back at her. "You need to stop with the thoughts. People will start to think you're legitimately crazy."

"I know. You should answer my texts more often. It'll help."

"All right, I got it. I'm sorry for not picking up the phone. I'm sorry for making you think I was possibly dead in a ditch or whatever. I have had a lot on my mind so I haven't been talking to anyone. And I did mean to meet up with you Friday but other things came up."

"Like what other things?" Her eyebrow perked up. "Man things?"

"Like investigative things. And then I passed out at some point." That technically wasn't a lie. Connecting with the Nethergate knocked me out cold and then Jack had to take care of me. Sarah would love the last little tidbit. Not that I could really explain any of this Heaven and Hell stuff to her. I was still coming to terms with it myself.

"You are such a workaholic," Sarah said, her earlier anger or concern having deflated. She sank into the couch next to me. "You are on medical leave and yet, you still somehow manage to get involved with an investigation. How does that even work?"

"He approached me and asked for my help."

"So that's a man's way to your heart. Bring up

work. I'll let David know."

"David hasn't even met me. What makes you so sure we're going to hit it off?" David was a safe topic. Talking about David wasn't going to reveal to Sarah that she might be the least crazy person in this apartment.

Sarah smiled. "Gut instinct. Pringles, please."

I handed her the canister and settled back into the couch. When she didn't elaborate, I unmuted the television and we watched *A Wedding Story* together in silence. I wasn't convinced by Sarah's gut instincts. I could barely trust my own these days. But reality television, my friend, and her threats to set me up with her dorky twin brother took my mind off the heaviness of the Banner case for the rest of the afternoon.

FIFTEEN

Sarah's visit made me think about other friendships I had neglected during my recovery, specifically a certain partner of mine.

Julia Robichaux answered the door when I arrived at Charlie's house for the first time in a few weeks. Sunday dinner with the Robichaux family used to be a standing date on my calendar, after I earned an invitation by his wife.

Now I stood on their front doorstep, a sheepish expression on my face. Julia looked me up and down, like she was taking inventory. She made a face a mother you've been avoiding for no good reason could make. The Robichaux girls would have a hell of a time as teenagers living in this woman's house.

"Is Charlie home?" I asked. His car wasn't parked in the driveway, but it was the only thing I could think to say.

"No, but you can come in for dinner, stranger," she said. She opened the door wide and I stepped inside. Their house was dated but in good condition and nearly as familiar to me as the station after working with Charlie for a couple years. After we initially worked together on the Banner case, I wasn't sure if his wife liked me or tolerated me. Julia was a tough woman to read. Her mere presence kept people in line because she would call you out on your shit. I liked her as much as I was scared of her in those early days. Heck, I still felt a little scared of her as I followed her through her house and into the kitchen.

Charlie and Julia's daughters, Tessa and Jasmine, were sitting at the table playing with their dolls and mimicking something they must have seen on some cartoon. Tessa caught sight of me first, her face brightening.

"Phoebe!" Tessa squeaked. Her younger sister spun around and both girls were out of their seats in seconds.

"Where have you been?"

"Daddy told us you were sick—"

"Are you sick?"

"Did you stay with the doctor?"

"Whoa, whoa, whoa," I laughed, bombarded by the two small girls. "Give me a minute to catch my breath. Girls, hello. How have you been?"

Julia watched us as she stirred whatever was on

the stove. "The girls missed you, obviously."

"I'm sorry I haven't been by for dinner," I said to the girls but my words extended to Julia, too. "I've been busy."

"You don't look sick."

"Yeah, you don't sound sick."

"Girls, she's not sick. You know your father told you that Phoebe was in an accident a few weeks ago," Julia reminded them. "She was in a car crash and had to go to the hospital."

"Did you hurt yourself?"

"You don't look hurt."

"When I'm hurt, Mommy gives me a band aid and ice cream. Did you get ice cream?"

"Yes I got ice cream. My friend Sarah brought me some of my favorite," I said.

"Girls, why don't you put your toys away and wash up? We're having macaroni and cheese," Julia added that last part for me.

The girls squealed in delight and hit the table, scooping up their dolls and various accessories before parading out of the kitchen. I cleared the doorway to avoid getting trampled. Once it was just us adults, I neared the stove to see what Julia was cooking.

"How's everything been?" I asked, peering at the pots and pans on the stove. Macaroni and cheese, green beans, and sausage. My stomach rumbled.

"You know, the usual. Charlie's been spending most of his time down at the station these days. I know that temporary partner of his is driving him up the wall."

"How is Charlie?"

Julia blew out a breath, pouring the measured skim milk into the pan and then tearing open the cheese packet. She dumped the orange powder in and mixed everything together. "You know how he is. He doesn't want to talk about it or anything. He tosses and turns at night, if he comes to bed at all. I find him sleeping on the couch some nights. These murders have got him on edge, Phee. He could really use you right now."

Unease unraveled in my chest as her words brought back buried fears. After Julia and I had gotten over our strange stalemate at the beginning of my partnership with Charlie, we began commiserating with how he reacts to cases like this. We haven't had many like the Banner case in the time I've been in Harrow, but the few times it has happened, he sleeps, eats, and drinks the details. I would know. I was the same way. It was one of the few ways I bonded with her husband early on.

"I'm sorry to hear that. I know it can't be easy for y'all right now."

"I hope it doesn't get any worse. Besides the murders, I mean. I hope there's no more." Julia sighed. "It's already going to take him forever to get through all the evidence and testimony, while all of Harrow watches."

The girls stampeded down the stairs and Julia and I dropped the serious talk. Dinner with the Robichaux women was a breath of fresh air to an otherwise bleak week. The girls loved to laugh and tell stories, making fun of their teachers and the bus driver. Julia and I were their audience, though we were tough critics.

The girls were upstairs while Julia and I chatted in the kitchen. We were cleaning up the dishes when we heard a familiar car door slam and then keys in the door. Charlie appeared in the doorway of the kitchen. He stared at me for a long moment before he broke into a grin.

"You're here to tell me you're coming back," he greeted me, crossing the kitchen.

I barely had time to set down the dish before he pulled me into a tight hug. Julia and I made eye contact over his shoulder and she shrugged. Her husband wasn't the most affectionate person with people other than his family. I considered myself close to him, but he had his personal space as I had mine. I wrapped my arms around him and gave him a squeeze.

"Go say goodnight to your daughters," Julia interrupted.

Charlie pulled back and delivered a kiss on his wife's cheek before he darted out of the kitchen. I swear I saw Charlie take those stairs two at a time.

I turned to Julia. "What was that about?"

"I told you. He's had it rough. I'm gonna see the girls to bed. Y'all can talk business all you want."

Charlie returned downstairs and found me waiting at the kitchen table. I had been scrolling through some of my messages on my phone, clearing them out. We chatted about my recovery, which I had been avoiding. Charlie didn't need to know that. He told me generic stuff about the girls and Julia and I told him I had been following doctor's orders.

When there was a lull in our conversation, I cleared my throat and broached a more important topic. "Can I ask you something about your case?"

"Depends on what that something is," he said as he spread a napkin out over his knee. He mixed his green beans and sausage into the cheesy pasta.

"Do you remember how I asked you if you found those markings at the Henderson scene?" I asked.

"Yes."

"Did you find it in the Lance murder?"

Charlie's expression turned to stone and he looked through me with his dark eyes. "You know I can't talk about that with you, Phoebe."

"I know, but that's all I need to know. Did you find the markings at the crime scene for the Lance murder?"

He sighed, measuring his thoughts. "Yes. But that's the only thing actually linking any of these murders back to the Banner case. Never could link the Henderson case, aside from the manner of the death."

"The circle wouldn't have been in the Henderson home," I said. "Aaron had moved back, remember? I went and looked at his old apartment in Dundee. He used to live in Magnolia Plains, you know. The property's about to be demolished —"

"What do you mean you went to his old apartment?" Charlie's voice changed, his volume dropping. That wasn't a good sign.

"It was a hunch that happened to pay off—"

"What the fuck, Phoebe," Charlie groaned, putting his head in his hands. "Don't tell me you've been investigating the case on your own."

"No, not the Henderson case. Do you remember Emily Banner, Travis and Kyle's cousin? She hired a private investigator to look into her aunt's disappearance," I explained before he could launch into a lecture. "The guy asked me to help with the case."

"Then why the hell are you looking at Aaron Henderson?"

Not really sure how to answer that one. I couldn't tell him about Jack's hunches. Nor could I explain to Charlie everything I had seen. Angels? Demons? Human sacrifice if that's indeed what was happening? Or what about demonic persuasion or possession? My face scrunched up as I shrugged a shoulder. "The timing? And brother killing brother. There was a coincidence."

Charlie wore the expression he always had when he could tell I was bullshitting. "Uh huh. Next question, why didn't you come to the police with this hunch? Why didn't you let us do the work?"

"I've... I've been busy."

"Fucking hell, Phoebe. You find a break in the case, one that you're not even supposed to be investigating, and you don't even tell us. You know how this fucking looks."

"We just found it," I defended myself, leaving out that we went on Friday. It was a long weekend. I wasn't even sure how to bring it up. Being swept up into Jack's investigation gave me a different outlook on the crime in Harrow.

"You'll get your gun and badge taken away for playing cop when you're supposed to be on leave. Resting. Getting better. Whatever happened to that?"

I frowned at him. "I'm not playing cop. I'm acting as a consultant to a private investigation. And our cases happen to overlap."

He snorted. "Right, whatever."

"Don't be like this."

"Don't be like what? Upset that my friend is throwing her career into jeopardy? Pissed that she's not taking care of herself? Too damn bad. You don't get to tell me how to act. I'll be however I want."

His words cut through me, reducing the size of my lungs. I know I messed up. Sure, I might not have thought about it until I was sitting across from him but I knew that now. My flight instinct was kicking in because I didn't want to get into a fight with Charlie.

"I didn't come here looking for a fight, Charlie. I came here to see you. I'd like to tell you what we've found because you'll need it for your investigation. I want to help. I want to give you information." Inhaling slowly, I weighed my next words. I drew out the business card Jack initially gave me a few nights ago. I placed it on the kitchen table. "If you change your mind, here's his card. I'm going back to his office in the morning if you want to swing by. We could really use your insight... and maybe we'll have information we can share with you, too."

Then I stood up and controlled my movements as I made a beeline to the front door. No need to wait for someone to show me out. Julia didn't interrupt but I could feel her watching us. She came out to the foyer as I stormed through, pulling the door open and launching myself onto their front porch. I couldn't look at her. I didn't want her to see the expression on my face. I wasn't sure if I could hold my composure until I got to the car. Tears burned in my eyes.

You're doing the right thing, I told myself. *You're doing the right thing. Charlie doesn't see it yet because he can't.* My hands were shaking against the steering wheel as I measured my breaths.

Did you really come here tonight to help him?

I don't know. Maybe. He's my partner.

He doesn't want you working on the case.

He wants me to get better.

That's not what he wants from you, girly.

SIXTEEN

The next morning, I found Jack's building was unlocked. I showed myself in while balancing a stack of
files and newspapers against my hip. The tax accountant in the front office looked deserted — no
doubt, he or she had less to do without the impending
doom of a tax deadline. Jack's office looked dark behind the frosted glass at the end of the hall. Not
surprising, since his truck wasn't even parked outside.
I lugged my bounty to the end of the hall and leaned
against the wall, sliding until I hit the floor. Exhaustion weighed heavy on me or maybe that was the
paper. From my spot on the floor, I started flipping
through newspapers, trying to organize the mess I
brought as evidence.

When Jack finally came through the front door
half an hour later, he froze when he saw me sitting

outside. He approached his office door, prodding a folded newspaper with the toe of his boot. "You've been busy."

"Nice of you to decide to come to work. I've been waiting for you to show up," I countered, stacking the papers before I scooped them into my arms. I stood, using the wall for support as I got back up on my legs. "Do you have a printer?"

He nodded, digging out his keys and letting us in. He held the door open for me and headed to the far side of the office, opening the blinds. The morning light filtered in, catching on dust motes as I went straight into his office. Dropping my work on his desk, I fell into his chair before digging out a thumb drive from my back pocket. I jabbed the power button on the tower, his desktop computer churned as it came to life. While I waited for it to power up, I organized the newspaper articles. I snatched the scissors from the cup on his desk and began clipping away.

Jack eventually emerged, standing in the doorway of his office as he sipped his coffee. He said nothing about me taking over his desk. In fact, he hadn't said much to me at all this morning.

"This thing is ancient," I commented, tapping my USB drive against his desk.

"I don't like computers," he said.

"So you haven't upgraded in about five or more years?" The boot-up screen finally passed and his desktop wallpaper appeared. Some nondescript picture of Harrow architecture. Maybe even the Bellemeade House. I plugged the USB stick into the computer tower and waited for his computer to recognize the drive.

Jack entered the office and took a seat across from his desk normally reserved for his clients. "Computers are marginally useful in my line of work, if at all. If I need anything that I ultimately need a computer for, I can go to Victoria."

My nose scrunched up as the external drive's folder opened up on his screen. I opened the images one at a time, sending them to his printer. His printer chugged along, loud and jarring. I jumped back up and sifted through the newspapers articles I had carefully cut out, plucking certain items from the pile. Once the pictures of the boys were printed, I snatched up the tape dispenser and started tacking up the pictures on his white board. The Banner boys were to the far left. I put Kyle, the confessed killer, above his brother Travis. Next to them, I put the Henderson boys. Aaron, on the first row. Blair, on the second. Then, the Lance boys — Curtis on the first, William on second.

The top row had the killer brothers above their victims. The night before, I had scoured different newspapers for details and used the internet to the best of my ability, finding information such as when the boys graduated high school to calculate a year of birth if I couldn't find that information in their obituaries. I took the whiteboard marker off the tray, uncapped it and started writing out dates and other vital information.

Three sets of brothers. There had to be a pattern and I would find it.

Jack sat back in his spot and didn't stop me during this. He watched, almost seeming fascinated as my evidence exploded all over his office. I felt his eyes on me. Once I was done scribbling data next to the photographs, I taped related articles around the boys' pictures.

Jack cleared his throat and set his mug on the desk. "How much sleep did you get last night?" he asked.

I shot him a look.

"All I'm saying is, your lack of sleep is becoming increasingly evident."

"How can I sleep at a time like this?"

He opened his mouth and I brace myself for a smart retort. Instead, he asked, "Coffee?"

"Yes please. I should be upset you didn't offer sooner."

"You seemed plenty caffeinated already. I didn't want to add more fuel to the fire," he said.

Jack handed me the coffee after he returned from the small break room. I took the mug into my left hand as I finished jotting information about the brothers. Dates of the crime, names, even the part of town they lived in. I was onto something here. I need to lay it all out and have someone else's eyes on it. That's why I brought my case to Jack's office. He was the unlucky volunteer who didn't get a say in the matter. He stood next to me, examining the work I put up.

"So three sets of brothers. The Banners, from a couple years ago. The Hendersons from Friday. And then the Lance brothers from Saturday. I had to glean some of it from any online profile or memorial page people set up. But from this, we can see similarities with the Henderson and Lance murders. Older brothers killing the younger. Charlie told me they found a Nethergate at the Lance household—"

"You saw your partner?" Jack asked.

"Yeah, Sunday dinner," I said, as if the answer were obvious. I didn't meet Jack's eyes. My confrontation with Charlie fueled the casework that kept me up most of the night. Now I felt I had a lot to prove. I didn't let Jack in on that. "Anyway, so all three crimes had a Nethergate, either at the scene of the crime or somewhere else, such as Dundee. But Kyle Banner doesn't fit the new profile. Older brothers killing their younger brothers. Kyle was the younger brother. He's alive."

"Maybe it's not supposed to be a new profile. You said yourself you weren't convinced by Kyle's confession."

"I didn't think he was capable of committing the crime and after running with you this week, I'm more inclined to believe he was possessed or something took over. But even then, something isn't right about the Banners."

Jack took a moment to turn that information around in his head. He scanned what I wrote and the paper I tacked up. "According to the new pattern, Travis would've been the one to kill Kyle," he reasoned.

My mind raced as I pieced together speculation. Kyle couldn't have killed Travis. But maybe Travis was supposed to kill Kyle. The initial investigation of the Banner murder came rushing back to me. Kyle's strange behavior, confessing though terrified, clicked. "Of course," I muttered, my eyes darting between the two Banner boys. I turned to Jack. "Do you think Travis resisted the influence of whoever is behind this?"

Jack sat back against the desk and considered my question. "It's possible. Maybe something went wrong with the killer's plans and that's why there's so much time between the Banners and the later two crimes. Maybe he had to regroup."

The pieces fell in place from what I had absorbed. I peeled Kyle and Travis's pictures off the board and repositioned them so that Travis was on killer row and Kyle should have been the victim. "Travis was supposed to kill Kyle. But he resisted because he still had some control, or maybe whoever was pulling the strings didn't quite know what he was doing yet. Whatever demonic entity hadn't gotten his claws into Travis completely. They fought. Travis had enough control to keep from hurting Kyle. The two latest Nethergates markings were coal, but not with the Banners. The bad guy used Travis as the ink for the Nethergate and hightailed it."

"And Kyle's gone missing as other boys are now being killed," said Jack.

"If Kyle, not Travis, was supposed to be the one who died, what's stopping whoever from completing the task? That is, if his end goal is for the younger of the brothers to be killed."

"You can't be too sure what he's using them for," he said.

Tortured, mangled images flashed in front of my eyes. Travis Banner's body crumpled on the floor with his brains on the wall. "Someone — or something — is making those boys kill their brothers."

The door to the outer office creaked open, cutting off our conversation. Jack jumped up from his perch on the desk and he stalked into the other room. I capped the marker and tossed it onto the whiteboard tray before following after him.

In the lounge of the office, a tall, exhausted detective stood. Charlie. He looked more haggard than I'd ever seen him before, much more than he was last night. His usual tie was missing and his shirt was unbuttoned at his neck. Heavy bags hung under his eyes. His sleeves were rolled up unevenly and his khakis were wrinkled. But he was here. After our confrontation last night, I was sure he wouldn't have shown his face, much less like this. What happened in the night?

"Can we help you?" Jack stood proud, his hands resting on his hips as he examined the man standing in the office.

Charlie didn't look at him because he was focused completely on me. I pushed myself past Jack and stood between the two men.

"You came," I said, growing concerned.

My partner's gaze scrutinized me from the crown of my head to the sole of my shoe. He then looked around the office. "You wanted me to stop by so I stopped by," he said, his tone dry.

I hesitated before introducing the gentlemen to each other. "This is Jack, the guy I told you about last night. He's been looking into the Banner family," I said to Charlie.

"I figured," he said.

Jack was motionless behind me. "You invited him here?"

I shot a look at him from over my shoulder. "In case you forgot, I'm a detective here. Some stuff I can't keep from the Harrow PD." Meeting Charlie's gaze, I continued. "Besides, I thought maybe we could share some information."

When Charlie let out a laugh, the amusement didn't reach his eyes. "Share information. That's an interesting way of phrasing it. Here I thought I'd give you a chance to explain this mess you've dug up. You gonna tell me what I see in the other room, with photographs of all the boys involved with this mess, or am I gonna have to go in there and tear it all down?"

The intent in his voice sliced through my veins.

"We're on to something, Charlie. I told you that. Something that may blow the top off this whole nightmare," I said.

Jack grabbed my arms and pulled me back against his chest. I ignored the jolt of adrenaline that shot through my body. His breath heated my skin, his words delivered right into my ear. "You really should've consulted me before you brought him into this."

"She doesn't have to consult with you on shit," Charlie barked. "This girl needs to be taking care of herself so she can come back to her real job, do some real work, and not chase ghosts."

"How about you fucking talk to me when I'm standing right here?" I snapped right back at him.

Charlie ignored me. "Take your hands off her."

Jack's grip on my arms tightened. I wasn't sure if it was because he was protective of his job or me. The core of my bones could feel the tension radiating from him. "Do you want me to take my hands off you, Phoebe?"

Goddammit. I didn't dare look back at him. Jack might as well have been taunting Charlie with a red cape because my partner looked like he was about to charge. And if Jack was the torero and Charlie the bull, I guess that made me the cape. His voice was teasing, and I could hear the underlying threat. This playground posturing didn't distract me from how solid Jack's body was behind me or how strong his hands were when keeping me close.

I stood rigid, jerking my arms back from him and elbowing him in the chest. "Quit it."

Jack loosened his hold on me. He let out a husky laugh and disappeared into the depths of his office.

Charlie didn't look happy. His eyes followed Jack and didn't come back to me until it was just us two in the lounge.

"What the hell is going on here, cher? These murders got us scrambling. The boys are confessing. Same with that damn Banner boy. No one's connecting it back to him yet, but the media is starting to shout murder pact. And you were saying that these were connected. But I come here and you're playing house?"

"Okay. One, who says playing house anymore? We're adults. And two, we are not playing house or anything for that matter," I shot back. Everyone needed to shut their mouths about Jack because I feared they may start being right. I took a deep breath and continued. "The Banner case is connected to the latest ones. We've been putting together the pieces between the three, trying to solidify a pattern."

"And you said the Banners hired this guy?" Charlie asked, nodding in the direction of Jack's office.

"Yeah. Emily Banner. Her aunt Karen disappeared

but Logan won't report her missing. And now Kyle was taken from the hospital. We're thinking someone is trying to use the murders in some kinda dark magic sort of way." Describing it as magic was easier than explaining Hell or the Nethergates and it was a theory we had kicked around with the symbols found at the crime scenes. Charlie was from New Orleans. Hopefully that wouldn't seem too outlandish to him. "The Banner crime doesn't match the others, so it's possible someone is targeting them again to finish a job."

Charlie was quiet for a long moment. It was much better than being told outright he didn't believe me. "Find any evidence supporting that?" he asked.

I led him into Jack's office. Jack himself was sitting behind his desk, staring at something on his computer screen. Most likely files on the USB drive I left connected to his computer. Not that it mattered. All data on that drive was related to the case at hand.

Charlie's attention went to the whiteboard on the side of Jack's office. His eyes ran over the news clippings and printed photographs, connecting the points. He lifted a hand and grazed his thumb along the edge of Travis's picture. He then rapped the whiteboard with his knuckle. "Travis is lined up with the killers."

"Yeah, I'm thinking he meant to kill Kyle but couldn't go through with it. So he got killed instead and Kyle took the fall," I said.

"That kid," he said of Kyle. "He didn't have it in him."

A spark of hope ignited in my rib cage. Maybe it wouldn't be too hard to convince Charlie of what I had come to find out by working with Jack Gregory. "I know. I also can't imagine what it'd feel like to watch your brother get killed because he wouldn't harm you."

Charlie nodded. He then took a deep breath, running a hand down the front of his shirt where his tie should've been. I recognized the nervous gesture. "Travis Banner's body was dug up during the night," he said. "And not by us."

He might as well have punched me in the gut. I gaped at him, turning around the information. "I didn't see that on the news," I said, wracking my brain. I would have remembered seeing anything when I had spent last night looking at news and obituaries.

"Because we didn't let the news find out. They've been too preoccupied with the Henderson and Lance connection anyway. Best they don't find out the Banners are going missing," Charlie said.

Missing. Three of the members of the Banner family had gone missing. Vanished. Karen from her home, Kyle from the hospital, and now Travis from the grave. "Why didn't you tell me sooner?"

"I don't know. I had to see... I had to see something."

I stared at Charlie for a moment, waiting for him to elaborate. But he was too busy studying the whiteboard. When he remained silent, I looked back at Jack. "Why would someone dig up a body?"

"Why would you ask him?" Charlie said, snapping out of his thought.

"Because if we're trying to profile the person that is using the boys or influencing them or whatever, maybe it's part of their established M.O."

Jack cleared his throat. "There could be a few reasons someone may exhume a body. But in this case, I imagine it may deal more with a ceremony or reanimation. As Phoebe mentioned, maybe the individual behind all these crimes has returned to finish the job or correct old mistakes."

One word stuck out to me. "Reanimation," I repeated to myself. Turning back to the whiteboard, I stared at Travis. It wasn't possible, was it?

Charlie watched me. "Are you fucking kidding me? Phee, don't listen to this guy. That's bullshit."

A few weeks ago, I would've said the same thing. But I had always had powers and a hunch that there was something more to them. And if there was something more to me, then why couldn't there be something more to everything else?

"Doesn't matter if it's bullshit if the bad guy believes it. If he truly thinks he can reanimate a dead person, does it matter if he can or can't?" I said.

"If there *is* someone else behind this," my partner countered. "Which maybe there is, but evidence that Harrow PD has collected hasn't linked those scenes together."

"You haven't even taken a look at Dundee. That's the connection right there! Those Nethergates—" I shut my mouth as soon as the word tumbled out. That was the last thing I wanted to do, was mention anything about Hell or demons.

"Those what?" Charlie asked.

Jack sighed. "The particular configuration of symbols found at the Banners, in Dundee, and at the Lances."

He looked from Jack to me. "Phoebe, don't tell me you actually believe the shit he is saying."

"He weaves a convincing story," I said, half-hearted.

"It's one thing to hypothesize that's what's going on, Phee. It's another to actually believe it," Charlie said. "How hard did you hit your head?"

Wrong thing to say. That was the wrong thing to say to me. After a lifetime of being different and knowing my head wasn't normal… that was the wrong fucking thing. Red flashed before my eyes. Now I was the bull, angry and rearing. "You gonna tell me the churchgoer doesn't believe in a little evil?"

He's lying to you. He lies. He believes. He can't see the dark as you do.

The voice, nestled in my head, fueled my rage and pushed it out. "Or maybe you miss having me on the case so I can tell you all the things I can read that you can't see? Sure, I've been gone a few weeks, but have you already forgotten how I can get a reading from the evidence? You've known all this time I'm different, that I somehow know things others couldn't find out. But you believed me then. I trusted you and you trusted me. We're partners. After all those cases, all those hunches, you choose not to believe me now? When I'm on the verge of something huge? When there might be something out there scarier and more demonic than me? And you won't even listen to me after I've proven myself to you over and over, after everything I've given to you?"

Charlie's dark eyes found mine. The silence throbbed between us. This wasn't the partner I had grown to trust. But now, trust was missing from the way he looked at me. His gaze was hollow. He made his judgment and squared his shoulders. "You shouldn't be working this case and you know it."

His words struck me hard with a strange finality — proof that I wasn't getting through to him. If he could easily cast me aside, I would do the same to him.

"Too bad," I said through gritted teeth. "Can't tell me how to act."

His expression flinched after I echoed the sentiment he threw in my face last night. We've gotten into fights before over a case. We're both stubborn and passionate. But we burned in different ways. It never got personal until last night. Until now.

Charlie stood across from me, searching my eyes.

184 · KATE NEWBURG

I wouldn't give him the satisfaction of finding anything. I gave him the coldest, blankest stare.

He turned and left without a word. When the office door clicked behind him, I let go of the breath I
had been holding.

Jack returned to the office after making sure we
were alone. "You shouldn't have invited him here. I
don't like having the police in my business," he said.

I scoffed. I was the police and already in his business. "And you shouldn't have grabbed me like that.
Not in front of him."

"Perhaps we should just call it even."

"Fine by me," I said.

Jack moved behind me, his hand grazing my elbow before resting on my upper arm. I squeezed my
eyes shut.

"Phoebe," he said my name, his voice offering me
something. A chance, an opportunity, an olive branch.

I wouldn't take it. I wouldn't break down over
Charlie in front of Jack. He was gone. Emotions
racked through my system, threatening to explode.
Charlie hurt me when he reprimanded me for my recent behavior. I didn't need his judgment either. I
needed my friend to believe me.

*Why do you need anyone else when you have
me?*

SEVENTEEN

After Charlie's visit, I crashed on the couch in Jack's office. The mixture of sleeplessness the past few nights, physical exhaustion, and my confrontation with Charlie was way too much for caffeine to battle. What started out as resting turned into the first dreamless nap I had in a long time. I couldn't normally nap. But dammit, I napped the hell out of that couch and afternoon.

My cheek was smashed against the fake leather upholstery and I may have been drooling when a distant phone ring broke through my sleep. I grumbled, rolling over and repositioning myself on the couch with the intent to put off the world for a little while longer. But from the corner of my eye, I saw a girl at the coffee table, scribbling away at some printer paper. I pushed the hair off my forehead.

Tabitha Gregory looked up from her drawing at me, breaking into a grin. "Daddy! She's awake!"

Jack emerged from the break room, a plate in one hand and a mug of something in the other. He set the plate in front of his daughter and she plucked the quarter sandwich off it. She munched away, careful to avoid the crusts.

I could feel Jack's eyes on me and I peeked at him with one of my own. "Posted your daughter on guard duty?"

"She asked to sit with you. I asked her to alert me when you woke up."

"I told him," Tabitha mumbled between bites.

"You've been sleeping all afternoon," Jack said, sitting on the edge of the coffee table between his daughter and me. He sipped away at the beverage in his mug.

I narrowed my eyes at the drink, considering snatching it if it happened to contain caffeine. The creases on my cheek felt deep and fresh and a spur of the moment realization made me check the neckline of my shirt to make sure it was properly covering me. Considering the sides of me Jack has seen since this case opened up, modesty was becoming moot.

"Must've needed it," I said. If it weren't for the present company, I probably would've fallen right back to sleep. I'd sleep well tonight.

"I've been thinking about your theory from earlier," Jack continued. "If whoever is behind this is trying to fix the earlier failure."

My nose wrinkled. "You mean actually kill Kyle because Travis couldn't?"

He gestured for me to cut it. Oh, right. Probably shouldn't talk about murder in front of the six-year-old. I really did need my sleep.

"He's playing with his brother," she said.

My eyes locked with Jack's and for a brief second, we shared our surprise. He turned toward his daughter as she sat at the table behind him. "What was that, pumpkin?"

"You're looking for someone. The police always want to find people and help them," Tabitha explained. She dropped her final crust on the plate and pushed it away, picking her crayon back up. "But he's not missing. He's with his brother."

"Is he with his brother or playing with his brother?" I shot back, bracing myself against the couch and pulling myself to sit up straight.

She shrugged.

"Which one is it?" I urged her to clarify. "There could be a big difference."

Jack held out a hand in my direction, silencing me. "Tabitha, pumpkin, we need to find him. He may not be missing, but we need to find him."

"Why? Is he in trouble?" Concern laced Tabitha's features as she weighed the dilemma, similar to the worry she had on her face when she told me the good news about not dying and set me down this whole crazy path.

"No, but he may be in danger," I answered.

She grasped for words. "He's playing with his brother. He's scared, but he's with his brother now. So he's not alone anymore," she said, chewing on her lip. "Their mommy won't be able to find them."

Jack stood up fast and ducked into his office. I jumped up and followed. We left Tabitha in the lounge and Jack shut his office door behind us.

"What the shit?" I hissed and he pressed a finger to my lips.

He listened near the frosted glass, waiting for some sign. My breath stuck in my chest. After a moment, a faint humming of a playground song could be heard from the other side of the door. Jack's shoulders relaxed and he motioned for me to join him further in his office, moving right past his desk and into the old bank safe.

"What the shit," I repeated, my voice not so quiet as before.

"She couldn't know what we're talking about," he rationalized.

My eyes widened and I gawked at him.

"I don't want my daughter involved in this case," he shot back.

"Too bad! She contributed whatever she saw. I'm not saying we gotta pump her for more information, but if she saw anything else, her vision could be our best lead."

"No," he said, his tone firm. "Absolutely not."

"Fine then. What about Kyle playing with his brother? He didn't have any other brothers, and Travis is dead."

"I know what she said and I know how it sounds."

"Do you think Tabitha means Kyle's dead? That he's with his brother as in they're both dead?" I asked, my questions derisive.

Jack poked his head back outside the safe for a moment, leaning a hand against the edge of the steel. He listened for his daughter's humming before returning his attention to me. "I don't know. If their mother won't be able to find them, maybe Karen was too late."

"Maybe Karen killed him," I said, trailing off as my mind weaved an idea.

His head whipped toward me. "What do you mean?"

My words were careful and neat. "Maybe their mother's been behind all of this. Emily said that she had taken to unconventional methods to communicate with Travis after losing him. Maybe she's been tainted somehow. Touched by the same thing that corrupted Aaron or the other boys."

Jack grew silent. His jaw steeled as he considered the information. After a moment, he spoke. "Kyle went missing after Karen disappeared."

"Maybe she made the arrangements and took him away from Harrow. Maybe it was to protect him.

Or—"

"Maybe she's finished what her son couldn't do," Jack completed the dark thought.

We stood in silence in the safe, far from the innocent humming and coloring of his daughter. I leaned against the shelving, shaking out my hair from the dislodged elastic. Part of me wanted to touch Jack, even briefly. Something small and insignificant would be comforting. Too many thoughts ran through my head. His unique energy could clear my brain from those darker thoughts.

As my next thought popped into my head, I spat it out. "Karen also disappeared before the Henderson murder took place."

Jack cursed under his breath, punching against the safe's doorframe. I winced at the impact but he didn't flinch. He stretched out his fingers and flexed his knuckles.

"We can't tell Emily that her aunt has potentially murdered Kyle, much less played a hand in the other two murders."

"Then we don't. We don't have enough evidence anyway."

He inhaled deep. "If Karen was involved in this, if she did kill her son, she had to be have been under the influence of the Netherworld. Those Nethergates were too complex for someone with a casual demonic connection to build them."

"We don't know a lot about Karen either way. Only what Emily has told us and what I remember. Who knows what she's capable of?"

Jack looked away sharply. He then exited the safe and headed back into the lounge, leaving his office door open.

Emerging from the safe, I hovered in his office before approaching the whiteboard where I had taped up the pictures of all the young boys. The Banners, the Hendersons, the Lances. My eyes lingered on the Banner brothers and my heart lurched. Could Karen have been involved in Kyle's possible death? Could she have somehow been instrumental in Aaron Henderson and Curtis Lance turning on their respective younger brothers?

Such behavior would be far removed from the mother I met during her sons' murder investigation. But this potential revelation cast a more sinister shadow on the first impression I had years ago. What if Karen did more than finishing the job by killing her son and maybe even influencing the new murders as Jack and I had speculated? What if Karen wasn't the grieving mother who lost her sons, one to death and one to the judicial system?

What if Karen was involved at a much earlier time?

What if, years ago, Karen tried to influence her son Travis to kill his brother?

"How many more?" I asked, loud enough for Jack to hear me in the lounge. He reemerged in the doorway. I hoped Jack didn't notice the hitch in my voice.

He contemplated my question. "I'm not sure what you're asking."

"How many more is this thing going to target?"

"We can't be sure until —"

"Wrong — the answer is none."

EIGHTEEN

My phone blinked, a message waiting for me as soon as I stepped foot into my apartment that evening. I tossed it aside anyway, slinking off to my kitchen to make something loaded with carbohydrates and possibly cheese. Or maybe eggs. I raided the kitchen for any sustenance to put into my growling stomach. Ten minutes later, I emerged from my kitchen. I stared out at my phone and stuck a forkful of spaghetti into my mouth. Then I remembered how Sarah stopped by unexpected last night because I didn't answer her calls. I carried my bowl of pasta and sauce over to the couch and picked up my phone with my free hand.

But my message wasn't from Sarah. I pressed play.

Jack's voice filtered through the speaker.

Hey, Phoebe… I got some bad news this evening.

Shouldn't talk about it over the phone. Let me know when you can meet up. It's urgent.

I groaned, but a very private part of me was eager to see him again. I pressed the command to call him back, setting the call on speaker and the phone on the coffee table. I curled up with my bowl of spaghetti by the time he picked up on the second ring.

"Hey," I said. "Saw you called."

"So you must've received my message," he said.

"Yes, I received your message." I rolled my eyes. "What's up?"

"If you listened to my message, you would know telephone is not the best medium for this conversation."

Now he was just being difficult. I narrowed my eyes at the phone. "I listened to your message which is a lot more than I can say for most people," I said, enunciating each word. "Guess it can't wait till morning?"

"Not really, no. There's been a development and we may need to mobilize tonight."

Mobilize? Dammit. I stared at my bowl of spaghetti and whined before shoveling another bite into my mouth. Chewing fast, I swallowed and tried not to inhale the bits of pasta down the wrong tube. "I can be at your office in about twenty."

"No good. I can't leave Tabitha right now. I've already exhausted my sitter privileges working this case," he said, with a quiet chuckle.

Oh, right. School night. Disappointment clenched in my gut and surprised me. I pushed it aside. "No worries. Totally understand. Should I swing by your place if that works? Should I bring anything?"

"Just yourself and a grim outlook on society," he said.

It was meant to be a joke. Neither of us laughed.

Half an hour later I was sitting in the driver's seat of my rental car, unable to force myself to climb out of the vehicle. I drummed my fingers against my steering wheel as I watched the trees, dim light from the street lamp getting tangled in its moss. Part of me wasn't ready to go inside — as if I could delay any more bad news simply by not receiving it. The other part of me was nervous to see Jack because, well, I wasn't sure I could behave myself around him for much longer. Out in public or working in his office was one thing. Being in the privacy of his home — and conscious for it — was something else entirely. Six months had gone by since I last… yeah. And I had a feeling if I kept his company, with the banter and the touching, my bad ideas were going to get worse.

Perhaps you need to get each other out of your blood.

That thought had been kicking around in my head since earlier this weekend, I mused in agreement with the voice.

You should teach him a lesson.

I laughed. There was something twisted about the voice's suggestion. It was hard for me to pay attention to her when so much was going on. In a way, being too busy to deal with the voice in my head was a welcome change. But in times like this, when I didn't know what else to do with myself, I could appreciate the voice's verve.

Then why was I so nervous? What did she know, anyway? The voice was cryptic and sometimes insightful. In the last few weeks since she had moved into my head, she had enabled some of my less appropriate responses. But at least her commentary melted my nerves away.

I climbed out of my rental car. Heading up the driveway, I moved past the front yard and surveyed the outside of the house. Nothing too crazy it seemed.

Jack swung open the front door before I even reached the top of the steps. My heart jumped into my throat and he held a finger to his lips, indicating the need to be quiet. When I satisfied that requirement, he motioned for me to come to the door.

"Phoebe. Hey," he said, glancing past me.

"Hey." I shifted the keys to my other hand and turned to look behind me. Nothing strange was in the air from what I could tell, nor was anything out of place. He grabbed my elbow and ushered me inside. He did one final sweep of the front yard and locked the door behind us.

Could he see something I didn't? The possibility

was a strange feeling. I had always been the one to sense or read things others couldn't. Turned out, I didn't like being left in the dark.

"What's with the paranoia?" I whispered, even though we were tucked in his living room.

Jack excused himself to go check on Tabitha. I wandered into the kitchen and took a seat at the kitchen table. The room looked very different at night, dimly lit by the fluorescent light from over the sink. On Saturday, I was in this kitchen after waking up with no recollection of how Dundee turned out. The time between those days felt stretched into decades. My body and brain wouldn't know how to readjust to regular time once all of this was over.

After Jack returned from down the hall, he went to the refrigerator, scanning its contents.

"Beer?" he offered.

"No, thank you."

Jack extracted a beer from the back anyway. He kicked the door shut and grabbed a magnetic bottle opener from the side of the fridge. He popped the cap off and set the beer in front of me. Well, it would be rude of me to refuse it now. I took an initial sip, which turned into a gulp before setting the bottle back on the table. Jack settled back against the counter, his arms crossed in front of his chest, as he appeared deep in thought.

"So what's the news that can't wait for the morning?" I said, propping a foot on the edge of my seat and draping an arm around my bent leg.

"Emily called me tonight. Given our run-in with Logan Banner, I thought it was best we talked about this in a warded place," he said, gesturing around his kitchen.

I followed his hand, my attention drawn to symbols I hadn't seen earlier in the week. Maybe they were new. Any curiosity I felt for them was trumped by Banner news. "You think someone could be watching us, too?"

"Not in here," he said. My eyes fell back on Jack as he continued. "Karen Banner's body has been found. Harrow police found her in some abandoned shipping crate down at the docks and notified the family."

In the span of a few seconds, my theory that Karen Banner could've been pulling the strings behind all these crimes dissipated. "Shit," I breathed. My foot dropped to the floor and I leaned forward in my chair. "Any sign of Kyle?"

"No, not from what Emily told me," he said. Jack rubbed a hand over his face and exhaustion rested on his shoulders. Something uncurled in me, wanting to reach out to him. I stood up from the kitchen table and set my bottle on the counter behind him near the sink.

"Did Emily say anything about Logan? How he's reacting to the news?" I asked, searching his face.

Jack didn't say anything, gave one shake of his head to indicate Emily didn't tell him anything about that either. I recognized that expression on his face.

After so much after the last few weeks — so much change, so much knowledge, so much death — I was becoming numb to it. I didn't want to think about it anymore. I wanted to feel something else. Maybe my judgment was impaired. Maybe the dimness of the light over the kitchen sink set the mood. I couldn't pinpoint my motivation, even if one of my fellow officers interrogated me. All I knew was one moment I stood in front of Jack and then the next I leaned forward, planting a kiss on his bottom lip.

Jack didn't open his mouth to kiss me in return.

This was a bad idea. I pulled back quick, feeling the heat rise in my cheeks and any sense rush back into my head. What the hell was I thinking, kissing him in the middle of his kitchen and all this bad news?

"Sorry. I… that was highly inappropriate of me," I stammered.

"Why would you do that?" he demanded, his words deliberate.

"I need a reason?" I thought it was pretty obvious.

"You need a very good one," he said, his voice dropping low. He stood straight and loomed over me.

My head tilted and I stared up at him in confusion. Where was this coming from? I only kissed him. It wasn't like I threatened his livelihood or anything. If he didn't want me to kiss him, he could have just said so. I pressed my mouth into a thin line as my eyes focused on the cabinetry behind Jack's head.

Did I completely misread the signals before now or our flirting while out in the field? Did I misinterpret the vibes I got while in his office? He had been giving me bullshit the entire time we worked together. He pulled a prince charming and rescued me out of some very unsavory situations like the Nethergate in Dundee. He felt it appropriate to grab me at any time he well pleased. But if I kissed him, he was going to get self-righteous? Oh, hell no.

I needed to diffuse the situation and fast to save face. I ran my hands over my hair and laughed at myself. "I'm sorry, I guess I thought it would be a lot better than talking about all this death and work and—"

"You shouldn't kiss men you don't want kissing you back," he said.

"If I didn't want you to kiss me back, I wouldn't have done it," I snapped at him. He didn't flinch and I looked away. I was an idiot. "I shouldn't have come here tonight. Maybe you shouldn't have invited me. Not much we can do anyway, not until we get more information from Emily. I'll see you tomorrow."

"Phoebe—"

The closest exit was the back door. I grabbed my keys from the table and headed right for it. I've never taken rejection well and I certainly didn't want him to see whatever look was on my face. Whatever. Jack Gregory didn't know me and he didn't want to kiss me back. In the larger scheme of my life, this moment was insignificant. I'd get over this blunder soon. But right now, in the moment, I didn't want to be near him if he was going to be like that. There had been too much happening in Harrow. I wanted a distraction. And if distraction came in the form of Jack Gregory, paranormal investigator and single father, well... who was I to deny what the body wants?

Well, Jack could.

Except he didn't let me make it to the door. He caught me by the elbow and spun me back to him. For a second, I thought he would tell me I couldn't leave out that door but then his mouth crushed against mine. I went to push him off me and stumbled. He steadied me, guiding me away from the door. If he was trying to make it up to me or simply make me stay, damn. His fingers twined the hair at my nape, melting my pride as my mouth opened wider.

As I bumped back against the edge of the kitchen table, he continued to kiss me deep and erase any of my wounded ego. I hopped up on the table's ledge and his hands moved from my neck, over my shoulders, down my arms to rest on my thighs. Not knowing what to do with my hands, I held onto his shoulders, pulled him closer, cupping his face. Soon my hands gripped his shirt, holding him close as he leaned me back on the table.

Then I stopped. I needed to check something since the reason I was here and not meeting him at his office was in the other room. Pushing my hair out of my face, I asked. "Tabitha?"

"Asleep."

That was all the permission I needed. My fingers moved down his shirt and curled around the bottom hem. I tugged the cotton shirt upward and over his head. He lifted his arms and let the shirt fall somewhere out of my periphery. His shirt or its location didn't matter because my hands were on Jack.

He watched me and let me feel his skin. My hands pressed against his stomach, inching upward as I read him. I slid my fingers over his chest and then moved my hands down his arms, drawing out energy. His skin wasn't coated in inconsequential thoughts, memories, or anything like I usually found. The vibration at the edge of my consciousness mingled with an electric hum. Cobwebs cleared from my psyche. For a moment, my evening, the Banner case, and even the accident disappeared. My head swam with Jack.

Even the voice yearned for a taste.

He knew his energy was different from what I felt from other people. In Dundee, I told him he felt different. Deeper. Raw emotion. But when he was like this, all focused and aroused, his energy felt like the force of a hurricane. He could see how I was reacting right now, probably written all over my face. My eyes slid closed and I focused on where my hands met him.

"What are you feeling?" he asked me, his voice husky.

My face broke out into a grin. The energy was intoxicating and nothing like I felt from other men in my past. Almost musical. But I wasn't going to tell him those precise words.

"Something entirely new," I whispered back, opening my eyes to look back at him.

Jack gripped my waist hard and pulled me against him. He then hoisted me up off the table and I pressed against his chest, grabbing onto his shoulders and pulling myself up. My legs wrapped around his waist on instinct, my hands lodged in his hair as I refused to let our kiss end. He groaned into my mouth, circling one arm around me, maneuvering us around the kitchen. I wasn't sure where we were going until he planted my ass on the counter. I scooted to the edge, wanting to feel him closer. He hooked his hands under my knees and yanked me closer still. Snaking my arm over his shoulder, I pulled him in and we were kissing again. If he kept kissing me like this, kept pressing against me, I hoped to hell that his daughter was a heavy sleeper because I wouldn't be able to keep quiet.

He gripped my chin between his fingers and thumb. He turned my head and pressed kisses against my jaw line, running the bridge of his nose against my ear before his lips grazed the side of my neck. I shivered and caught sight of us in the reflection of night through the kitchen window. Etched across Jack's bare back were two large rows of tattoos along his shoulder blades. I didn't have any tattoos myself, but I loved them on men. I wanted nothing more than to trace the lines of the ink, memorizing them with my own body. Tattoos were yet another story for me to feel through my hands.

Maybe underneath all that heaven and hell bullshit and apart from him having a daughter, Jack was more my type than I anticipated. What else was waiting for me under the rest of his clothing? What other lines could I trace? What energies could I read?

My hands ran up his back and over his shoulders, grazing his ink and for a moment, white flashed in front of my eyes. Sunshine and green was all around us. No, not us. We weren't alone. Everyone around me was dressed in black and focusing on a box. A casket. The recitations of a preacher tugged at my consciousness and I saw myself. No, not me. A younger version of me. I had been twenty-two. Twenty-two when my dad died. His funeral was held here in Harrow.

What was I seeing?

Wrong question.

She's right — what was I *missing*?

The vision, however brief, pulled me out of the heated moment on Jack's counter. I pushed against him, needing to breath. "Wait—"

He must not have heard me because his mouth continued its attention on my neck. I shoved at his chest, wedging my arm between us. I needed space.

Not enough oxygen was in my lungs. That intoxicating, vibrant energy became the same rush clogging my senses.

Something wasn't right. No, no. Something was very wrong.

He's not the only one keeping secrets from you.

"The other day when you saw me at the school," I blurted. "You knew my name."

The accusation sobered him up, a lustful haze lingering in in his eyes. He pushed his hair out of his face, clearing his throat. "What are you talking about?"

"I convinced myself that you must have heard it from your daughter or maybe her teacher. I went to her, you know. Wasn't sure if something was wrong at home. But you didn't hear it from her or Ms. Jennings, my name—"

Whatever I thought had been butterflies were suffocating me now. My head throbbed. My ears weren't working right. Bright spots were burned into my vision.

"Ms. Jennings?" he asked, confusion spreading across his features.

Droning filled my head. I shook my head, trying to get it to spill out. "Tabitha's teacher," I snapped.

Jack stared at me. His mouth moved but I couldn't hear the words. No. The room began a slow spin. Colors blurred. No, no. Stop. My fingers dug into his arms to anchor myself, trying to extract anything to keep me from falling. I stared at his mouth and tried to focus on the sound coming out.

"Huh?"

He repeated his words. "Tabitha's teacher is Ms. McNamara."

It was the only way I knew how to talk to you before.

"I don't feel too—"

I'm so sorry, girly. It was for your own good.

"—good."

"Phoebe... Phoebe, stay with me — Phee!"

My body slumped, a strange looseness injected into all my joints and muscles. Jack shook me, the last thing I felt before nothing.

It's for your own good.

NINETEEN

A sharp pain of my wrists and the weight of my arms welcomed me back to consciousness. My hands were bound over my head. Hard concrete was under my ass. My head felt heavy, too heavy for my shoulders. When I managed to pry my eyes open, I saw nothing but blurred, dim shapes. Fighting to train my eyes on my surroundings, I focused on tools, buckets, a motorcycle, a lawnmower, some shit covered in a tarp. Jack's white truck sat outside of the garage, parked behind his house a good thirty feet away.

As my mind cleared and realization sank into the pit of my stomach, tension spread throughout my bound body. I tugged and tugged at the restraints, rope securing my hands over my head.

What the fuck was I doing tied up in Jack's garage?

"Jack!" I shouted, yanking harder at the ropes. "Jack!"

Then I shut my big mouth. What if something happened to him or Tabitha? Had I given myself away? I listened hard, waiting for any suspicious sounds to break through crickets chirping. My own breath was too loud. My pulse pounded in my ears.

I wracked my brain for what could have happened. Last I remembered, I was on Jack's counter and we were kissing. But the voice kept saying something and I couldn't understand Jack and —

Across the yard, the backdoor swung open and smacked against the side of the house. Jack appeared on the stoop under the porch light. Shadows cast across his face as he crossed the porch and stalked in my direction. I should have wanted answers. I should demand to know why I was tied up here. But the serious look on Jack's face caused my tongue to grow heavy and dumb.

Jack entered the garage. He pulled over a plastic lawn chair from one side of the garage to where I was secured. He didn't say anything for the longest time and neither did I as we sat across from each other in the dark. He watched me and I watched him. My palms were clammy and my arms were tired but he wasn't saying anything.

"What's wrong?" I cracked the silence, pushing the words out of my mouth.

"You haven't been entirely truthful with me,

Phoebe," Jack said in a collected, restrained voice. He stood from the chair and moved around the garage.

A chain clicked and a bare light bulb illuminated the space. My pupils contracted, blinded by the sudden light, and I squeezed my eyes shut.

"When you came to me, you never really said what was happening to you and maybe I should've asked more questions. Maybe I should've made you the focus of my investigation rather than part of it."

"I don't understand—" I started.

Something dark and angry rumbled in his chest. "Did someone send you after me?"

"What?" I gaped. "You invited me here tonight!"

"Before tonight. Has anyone ever encouraged or convinced you to seek me out?"

Yes. No. My face twisted and my mouth hung open.

"Is that why you tried your poor attempt to seduce me?"

Blood drained from my face. I struggled against the rope, leaning forward. My back arched, my shoulders aching as my arms hang over my head. "You were into it until —" My words broke off as our conversation from the kitchen came flooding back, no longer clouded in my memory. I had been making some powerful accusations and never got any answers. "No. No, you don't get to turn this around on me. You knew my name!"

"And you thought someone else was my daughter's teacher," he spat back.

That's right, he had said something like that before I… before I lost track of time.

He continued. "So I'll ask you again. Did someone send you to my house, where my daughter sleeps, in order to unleash some trap on me and mine?"

Daughter and *trap* jumped out at me. My face burned. "I don't—"

Jack jerked, sending the chair flying and crashing against the other side of the garage. My heart raced and I stared up at him. He loomed over me, heaving and furious. But his voice was low, calculated. "You tear through my home, chasing after *my* daughter during your rampage, Phoebe. And you don't remember it. So what am I supposed to believe? Tell me what the fuck I'm supposed to believe."

Dread cascaded down my arms and face, washing over my tense body. Jack's words made no sense to me but their implication and his anger made me feel the accusations he made were very, very real.

"I didn't hurt Tabitha," I said.

He didn't answer me. His face was hard as a stone.

No. I squirmed against the restraints, panic glinting in my eye. The idea that I had hurt someone, especially a little girl, twisted in my side and underneath my ribs. No, no, *no*. I was supposed to be one of the good guys. "Did I? Jack, I wouldn't hurt Tabitha. I didn't hurt Tabitha," I pleaded, not recognizing the desperation of my own voice.

Jack stood over me, sizing me up as I cowered under his scrutinizing gaze. "I'm not entirely sure what would've happened if you had gotten your hands on her," he finally said.

What would've happened to Tabitha or what he would have done to me? I swallowed back my apprehension and maintained my defense. "I didn't—"

"She got out of the way before you could get to her. So I'll ask again. Did anyone send you after me?" he asked.

My face contorted and I shook my head. "No."

The edge of his anger softened. The muscle in his jaw moved and he turned his back toward me. His shoulders rose and fell. "It's possible you're being manipulated and you don't even know it."

"No, I came here tonight because you invited me. And for whatever reason, I wanted to see you, too. I wanted to distract myself from all the shit you dragged me into. And I don't know, maybe it's dumb. Please don't make me say it." Even tied up in his garage and worried that I could've caused harm to his daughter, I didn't want to admit I wanted him. I didn't want to vocalize it.

He blew out a harsh breath and turned to face me. "Fine. Then let's talk about the fact that you don't remember the last couple hours. Have you been experiencing black outs before tonight? Maybe even before you returned to Harrow?"

Couple *hours*? My mind raced. No, no, it can't be.

Not since… Jack's words hit too close to home and I broke my eye contact with him. That was all the answer he needed, apparently.

"So you can't account for all your time in the last few weeks," he accused in a tone that I recognized all too well. I used it all the time in my line of work when I interrogated criminals.

"What do you mean?" My eyes narrowed at him, meeting his gaze again.

"Since the murders started, can you account for all your time?"

My nostrils flared and I gritted my teeth. "What are you saying? You think I had anything to do with that?"

"You were at the Banner scene."

"Because I'm a cop!" I shouted. "I told you about the news cast for the Hendersons. And when the Lance story broke, I was with you!"

"You may not remember everything you've done," he said.

He remained calm and I hated him for it, wishing I could shut him out. Wishing I could get something out of him other than accusations and calmness. What — did I want him to be worried about me? Scared? I had no idea. I didn't want this.

"Have you experienced any black outs since you've been in Harrow? How much time are you missing? Periods where you can't explain what you've done or where you've been?" He continued with his questions. His stupid, prying questions. He was trying to goad me. I knew it.

"No," I finally admitted and lifted my chin to look at him. "I used to have these headaches when I was younger, when I was learning how to read objects and people. But... but not in a very long time. Not until I met you." My final words stung him. I could see it in his amber eyes. Pushing the stake in further, I continued. "In fact, I only seem to have them in your company. So what does that say about you?" I sneered, petulant and turning this back around on him.

He crouched down in front of me, meeting my eye level. "Phoebe, tell me what's been happening. Tell me about what's going on in your head."

Alarms sounded in my ears. No, not alarms. The droning. The same droning from before when I was in the kitchen, right before I blacked out. I thrashed against the restraints, not wanting that to happen again. My mouth open and closed as I fought for words to tell Jack, thought of the words to tell him to help me keep the droning away. He didn't need me to tell him. He saw it all and grabbed my face, his hands wrapping tight around my jaw as he steadied my head.

"Are you hearing things?" he asked, looking into my eyes. "Is there a voice?"

No, no, *no*. "I can't..." I trailed off, feeling my mouth twitch.

"Yes, you can," he said. He stood up straight, leaning over me to untie the rope from around my wrists. I stared up at him, trying to make sense of the droning, his actions, tonight, and everything. When my hands were free, I clutched them to my chest. He knelt back down and took a seat in front of me. He grabbed my hands. The sensation of blood rushing back, mixed with his energy, forced the droning away. I stared at our hands as he maneuvered mine in his, rubbing my palms with his thumbs. Then he laced his fingers with mine, his grip tight.

The intent was clear. He was trying to help me clear my mind.

"I can't help you if you won't tell me what's going on, Phoebe," he said. He gave my hands a squeeze. "Tell me about the voice."

How could he know? How could he possibly know? I stared at him, unblinking, feeling the tears burn in my eyes. "I haven't told anyone about her," I said, the words falling out of my mouth as I focused on his eyes and the grip of his hands on mine.

"It's okay. It's going to be fine. You can tell me about her now."

I laughed and blinked, a few tears spilling. "How can you say that? I… I can't even talk about it. I can't even tell anyone about… what…"

"Do you want to talk about it?"

Anger laced my features. "Of course I do! I want to figure out what the fuck is happening to me! Why I even have this voice in my head! Why she tells me all these things. Why she wants me to listen and... and..."

"What sort of things is she telling you?"

I closed my eyes and lowered my chin. "That she won't let me die. That she'll never let me die. Only an idiot would be upset about that sort of thing, right? That was supposed to be a good thing, yeah? It was the first thing she said to me in the rearview mirror, when I was in my... my Jeep... And she was like me but not me, her eyes — Jesus, her eyes. That was the one time I saw her..."

My heart cracked and I felt like I was betraying the one person who sought to protect me, even in a creepy way. But she said nothing. Silence. Unnerving silence in my head mixing with Jack's energy. His beautiful and raw energy.

"Her name is Delia," he said after a moment. I lifted my head. He studied my expression before he continued. "After you lost consciousness inside, she possessed your body and lashed out at me."

Rampage was the word Jack used earlier. The voice had taken hold and I couldn't remember it. It felt wrong, having someone walk around in your body. Even if she'd been living in your skull for the past few weeks. "You talked to her?" My voice came out strangled.

"More like she talked to me. She's not very happy with me. She feels that I abandoned you in some way, that I haven't helped you as you need to be helped. I have a suspicion she's been connected to you for a very long time."

I thought back to the accident. "Three weeks?"

"Much longer than that."

I shook my head but asked. "How long?"

"You were about nine when you first were in a car accident, yes?"

I don't recall ever telling him that. Not that precise fact. But apparently the voice was talking to him through me and I couldn't be sure what she told him. "Yes…"

"That may have been the moment when she… joined you."

"No. No. She showed up the moment of the accident. She was in my rearview — I'd never seen her before…" my voice trailed off, as I recalled something said to me before I passed out. She said… she said I wouldn't listen before. Goosebumps ran up my arm and I choked back some tears. She — Delia — showed me herself in my mirror. She made me see someone else as Tabitha's teacher so she could talk to me. What else could I have seen? What else could she have fabricated?

"What is it? What is she?" I asked.

"Something more volatile than a demon and more rare than an angel. I need to do more research first to be sure. If she's with you, and she's been assigned to protect you, she will carry out that mission. She seemed… she seemed very loyal to you, Phoebe. Believe that it's a good thing that she's protecting your life."

If she had been with me for so long, had protected my life and was now showing herself, what other ways had her presence affected me? "Is she the reason I have my powers? My ability to read?" I had to know. I squeezed his hands, my nails digging into his flesh.

He shook his head. "No, I believe that power is entirely yours. But she may be helping shield some more frightful aspects of your abilities."

More frightful. I laughed sadly. "Why is this happening? Why now?"

"I don't believe in coincidence. We don't have all the facts so it's natural to fill in the gaps with happenstance," he explained. "But I told you at the very beginning, all of this is connected."

"And you haven't done a very good job at helping me understand why," I lashed out. "Just tied me up in your garage. Telling me all these things. I don't even know what to believe."

"Believe me," he said. A simple command. I wished it were that easy. My tears had dried and the information about the voice — Delia, I reminded myself, she had a name — worked its way through my mental gears.

Jack must have read my mind. "Your family lived in Atlanta, right? You were born here but moved to the city when you were pretty young."

"Mom still lives there."

"Then why'd you move back to Harrow?"

"What does that have to do with anything?"

"We've already established Harrow attracts certain attention. Did Delia convince you to move back here?"

The droning trickled back into my consciousness. Inhale. Exhale. Jack's energy. I focused on the strength of his hands.

Jack continued. "Forget why Harrow. Better yet, why a police officer? There are plenty of other professions you could have pursued to help people. Doctor, teacher, paramedic, counselor. Why not a fire fighter? Rescue kittens from trees. Pull people from burning buildings. Or better yet, if you want to protect people, why not join the military? You could've been fighting abroad, protecting all our best interests. No, that wouldn't have been close enough to the people. Here, in the city where you were born but you couldn't even remember."

My eyes narrowed on him. "What are you getting at?"

"Angels and demons flock to this town for asylum, trying to survive a very human existence. And here you are, serving and protecting them, without even a damn clue as to why you would possibly do such a thing."

I'd never thought of it that way since he introduced me to the reality of angels and demons. That the people I swore to protect could be anything other than human. Something greater than human. "If angels and demons are walking around acting like the rest of us, does it matter what they are?"

Jack stared at me for a long moment, the flecks in his eyes glittering. He cleared his throat and looked away. "Fuck, you are so very human," he muttered.

What an odd thing to say, as if it were a compliment. Maybe he thought with my powers... or Delia... that I wouldn't be as human? Or maybe angels and demons surrounded him in his line of work that working with another human was what he needed. With the Banner case and the connection to the Netherworld, our humanity was a solace.

"I moved to Harrow because I was looking for someone," I said, addressing his earlier question. After everything tonight, I should've been shutting my mouth. But I felt the words pouring out of me, wanting to tell Jack so much. "I didn't think much of it growing up. But when I took biology in high school, we had to fill out one of those charts about dominant and recessive genes. It was about eye color. My parents had brown eyes. I have blue. Blue's recessive so they must have been carriers, right? That's what I reasoned until I saw photographs of my grandparents. Guess what? All brown eyes. The possibility of me having blue was supposed to be nil. I asked them where the blue eyes came from, hoping that maybe there was some distant ancestor or something like that and they'd been carrying the recessive color for a few generations. But the look on my dad's face gave the secret away."

"You're adopted," he concluded.

I nodded. "I guess I'd always known that I was different from them. They told me that my birth parents had given me up, that I was born here in Harrow. After my adoptive father died, something clicked. I had to leave Atlanta. I had these powers and I thought that maybe if I found my birth parents, I don't know. I could get some answers. Haven't discovered anything new in three years of looking, until I met you."

"Phoebe—"

"Please let me finish." I took a deep breath. "I moved to Harrow to find my birth parents. And I became a cop because it was the best way I knew how to get to whatever truth there was. Like I'd find them and know as soon as I saw them. And it would all start making sense. The black outs. The voice. The energy I can read. Any parent in their right mind should've had me examined by a doctor but not my parents. No — my parents knew something but they helped me hide my powers for as long as I've had these abilities. They had to know something was up with my birth parents. Don't get me wrong. I'm grateful for everything they did for me. But there's something wrong with me. Always has been. I figured if I found my biological parents, that —"

"You'd be able to figure out what's going on with

you."

"So I'm here. Searching. Because no one else is offering up answers," I said. He opened his mouth like he was about to go on the defensive, but I shook my head. "I want to catch the bastard behind these murders. I'll help you. But if you're leading me on and got nothing to give me in return?" Inhaling a shuddery breath, I shook off that threat. "You have to help me, Jack. Because no one else has the answers. You're the only one I've found that can even begin to start explaining. Please don't lead me on."

Emotions replaced the droning and tears returned. I felt like I was going crazy and Jack was the only one giving me any information. Like he was the last life preserver flying past me in a hurricane and I was clinging to him. I stretched my fingers, untangling them from Jack's grip. I left half-moon nail marks on the back of his hands. When my emotions were under control, I lifted my eyes to meet his gaze. For a brief moment, he looked like he wanted to kiss me but he didn't. I was glad he didn't. Delia, the case, and even Jack had me so messed up right now.

Jack patted one of my thighs before he rose above me. He offered me his hand and I took it, letting him pull me to my feet.

"I'll help you for as long as I'm breathing, Phoebe Harris," he said.

"You plan on not-breathing before this is all over? Because that's going to be really inconvenient for me," I said, a small hitch in my voice.

Jack cracked a smile. Then he reached out and touched my hair, no doubt crazy from tonight. His hand ran over it and I could tell it was a mess. His expression was strange, transfixed, like he was looking through me. After a moment, he pulled me closer, wrapping an arm around my shoulders. I tensed, then relaxed against him. The droning was gone.

"I know none of this makes sense right now. But it will. Believe me. Harrow's a good place to start looking for answers," he said near my ear.

As he held me in a tight embrace, I peered around his shoulder. "You didn't tell me you had a motorcycle," I said. He didn't tell me to stop being a smart ass either.

TWENTY

Bed was where I should have been able to forget what happened last night, except I couldn't forget. Moments, like the flashes I read when touching an object or person, replayed in my mind. I was awake before the sun rose, trying to patch together each and every stray moment from last night.

Delia, if that was her name and Jack wasn't making shit up, wasn't lingering in my mind this morning. If Jack had taken care of her existence, surely he would've told me? Why would he have questioned me about her, told me about her, offering assistance to find out more about her, if he simply fixed me?

Last night changed the dynamic between Jack and me. Maybe it even changed us. I know it changed me. Despite the kitchen action and him tying me up in his garage, Jack crawled under my skin and got to a lot of the secrets I had held close and buried deep. While Charlie may have been privy to the benefits of my powers, he didn't know about why I had moved to Harrow in the first place — not that I would've prevented him from knowing. I didn't talk about it. It was no one's business. Now Jack held stock in my business. My parents helped me go unnoticed but I needed to find my biological parents to figure out why I was the way I was. At least, I convinced myself of that goal for years. Jack made me vulnerable and I revealed much more than I was comfortable with sharing. I figured if I stayed in bed and avoided going into Jack's office, I could somehow replace the closeness and scrutiny I felt with the distance I needed to do my job.

I stared at my ceiling, twisting my hair and replayed what Jack had told me in the garage. He had to do more research into what the voice was, but Delia wasn't an angel or demon. That part made sense. She was in my head, so how could she be another physical being? And the fact that any of this could make any sense to me made me want to melt into my mattress and never again show my face to the world.

"Delia?" My small voice broke the morning silence.

Delia? Hello? I prodded in my head.

Inhaling deep, I forced myself to continue past the ridiculous feeling welling up in my heart. "You said I wouldn't listen before. But I started. We were talking pretty regularly, right? And now you're not talking at all."

Or are you going to manipulate more of my perception of reality?

"Is that what you're doing because you think I won't listen? I'm listening now."

She wasn't taking the bait. Dammit. And even hearing myself made me realize how off-kilter I had become. Trying to externally and internally address a head voice, which apparently has a name and has been with me nearly my whole life? Someone, please institutionalize me.

"I wish you'd talk to me again."

What did Jack do to silence the voice in my head? What did he have to do to Delia to stop her attack last night? I should be grateful. On some level, I was. But there were so many unanswered questions — if Delia had been with me almost my whole life, did she remember my biological parents? Would she know why I have powers? For the last three weeks, I had wanted to get rid of her. But now that she was gone or not answering me, I couldn't feel more alone.

The feeling of lost hope was stupid. This whole thing was stupid. Delia wasn't my fairy godmother. She didn't magically have the answers, or maybe she did but now she wouldn't talk to me.

Something Jack said came back to mind. Guilt twisted underneath my ribs and I hated even asking this question. "Why don't you like Jack?" I whispered to Delia, hoping that for one last chance, she's answer me.

Nothing. Not even the droning of her presence. Idiot. I was an idiot. Rubbing my face, I sprung straight up from my bed. I had to stop wallowing and stop thinking about it. Maybe if I didn't try to contact her, she'd come back around. Did I even want her to come back?

On my dresser across the room, my phone vibrated for the fourth or fifth time this morning since I woke up. Jack had to stop calling me. I told him I needed a little space last night when he escorted me to my car. Maybe some coffee and waffles in my own damn kitchen. Then I could stroll into his office and pretend none of last night happened.

Dragging myself to my feet, I crawled away from my bed and scooped up my phone. The missed call wasn't from Jack. It wasn't even from Sarah. The phone number had the prefix of the Harrow-Creek Police Department.

Whoever was calling me from the station left no voicemail. I imagined Charlie calling and hanging up when he got to the automated message, sighing in frustration when I wouldn't pick up. But why would he call me from the station and not his personal phone? Did he really think I'd avoid his phone calls? Would I avoid his phone calls? I pressed the number to call the station back before I could rethink my decision. The phone rang and rang as I paced the space between my bed and dresser.

Someone answered and it wasn't the secretary. "Harrow-Creek Police Department. Chief Frank Roscoe speaking."

My heart stopped. Chief. Chief Frank Roscoe was on the other line. Surely that was a mistake. Surely someone else must have been calling me.

While I was on his payroll, I never really struck up a personal relationship with the Harrow-Creek police chief. And after the initial hiring process, I avoided Roscoe as best as I could mostly because I didn't want him to question how I found out information. Charlie usually acted as our go-between if I had any news or hunches I had to pass on to our boss. My partner somehow managed to make it all seem okay and not the product of my abilities. And based on the accuracy of our results, Roscoe never questioned the information we collected.

So why was Roscoe calling me now?

"Hey, Chief. I saw someone was calling me from this number and I was calling back," I said, running a hand through my hair and holding my bangs out of my face. "It's, uh, Phoebe Harris. Detective Harris."

Silence expanded on the phone line and I wasn't sure he heard me. But before I could say anything else, I heard background conversation. Then silence again. "Harris…" Roscoe said into the phone. "I need you to come down to the station right away."

"I haven't been cleared to come back yet, sir," I

replied and squeezed my eyes shut, embarrassed at how that sounded. He would've known that, right? Because as soon as I was medically cleared, I would've been beating down the doors of the station.

"I'm aware, Harris. Still, you should come in. Bring your badge and your weapon. We need to talk."

* * *

Gripping the steering wheel tight to keep my hands from shaking, I drove down to the Harrow-Creek police station. An ill feeling ate away at my stomach. When I first got off the phone with the Chief, I let myself think his call was about needing my help on the case. After all, I had been one of the leading detectives on the Banner case and if a series of new murders followed similar patterns, they needed me, right? The other detectives didn't have the insight I did if they were trying to link the murders together. I couldn't take an active role in the investigation until my doctor cleared me, but I maybe could work in the office if the Chief let me. I could look over the details and consult with the active detectives. I'd be on my best behavior around Charlie's new partner. Around Charlie, too, even though I was still angry with him.

Could I leave Jack though?

The stray thought entered my mind before I could snuff it out. Returning to the station didn't mean I was leaving Jack. I would be returning to work. My case with Jack was a temporary measure, something to help kill time and find answers. But as I drove from my apartment and pulled into the parking lot behind the station, I wasn't so sure about that anymore. I wasn't sure about a lot of things.

My rental car looked out of place among the regulars I was used to seeing over the last few years. As the Chief had asked, my gun was holstered underneath my arm and my badge was clipped to my belt. I made sure my shirt was tucked in as I approached the rear exit of the station. Nearly a month had passed since I stepped through these doors — the last time I left, I climbed into my Jeep and proceeded to the accident.

Anxiety crept up my throat and I swallowed it back down as the familiar smell of the station rushed to greet me. Stale coffee and newspaper. Lysol and someone's leftovers that had been heavy on the garlic. None of the uniformed officers turned to look at me. My attention snapped to the corner where the few detectives sat. My desk was empty and waiting for me to return. My eyes skimmed right over Charlie, refusing to settle on him.

Chief Roscoe's office door was wide open so I took the invitation to linger in the doorway. He spotted me and stood from his desk. "Harris," Roscoe said, gesturing toward his office door. "Go ahead and close that."

I did as he said, closing his office door. I approached his desk. In my three years, I avoided being called alone into this room. I wasn't good at concealing and I didn't want to be under his scrutiny in case he became suspicious about how I found out certain things. His office was various shades of brown, green, and beige with a large window overlooking the rows of desks and officers. Roscoe had also draped himself brown, green, and beige. He had been with the Harrow-Creek Police Department since he was a uniformed officer. Due to his knack for sussing out bullshit, he navigated the politics of the small town to be elected as police chief.

The chief didn't ask me to take a seat and he didn't take one for himself, either. We stood across from each other, his giant wood desk and its pillars of paperwork between us. He watched me and when I didn't say anything, he sighed. He straightened his brown tie and flipped open a folder in front of him. From where I stood, the file didn't look like anything special.

Roscoe cleared his throat and then began. "Word is, one of my officers has been harassing a member of our community."

Harassing? "What?"

"Harass. Verb. Intimidate or otherwise bother the fuck out of," he said.

"I know what it means, sir. I'm trying to figure out what you're talking about."

Roscoe pinched his nose and closed his eyes. Taking the opportunity, I glanced toward the blinds at the interior window overlooking the floor. Charlie's back was to glass but he wasn't working. He was sitting perfectly still. He couldn't hear our conversation but was he anticipating it? Did he know what was going on here?

"Tell me, Harris. Tell me you didn't go anywhere near Logan Banner."

Roscoe's voice brought me back to this room, this office, this conversation. Logan Banner? Anxiety rose back up in my chest like an aching case of heartburn. When I saw Logan on Sunday, I may have been a little rough. Maybe even harassed. But my intentions were pure. He even reached out for help and told us he was being watched. Was I imagining Logan's silent pleas? What about his note? I ran over the details of our conversation and I couldn't think of a damn thing that could count as harassment.

"I did," I admitted with careful words.

He crossed his arms in front of his large chest. "So how did you think doing any police work, much less with a family potentially associated with the media nightmare our murder investigation has become, was a good idea?"

"I'd been asked to consult with a private investigator that was hired by Emily Banner," I offered as fast and professional as I could. "Emily wanted us to investigate, sir. I know about Karen Banner's death. And that Kyle Banner has gone missing. Emily's wor-

ried about her family. She was worried about her uncle and her aunt and her cousin and—"

Roscoe held up his hand. "Be that as it may, the
Banner case is not for you to investigate. Especially
right now."

"It's not my fault that the cases happened to overlap. Logan Banner told me he was being watched and
his niece is worried about why he won't come forward—" I spat out as fast I could, trying to weave my
last minute defense.

"You're a decent cop, Harris. If it were me — if
Mr. Banner had come directly to me, detective — I
could maybe smooth this one over. But he contacted
the mayor directly. And with these murders in town,
it's got everyone on edge and the mayor wants to
know what's taking us so long," Roscoe said. He inhaled and picked up a piece of paper from the folder
in front of him. He continued with his deliberate
words. "You're a liability and I can't have liabilities.
Not now. Not during this investigation. Not ever."

Ice spread through my veins and I stared at the
chief for a long moment. My ears must not be working again. I shook my head. "No. No, I don't — what
are you saying?"

"I need your badge, Harris. And your gun. You're
suspended until further notice—"

"No," I said, shaking my head hard this time. "No
I can't give them to you."

"—Without pay, pending an investigation."

Goose flesh spread over my skin and the anxiety plummeted from the back of my throat down to the pit of my stomach. No, no I was a good cop. I was helping the Banners! Why would Logan report that I was harassing him? "No! Didn't you hear me? I said I was helping on a private case that was privately opened by Logan Banner's niece—"

"Don't make this worse, Harris," he said, putting a stop to my last rebuttal. Roscoe thrust a sheet of paper in my direction and I snatched it from him. My hands trembled and the words on the paper blurred. The tears burning in my eyes made it impossible to read the notice. Suspension. I was suspended.

In a swift, impulsive movement, I unholstered the gun and set it on the hardwood surface of his oversized and ridiculous desk. I unclipped the badge from my waist but stopped short of dropping it. My hand lingered, reading the earliest memories from the badge with a swift rub of my thumb. Images flashed in my mind. No more career as a uniformed officer in Atlanta. The first day I got to wear my own clothes to work. Shaking hands with Charlie after being assigned as his partner. The first Nethergate I had seen, before I even knew what it was, and the late nights we spent trying to decipher it. And then consoling the Banners after their sons were taken from them.

A lot of blood went into that badge. A lot of sweat. Now came all the tears. But I wouldn't let them fall in front of Roscoe. I lifted my chin and drew up the last ounce of composure I had left. "Goodbye, sir."

As I exited his office, I kept my eyes to the ground and weaved through the familiar desks. Did everyone know? Had they heard through the grapevine about Logan Banner's harassment report? Tears burned in my eyes and I ran right smack dab into someone's broad chest. My head jerked up to see who was in my way.

Charlie Robichaux. I backed away and pushed past him.

"Phee…"

"Don't you dare say a thing," I snarled, not stopping.

The back door swung open and slammed shut after me. The heaviness in my chest weighted me, every step away from the station becoming harder and harder to carry. Behind me, the door opened and shut, followed by footsteps.

"Phoebe!" Charlie called after me. The only thing that made me stop in my tracks was the hitch in his voice. I froze, the car keys in my hand. I refused to turn around.

"Did you run and tattle to the chief the first moment you could, Robichaux, or did you wait until you had enough of a case against me to rat me out?" I accused him.

"I didn't tell him anything, Phee," he said with caution. His shadow approached mine along the concrete and I could see his hands were held up as a truce. Spinning to face him, I narrowed my eyes at him and didn't hide the fact that my eyes were red and puffy. Charlie took in my appearance, the emotion etched into my face, the anger in my words.

"Phoebe," he said my name again. I hated the way he said my name. Like it meant something to him.

"No," I stopped whatever he felt from surfacing. "No, I was helping Logan Banner. I don't believe for a second he had any reason to report me for harassment."

"You remember how his wife was an old high school friend of the mayor? Small towns like this are all built up on that bullshit," Charlie reasoned. Then he added, "I didn't know you would get suspended."

"Right, you kept telling me I shouldn't have been helping Emily figure out what was going on with her family. Well guess what, Charlie? You were right. Once again, you were right. You always get to be right. When do I get to be right? How about that? I am so close to figuring out who's behind these murders. I could've helped you—"

"You shouldn't have been helping with that case or that Jack guy."

"And I bet you were more than willing to tell the chief about that."

"When Roscoe asked me if I knew anything, I couldn't lie," Charlie said, having the decency to lower his head in shame. "If it weren't for this investigation, I'm sure Roscoe would've suspended me for keeping it under wraps—"

"Your sacrifice is noted," I sneered.

Then I recognized the look in his eyes. That same concern he showed victims of the crimes we investigated together. That sympathy. His white knight syndrome. Except right this moment, any sympathy struck me as pity. I didn't want any.

"Fuck you," I said, jerking the car door open and climbed in. The door slammed after me and I braced myself against the steering wheel. I jabbed the key into the ignition and twisted it. The engine drowned out any noise or thoughts in my head.

Charlie continued to stand at the side of my car. He peered in and I refused to look at him. When he didn't move, I pounded my fist against the horn and held it. He jumped back at the jarring blaring and I didn't let go until he was a reasonable distance away from the vehicle and me. I reversed the vehicle, with a sharp turn of the wheel. My wheels squealed as the car pitched forward and I made my exit.

As I pulled out onto the main stretch of the road, I realized I was gasping for breath. My tears weren't tears of sadness but frustration as I steered away from the station, even away from Jack's office, and headed to the one place that had come to mind for more answers.

TWENTY-ONE

My rental car was the only vehicle in the parking lot behind Oakview Memorial. I stared at the brick funeral home, stewing in my own numb righteousness after the anger had melted away. No, that wasn't it. My heart was broken. Shattered. Crushed into a mortar by some asshole pestle. I didn't know if I could feel anything after that or how long I had been sitting here. Being a cop was all I had. Being a cop was what I needed to be in order to find the answers to make sense of myself — of my abilities and strangeness. And that had been ripped away from me by my own dumb-ass actions. As much as I wanted to pin my suspension on Charlie or Jack or anyone else, I only had myself to blame.

I had moved to Harrow for more answers. I thought if I could tap into the community, I might find more information about my biological parents, so I left the Atlanta to become a detective in a small, creepy town. And if I could find my biological parents, maybe I could find out more about who I was and why I had powers and apparently a mental sidekick named Delia. Everything had gotten so complicated in the last few weeks — hell, in the last few *days* — and I didn't know how to untangle the mess. I was benched from a job that was my ticket to finding my past.

Except... I had one more opportunity for answers.

I didn't want to see Jack after last night's debacle. I didn't want to see him when I knew I wouldn't have gotten mixed up in this case in all the wrong ways if it weren't for him. Yet my arrival here was related to something he said the other day.

A sleek two-seater convertible turned into the parking lot and glided into the parking spot closest to the exit door. The driver's side door opened and a pair of long, pale legs punctuated with black pumps swung out from her seat. Victoria extracted herself from the car and looked more like she was ready for a photo shoot than an autopsy. She looked in my direction and surveyed me over the frames of her sunglasses. She removed the glasses from her face, folding them up as she squared her shoulders and slunk over to my car. She came around the driver's side and rapped her sunglasses against my window. I rolled it down and looked up at her.

"If you're trying to be discreet, you're failing," she said.

"Good thing I'm not trying to be discreet."

A devious grin tugged at her heavily stained lips, a shade of red that matched her car. Victoria bent down, looking past me to survey the inside of my car. "Jack's not with you."

"Does that matter?" Nerves knotted in place of my heart and I was second-guessing my impulse to drive over here.

She raised an eyebrow at me and by the way she studied me, I was sure my number was up.

"I came here alone. I had some questions I thought you could answer. Questions about Harrow and your business." I inhaled deep and pushed the next works out. "And I need to hear it from someone who isn't Jack."

A soft cluck of her tongue and a Cheshire grin spread across her face, the dark redness of her lips contrasting against her white teeth. "Then we should take this conversation inside."

Stepping foot back into her morgue was one of the last things I wanted to do today, much less ever. The memory of seeing the dead angels waiting their entombment and Beatrix arriving and departing in a streak of lightning would haunt me for a long time. I didn't know if I was ready to go back there — who knew what else I would see? "Why?"

"I run a business, Miss Harris. I do have to get

back to work," she said. And then, as if she could read the green on my face, she continued. "I haven't left anyone out on the table this time. Though if you ask nicely, I'm sure I can retrieve a body for you."

"That's extremely unnecessary."

"Very well. Shall we?" Then Victoria reached down and gave the handle to my car door a tug. The door opened and I stared up at her. This was what I wanted, but now anxiety gurgled in the pit of my stomach. I twisted the key in the ignition, killing the engine before I undid my seat belt and stepped out of the car. She closed the car door behind me and then led me to the rear entrance of Oakview Memorial.

Victoria led me downstairs and through the hallway to her station. As she promised, no bodies were out on the slabs as they had been the other day. She went straight to her desk and dropped her bag before checking something on her computer. I used the opportunity to survey the perimeter, my eyes searching for labels or papers I could read. I didn't dare touch anything. I wasn't sure I could handle any vision this place could emit.

"You're not going to ask why I'm here?"

"You already told me you had questions. I assumed the inquisition would start when you were done snooping," Victoria said as she clicked around on her computer.

I took a deep breath. "Jack told me you're a demon."

She immediately let go of the computer mouse and swiveled in her chair toward me. She folded her hands primly in her lap. "Jack tells many stories. Is that the one that brought you out here today?"

"It's the one I'm starting with," I said, folding my arms tightly across my chest.

Victoria watched me, surely looking for some signal. "Yes, I am a demon," she confirmed.

"You don't look like one."

"And how exactly did you expect one to appear? Like those offensive media representations of hooves and horns?" She dismissed that idea with a huff and a wave of her hand. "I am trying to retain some sense of beauty and grace, Miss Harris, as long as I'm sentenced to exist among mortals."

Sentenced. Mortals. Victoria's words stewed in my head as I lowered my gaze to the examination table in front of me. "Does being a demon make your job easier?"

She leaned forward. "What an interesting question — what job is that, Miss Harris?"

"From what I understand, you prepare the bodies of dead angels."

Victoria laughed, throaty and clear. "Dead implies they were at one point mortal."

"Whatever. Fine, you prepare the bodies of angels. Does being a demon make it easier for you to do that?"

"Certain precautions do become easier because of

my nature, yes." She spread her hands out across her knees, straightening against the back of her chair. "Many angels and demons aren't that different, aside from how we manifest on this ground."

I nodded. "Jack told me there's different kinds of angels."

"Yes, but not dead ones," she said. I narrowed my eyes at her and a smile spread across her red lips. She continued. "As I said, demons manifest differently here on your ground than angels would. For example, the Nether population is greater here in Harrow. Creatures from the Aether rarely flock here, unless they are sent on a mission or otherwise committed. Mostly messenger angels, your typical guardian angel from lore."

"So... what? They live as mortals among us?" I asked.

Victoria nodded. "Angels get high playing at a mortal life – all those feelings and the possibility of death. They romanticize it. They'd abandon their posts, their obligations for a taste. They write some of the worst poetry. They envy every damn mortal. Demons though... Many of us are here on our own accord. Many of us are entrepreneurs. But demons that are forced from their homes to stand on these grounds, all they have left is what they bear when they leave the Netherworld."

"Forced from their homes," I echoed. "How does someone get kicked out of Hell?"

"Angering the right person, failure to perform your duties on behalf of the kingdom, repenting, relinquishing your vows," she rattled off the possibilities.

I stared at her for a moment. "What about you?"

"It's one thing to tell generalities. It's another to tell you about my past, my secrets." She smiled. "But what I carried with me from the Netherworld fuels my existence as you see it. It's all the years I have left. I burned a lot of my power during my first decade out of the Nether. One day I will become human and then I'll live until die. I can't think of a more disgraceful fate."

Disgraceful to grow old and die? Maybe angels had the right idea to fantasize about the human life. A knot twisted in my gut. "So then are messengers the only kind of angel you see around Harrow?"

"Not all angels here are messengers, but most. That hag Beatrix is one exception."

The angel's name trickled down my spine and I shot a look toward the door, expecting lightning.

"I wouldn't worry about her today. She tends to follow our friend around and since he's not here, we have our privacy," Victoria explained. She stood to her full height, approaching the table where I stood.

"Jack said she was like a probation officer," I said.

"Perhaps that's something with which you are familiar."

"I never served—"

"I meant in the sense that you also have something

to hide. And you have someone helping you hide it," she cut through my words. Her ice blue eyes narrowed and trained on me as she leaned forward, palms flat on the metal slab between us. "I imagine you didn't come here this afternoon to verify Jack's tall tales."

My teeth clenched and I focused on a spot past her head. I wanted answers about my birth parents, but since I started working with Jack, other questions have arisen.

"You prepare the bodies of angels here?" I choked out, returning to my earlier line of questioning.

Victoria was reading me like a billboard sign. She knocked her knuckles against the metal. "On this table, yes. Messenger angels specifically. After they've served their mission, they need to be extracted from this world and given a chance to heal before returning to the Aether."

Bile rose in the back of my throat and I felt like I was betraying my family. "But not mortals."

Victoria stood straight, her eyes unblinking. "Humans?"

"Yes! Yes, humans. Have you prepared any human bodies?" My voice cracked and the words came rushing out. "In the last ten years, have you ever prepared a human body in this facility? How long have you even been here?"

"Nearly ninety years," she said, her voice dropping low. Her eyes finally left my face and flickered down my body. "As much as I love a fresh human body, I have not serviced one here. Ever. This is a sacred place. I would not contaminate it with human blood."

My heart was turning to stone. I shook my head, trying to shake her words away. "No… no. Do you keep any records?"

Victoria tensed. She moved around the table, stepped closer to me and crawled under my skin. "Tell me, Miss Harris, why is the detective suddenly interested in my clientele?" she said before licking her lips. I stared at her as she asked the question I dreaded. "Who did you lose that ended up in my hands?"

Her eyes were death, ice, nothingness, and a thousand winters. An undertaker. A mistress of death. I had no idea what kind of demon she was — if there were different kinds of angels, there had to be different kinds of demons, right? She could lead anyone through the Netherworld, no doubt. Could she have really prepared — "Oliver Harris," I spat out. When her eyebrow quirked, I added, "My dad. My adoptive father. He was sent here, as were his wishes."

Victoria's shoulders deflated and her defenses softened. With one last trailing look, she turned away from me and returned to her desk. "An adoptive father," she said as she took a seat at her computer and began pulling up some search program. "My dear Miss Harris, you've suddenly become more interesting. It may even explain Jack's fascination with you. Oliver Harris, you said?" she said, paused in her typing to look at me. I nodded. She finished typing and pressed enter. "An alias, no doubt, but it's somewhere to start."

In all the time I spent in Harrow, hoping to find information about my biological parents, I should have started with my adoptive father. A messenger angel. On a mission. I stared into one of the fluorescent lights, conjuring up memories. Did he lie on that same metal slab under those harsh lights to be laid to rest by this ice queen? Were her eyes the last thing he saw? These thoughts crowded my mind, filling the void of Delia's silence.

"Why would they send a messenger after me?"

"Messengers serve missions," she said, her voice monotone as she repeated the information. "If one was assigned as your guardian, it can be assumed that you may be important in some larger scheme. The weight of that importance is neither known nor documented because, to be honest, I don't care. He may have been sent to protect and raise you or perhaps groom you for your fate. Maybe it wasn't even you — maybe your mother had something to do with it. Or perhaps your biological father was called away. The point is though, Oliver Harris was sent to you and yours to serve a purpose. He completed his mission so it was his time to leave."

"Leave? So what? Do they say it's time to go and call you? Who do they even get their orders from?" Shrillness teetered on the edge of my voice. The idea that my adoptive father decided to leave this ground, or whatever Victoria called it, twisted and scraped my insides.

"Those would be questions for Jack and Beatrix. I know very little of angels other than their bodies," she said.

"What happens to them after you finished whatever you do here?"

Victoria scrolled through her computer's search results. "You would know. We bury them at Rockhaven... just as we did with Oliver Harris. They stay entombed during the rejuvenation process. And eventually, when the headstone has grown dark and the family stops visiting, we set them free."

Last night, when I touched the tattoos on Jack's shoulders, I saw a flash of that mocking sunny day before Delia had taken over. I forgot about that flash until this moment. What was it that I was missing? On the day we buried my dad, I vowed to find out my heritage, because my dad had always been supportive of me and my abilities. I wanted to find the truth, so we could both be at peace. I thought if I had found my biological father and got answers for my abilities, everything would suddenly make sense in the world and my dad, in whatever afterlife he found himself in, would know and feel it. But maybe he knew this whole time. Maybe he knew from the very beginning...

"What does that mean, set them free?" I asked to

keep from dwelling on the implications of my dad's status in the community. If I could focus on facts, find out more information, I could sort it out later when Victoria or anyone wasn't near me.

"Oakview is my day job. Rockhaven is my night job. If you ask really nicely, I can take you on a ride along. I have one such appointment tonight if you would like to see with your own eyes."

"I'm sorry. I found out my adoptive father was a messenger angel. I could do without the invitations," I muttered, pushing my hair out of my face.

"Perhaps you should be less concerned about who Oliver Harris *was* and more concerned with whom you *are* currently spending a great deal of time."

Stopping mid-step, I turned to Victoria. Her meaning was clear.

"He tells you all these stories and you two go on your little adventures. Haven't you wondered how he knows all this?"

"He did his work," I said, growing doubtful. "He learned like I'm learning."

Victoria laughed. "Charming idea. But you haven't begun to scratch the surface when it comes to Jack Gregory. You should pay more attention to the company that you keep."

Delia told me the same thing. And now I was hearing it again from Victoria. My phone interrupted our conversation with a melodic ring tone. Extracting it from my pocket, I found Jack's name on the screen.

Speak of the devil.

"This is Phoebe," I greeted him with my most professional voice, faking any composure I had to right now but grateful for the distraction.

Except the person on the other end of the line definitely wasn't Jack. The sniffling was definitely not that of a grown man, but a little girl. His daughter.

"Tabitha?" The small whine told me I was right. Victoria was out of her seat and approaching me fast. I gripped the phone and dug out my car keys. "What's wrong?"

"My daddy isn't here. He supposed to pick me up from school, but he didn't get me today," she blurted out. "And he's not home."

My eyes searched for the wall clock I had seen earlier and checked the time. It was a couple hours after school would've let out. "Does he ever stay late at the office? Do you have that number?"

More crying came over the phone. "I don't know."

I made eye contact with Victoria, which was a mistake. If I thought her eyes were ice before, they were full on winter storm now. "Okay," I said to Tabitha as I stepped back from Victoria. "Okay. Make sure the doors are locked. Keep this phone with you. I'll be there soon, Tabitha."

As soon as I hung up the phone, Victoria was in my face and her voice dripped with venom. "Why on Earth would she call you?"

"Perhaps because she wants a cop and not a morti-

cian to be able to find her father," I said, sliding my
phone into my back pocket before making my exit.

My confidence was shaken. The truth about my dad
— my adoptive one — rattled around in my head as I
approached the Gregory house. Unemployment
loomed for another time. Despite all of this and a
hundred other bad feelings, I had to help Tabitha
Gregory.

Not wanting to alert anyone or anything to my
presence, I parked my rental car down the street. All I
focused on was the fact that Tabitha called me for
help. And even with that, I wasn't sure what I was
getting into.

I approached the house quietly, scoping out the
yard and the neighbors before ducking along the side
of the house. Walking as briskly as I could without
drawing attention, I made my way up the driveway to
the back porch. I squinted at the tree line behind the

detached garage where I was tied up the night before. Jack's white truck was nowhere to be seen. I inhaled deep, spreading my fingers out and sought to detect any strange energy in the air. Whatever Jack was facing wasn't near his house from what I could tell.

I stalked up the back steps, onto the porch. Banging on the door, I spoke up. "Tabitha, it's me, Phoebe. You can open the door."

And then I waited. A moment passed until I saw the mop of hair and one dark eye peek out at me from between the blinds. I waved at her and she stared for a long moment before dropping the blinds. With a small struggle, she undid the lock and opened the kitchen door.

"Hey, girl," I said with a small smile. "Your dad home yet?"

Tabitha shook her head, pressing her mouth together and wiping her nose with her wrist. Tears had dried on her face.

"Can I come in?" I asked.

She hesitated and then I remembered. Jack said I — or Delia, to be precise — had torn through the house the night before and gone after Tabitha. What was it that Jack had said? That he wasn't sure what Delia would've done if she had gotten her hands on his daughter? I felt so guilty over the possibility of hurting her, even if it wasn't *me*. Of course she's nervous at the sight of me.

I crouched down to her level, stealing a glance to

the garage before meeting her wide-eyed gaze. "Hey, I don't remember what happened here last night. Your dad told me about it a little bit, but I don't know what I did. So if I hurt you in any way—"

"It wasn't you," she said, fiddling with the bottom of her shirt. "It was some other lady that looked like you. She went away. My daddy scared her."

That was a big chunk that was missing for Jack's story about last night. He didn't tell me what he did to silence Delia. He had to have done something — she was absent from my mind this morning and she hasn't nagged me at all today. "Is there anything I can do to prove to you that she's not coming back?" I asked.

Tabitha stared at me with her big brown eyes like she was reading something deep inside me. Maybe that's how she knew about my earlier accident — she could sense it when she saw me.

"Count to fifteen so I can go back to my room?" she requested.

I stood up straight. "All right. I can do that. One, two, three…"

She turned and ran from the kitchen as I counted, banking right down the hallway and into the direction of her room. While she scurried, I opened the door wider so she could hear me counting and so I could survey the damage done to the kitchen. A fight had broken out here the night before. The table was on its side, as well as a couple of the chairs.

"Seven, eight, nine…" I continued to count down,

pacing myself as I stepped into the kitchen before reaching fifteen. Closing the kitchen door behind me, my eyes ran over the knocked over furniture and debris littering the floor.

I reached out to the table's edge, curling my fingers around it and focusing. An image jolted into my brain, more of a feeling than anything concrete. Lashing limbs and taunting. Something was wrong with my eyes. But nothing else came of the vision. I gripped with my other hand, squeezing the table's ledge tight for any more information. Nothing but silence.

"Phoebe?" Tabitha's small voice broke through my concentration.

"Twelve, thirteen, fourteen, fifteen," I spat out quickly. I exited the kitchen and turned down the hallway. The damage from the fight extended here. Books and picture frames littering the floor. More disturbingly, claw marks were burned into the wallpaper. I pressed my palm against the marks and tried to concentrate, but nothing. Maybe even in her muted state, Delia was altering my perception so I couldn't find out more about her.

I felt Tabitha's eyes on me. Yeah, I was acting strange but at least I wasn't tearing through her house. She watched me as curious as I felt about the wall.

"What was she like?" I asked, running my fingertips over the claw marks, which originated halfway down the hall and dragged toward the bathroom.

Tabitha's head peeked out from the door and when I looked over at her, she disappeared back into her room. "Scary. Mean. Loud."

Maybe I shouldn't have empathized with Delia. Sure, she was a voice in my head and Jack said she was loyal to me. But what did it mean to have a monster loyal to you? She wasn't an angel or demon. She wasn't even human. Was Delia the reason why my dad was assigned to me as a messenger angel?

My hand trailed the wall that Delia had destroyed the night before as I moved down the hallway to right outside Tabitha's room. Her doorframe was littered with symbols carved into the wood. If I didn't know better, I would say the symbols protected her.

"Those are my runes. Daddy says that if anything scary ever happens, all I have to do is get to my room and I'll be safe," Tabitha said, as if she could read my mind. I looked down at her and saw she was also looking up at them, almost proudly.

My eyes went back to the runes. They didn't look anything like the kind of symbols used to make the Nethergates. The runes lining the threshold must have been a different language. "Did you hide in your room last night when Delia showed up?"

She chewed on her bottom lip and then nodded.

"I am so sorry, Tabitha. You have to know, I wouldn't have done that—"

"You didn't do it. It wasn't you. She looked like you but not. And Daddy fixed it."

Once this whole case was over, I would explore more into what Delia was, especially if she was able to take control of my body. She was dangerous. I was dangerous. And if she was the reason my dad had to watch over me, then I needed to take responsibility for her and learn as much as I can. But for now, I had to find Jack.

"You called me from your dad's number," I said, focusing my attention on Tabitha now. "Do you have his phone?"

Tabitha's face lit up and she ran to the other side of her room. She grabbed a phone off her dresser and returned to me. She tentatively stuck her hand past the threshold of the door. I held out my hand and caught the phone when she dropped it.

"I tried calling him when he wasn't home. And then his phone was ringing on the couch," she explained before chewing at her lip again.

"Good detective work," I said, flashing her a small smile.

Turning the phone over and around in my hand, I flipped it open and blew out a breath of relief when it wasn't locked. I wasn't even sure an older model flip phone like this would have a security feature, but thank god, Jack didn't think to do that. I navigated through his voice messages, seeing one from earlier today. "Do you have any relatives nearby? An aunt or uncle?"

Tabitha shook her head. "No, but I have a grandma."

That's right. Jack left Tabitha in her grandmother's care a few nights ago. "Do you know where she lives or how to get there?"

"Sometimes Daddy leaves notes for the babysitters with grandma's number," she offered.

"Don't worry. I'll find it," I said. "I'm going to take a look around and see what I can find. How about you pack a bag to stay with your grandmother, okay?"

As Tabitha gathered her things, I headed into the living room. I rummaged through the drawers on the coffee table and side tables. After some digging I found an index card with emergency numbers written on it as well as a name, phone number, and street address for Tabitha's grandmother. Excellent.

I dug out my own phone and dialed the number, figuring if I needed it later, I'd have it saved in my call log. The phone rang for a moment until a soft click. "Hello?" An older woman answered.

"Hello, Nancy. My name is Phoebe Harris and I'm with the Harrow-Creek Police Department," I introduced myself. "I'm also a friend of Jack's. Your granddaughter called me because her dad hasn't come home yet. I'm sure he got wrapped up in work, but could I drop her off with you while I take a look?" Silence stretched on the other line, so long I thought I had lost her. "Nancy?"

"Yes, of course. Of course you can," she said.

Nancy verified her address for me and we said our goodbyes.

Any number in his recent call log could potentially point me in the right direction of finding Jack. The first entry was an unsaved number. When I called it back, there was no answer so I began scrolling through the few more recent names in the call log — Emily Banner, obviously. Vic — must've been Victoria. Jealousy panted in my gut and over what? The fact that he has a demon in his phone under some nickname? I rolled my eyes at myself and continued to scroll, freezing on a certain name. A name I never in a million years would have imagined I'd see in Jack's phone.

Justine Harris.

I stared at the screen, flipped the phone closed and re-opened it as if I were seeing something and that would reset reality. My mom's name remained in his phone. Without a second thought, I jammed the dial button and his phone started calling. It rang twice.

"What do you want?" a familiar woman answered the call, disdain in her voice. That was how my mom had answered a call she believed to be from Jack? Chills spread across my skin and froze any blood in my chest. Mom let out an impatient breath into the phone, a sound I knew very well. "I told you, Jack. You can't call me. She's out of our hands now. We tried keeping her away from Harrow but she's an adult. You should talk to Beatrix—"

Before I could hear another word, I snapped the phone shut.

The numbness stretched into minutes. My mom. My *mom*. She didn't only know Jack. She knew him well enough to answer like that. Jack had called her about me before. She... she knew about the angel Beatrix.

What was going on here?

My dad was a messenger angel. My mom was somehow in contact with Jack and apparently Beatrix. Oxygen couldn't thaw out my lungs fast enough. I inhaled deeply, unable to get enough air.

Focus, Phoebe. Focus on why you were called here — to get Tabitha to safety. I shoved the revelation of my adoptive parents far into the recesses of my mind, where Delia used to take up residence. I had to focus on helping Tabitha or I would vomit. For years — for nearly ten years I had searched for information about my biological parents. For fucking years. And now the ones who raised me were equally suspicious.

No, I can't focus on those thoughts right now. I had to help Tabitha. Then I could find Jack and when I found him, I wanted answers, I didn't care if I had to beat them out of him and I meant that down to my bones. Victoria had told me I hadn't begun to scratch the surface of Jack yet. Delia had warned me about Harrow. And my mother's phone number was in his phone. Jack knew much more than he was letting on and he was holding out on me.

But right now, in this very moment, I had to help Tabitha.

First, I deleted the call to my mom from the phone's log, removing evidence that the phone call had taken place. Then I searched through the phone. Jack didn't have many other contacts beyond what was already in his call log. The temptation to erase my mom's number had to be tossed aside. I didn't want Jack to know what I knew until I knew what he did.

Glancing around the room, my eyes landed on a pair of double doors leading from the living room. The doors, with large windowpanes, were ajar. From this side of the glass, the room appeared to be Jack's home office. I stood up, shoving his phone into my front pocket and mine into my back pocket before I wandered into the other room.

Jack's office was large considering the rest of the house. Bookshelves were crammed with leather-bound books, the binding worn from constant reading. Small paintings hung on the whitewashed paneled walls. Dust had not settled and Jack's familiar vibrations lingered in this place. Yet there were no pictures of his late wife, Tabitha's mother. Perhaps it was too hard for Jack to look at her on a regular basis, since it was apparent he spent a lot of time in here. But that would explain why he didn't keep a picture of her at work. Her absence in his home office struck me odd.

My eyes were drawn to a wall safe, the door ajar

and hidden behind some framed folk art. The contents of the safe were emptied, most likely with Jack or spread across this desk. I examined the inside of the safe anyway, a trace of Jack's energy on the metal. However, when I moved the door to take a look at the painting, a memory sparked — not Jack's, no. But his late wife's.

A glimpse of Jack purchasing the painting from a street vendor on a square. The warmth of new love. Infatuation. Then cardboard boxes and an empty house. This house.

My hand drew back, disconnecting from the vision before I saw more than I dared.

She must have loved that painting for me to find that memory years later.

I stood there for a moment, staring at the swirls of blue and yellow paint. I shook my hand, trying to rid myself of the feeling that accompanied the painting. Jack didn't have photographs of his late wife but he used mementos, evidence of their relationship, guarding whatever he deemed important enough to conceal in a wall safe.

I went to Jack's desk to find what he could have pulled from the safe. His desk was cluttered, the resting place of several haphazardly stacked books and a smattering of papers, proving that his home office was much messier than his desk at work. He was obviously working on something but as I scanned the surface pages, not a damn bit of it in English. I lifted books and pages items to reveal more underneath. There had to be something that told me where he went or what he's doing.

My fingers shoved electrifying pages aside as their soft vibrations beckoned me, trying to tempt me away from my mission. I imagined Jack had a lot of interesting items here beyond our current case. I couldn't tell what. There seemed to be nothing for me here. No words I could read. No diagrams I could decipher. But then my eye caught on one word I recognized — Phoebe.

Reason would tell me it could've been about anybody named Phoebe, but I launched into a frenzy. Abandoning my search for information about Jack, I snatched the stack of pages off his desk and shuffled through them. The handwriting was similar across these dated entries but they were in different languages. I stared at the words, willing them to tell me what they meant. I flipped through the languages I couldn't understand, scanning for words to derive their meaning. My name littered the pages. My mind was spinning. What was it that he asked me when he had me tied up in his garage, at the mercy of his interrogation?

How much time have you lost?

He never told me how he knew my name.

"Phoebe?"

I jumped, spinning to look at Tabitha. My mouth ran dry and I didn't know what to say. She had her pink backpack at her side and a stuffed animal hugged to her chest. A tiger. She had a stuffed tiger. I seized a breath and focused my attention on her.

Clearing my throat, I dropped the notes back on Jack's desk. "You ready to go?"

She nodded.

I hated to leave Jack's home office. I wanted to pour over these pages. I wanted to know why Jack was investigating me or someone who shared my name. Was this because of Delia's fight last night? If so, he must have been busy throughout the night because the sheer amount of material here was intimidating. But something in my gut, something that felt entirely Phoebe and not at all Delia, told me he had been looking into my background a lot longer than that.

How the fuck did he know my name?

I scoured the desk for a scrap piece of paper, finding a return envelope for some bill or something. Plucking a pencil from a mug on his desk, I scrawled a phone number onto it then handed it to Tabitha.

"This is my number. I'm going to hold onto your dad's phone for a little while. But you can call me if you hear from him, okay?"

"Okay," she said. She took off her book bag and slipped the envelope inside its front pocket. She patted it once, twice to make sure it was secure then looped the bag's straps around her arms. She tightened her grip onto the tiger.

Holding my hand out to Tabitha, she took it and we left the house for my car. Her energy surging up my arm was similar to her dad's, rather than the feeling I got from her mom's painting on the wall. The familiar feeling was there, but fading.

TWENTY-THREE

The Banner residence was the last place where I should be. But after I dropped off Tabitha, I drove straight to the Ivy Heights neighborhood. Loose revelations rattled in my head and I focused on the pavement in front of me. Couldn't dwell on what I found out today. Had to push forward. Had to find Tabitha's father. Had to find the asshole who was keeping more information from me than I realized. Only after he was safe and sound would I beat him for keeping me in the dark.

The neighborhood was pitch black. My headlights pushed against darkness. All the streetlights were out. All the houses were dark. Most of the cars were missing from the street or driveways. Suspicion prickled in the back of my mind as I parked the car on the side of the road, about two blocks away from the Banner house.

As soon as I opened the driver's door, the thick, pungent air seized me. The strange air seeped deep into my nostrils and mouth, wrapping tendrils around my exposed skin. My stomach lurched and I started hacking, fighting off the biological urge to spew what little fast food I could stomach for lunch. A few moments passed and the warm nausea settled in my chest. I slumped against the car until I could stand on two feet.

My eyes settled on an empty driveway. I blinked before scanning the front of the connecting house. The front door left ajar. Then I look at another house. The garage was left wide open. I turned, surveying the houses around me. The neighborhood wasn't missing electricity. Its homeowners had abandoned it in a hurry. The air — they must've been driven away by whatever was in the air. The thick energy tasted poisonous and settled in the bottom of my lungs.

The air must have driven the residents away. I imagined the energy should have dissuaded outsiders from approaching. I came too far to turn back now. If the neighbors evacuated themselves, then there was the silver lining. Hopefully, Jack had stuck around.

I reached back and extracted the handgun from my shoulder holster. The gun was a comforting, familiar weight that hung heavy at my side. My free hand flexed, trying to get any reading I could from something I couldn't touch, to absorb any feeling from the air. A sense of something frigid, something dreadful. My fingers curled and unfurled to extract more information but I couldn't pinpoint exactly what awaited me.

Quiet as I could, I shut the car door behind me and moved in the direction of the Banners. I stuck to the middle of the street. No one could sneak up on me that way and I had a better view of the neighborhood. Passing a few more houses before clearing the block convinced me that the neighborhood was empty. Here I was, going into a potentially dangerous situation to find a man I wasn't not even sure I liked very much right now and no one could come to my aid.

Charlie flashed in my mind. Nope. Not going there. I shoved the idea far away. This was my mission. He already showed me what side he fell on.

As I drew closer to the house, the pit of my stomach widened and swallowed the shaky confidence I brought to the street. The energy radiating from the Banner house made my heart twist and turn, made it feel inverted and squeezed. Darkness invaded my blood, poisoning me in a way that the air couldn't. Strange blue light flickered throughout the upstairs of the Banner house. Too much light to be a television in one room. The sole source of light in the neighborhood. My gut told me it was the source of the strange energy permeating Ivy Heights and turning my blood into dark sludge.

Jack's truck sat in their driveway.

I crept up the driveway until I stood beside the familiar vehicle. One eye and ear focused on any sign from the house while I quickly scanned the cab for any sign of him. His toolbox was on the bench and open, ransacked. With careful movements, I opened the driver door and slid into the seat. I leaned over the toolbox and took an inventory. Satchels, vials, some sticks of varying width and girth. Some trinkets that looked old. Nothing but a few knives and candles made any sense to me. I took what I could and what I knew how to use: a knife sheathed in some leather casing.

Extracting the blade, I saw deep markings carved into the metal. The markings looked similar to the runes on Tabitha's door. That had to be a good thing, right? Either way, it had a sharp blade and that was good enough for me. I sheathed the knife, tugged up the pant leg of my jeans, and secured it within my boot as best as I could.

Gun? Check. Knife that may be protective even if it wasn't deadly? Okay, sure.

I slipped out of the truck, lowering myself behind it then pushed the door shut as silent as possible. One breath. Two breaths. Under the cloak of the darkness, the blue light waxed and waned, throbbing against the curtains. My eyes had adjusted to the level of darkness and I saw a direct route upstairs. A staircase connected to the back deck that led up to the second level of the house. Nope. Not ready to go crashing right into the crazy yet.

Sticking close to the house, I tested windows and doors to see if anything was unlocked. Everything seemed secure. Okay. I settled for the downstairs door with a window, underneath the porch. Peering inside, it looked like a mudroom or some sort of space connected to the garage. Gritting my teeth, I smashed my elbow against the windowpane, once and then twice until the glass shattered.

I held my breath, waiting, listening to see if anything heard me. When nothing happened, I reached through the broken glass and unlocked the door from the inside. My sleeve caught on the glass as I pulled my arm backs out. Slowly, slowly. Once my arm was free, I turned the doorknob, pushing the door open a smudge. The room was dark. Flicking the light switches provided no light. A moment passed as I oriented myself and let my eyes adjust further.

Sticking to the shadows, I entered the living room with my gun ready. The dim light from outside filtered in through a large picture window. This was where Jack and I had talked to Logan Banner the day before.

Somewhere upstairs, stomping turned to crashing and grabbed my attention. The light flashed from the top of the stairs. Moving fast, I froze when I found Logan Banner in a crumpled heap at the bottom of the stairs, propped up against the wall.

In his hands, he cradled something dark. As I

moved closer, I realized it was blood. His shirt was soaked through and the wound gaped in his chest. I lowered my gun and knelt down next to him.

"I tried," Logan croaked, barely audible. I leaned in closer to hear him. His wound was bad. He lost too much blood already. He rasped, "I'm sorry… I tried, Detective… He got my son. He got both my sons. He killed my wife."

"Shhhhh," I soothed him as I surveyed the damage done to his body. Something ripped into him. Was that something lurking upstairs?

"I… I went along with it because I didn't want him to hurt anyone. It's too late. It's way too late," he babbled.

"Too late for what?" I prompted him. If he kept talking, I could figure out how to help him. I didn't know how to help him right now. I searched for my phone to call an ambulance, a fire station, anyone but Logan grabbed my hand. Images seared into my mind's eye — his wife leaving. Emily begging him to file a report. The hooded man. Kyle. Kyle's here? But not Kyle. Red eyes burned beneath the hood.

"I'm sorry. I'm sorry. Please… forgive me," he said, barely breaking through my vision. I jerked my hand out of his and as my mind cleared, Logan Banner came into focus. He no longer moved. His eyes. The life was gone.

Gently, unlike the way he received the wound in his gut, I closed his eyes. Remorse and the failure of being too late clung to me. I couldn't find his wife. I couldn't save his boys. I couldn't help his family. I got mad at him when I was suspended but now, too late, I realize it couldn't have been him.

I'm so fucking sorry.

Something watched me pay last respects to Logan Banner. Its eyes bored into my back as I stood. I stepped over his body and onto the stairs, balancing myself with the bannister. Launching myself up the stairs at a time, I peered over the top stair. Two figures grappled at the end of the hall. The light flashed again and I made out Jack's face. He struggled against the thing clawing at him. The second figure must be what tore into Logan Banner.

Lifting my gun, I aimed as best I could. The thing wouldn't stay the shit still. I crawled up the remaining steps. The floorboards under the carpet creaked and alerted the two to my presence.

My heart stopped as the unknown thing froze. Its floppy head twisted on its shoulders, looking in my direction. Its red, hollow eyes dilated and focused on me.

Holy shit. That face…

Travis Banner.

Kyle's older brother. The one who was killed years ago. The one who Charlie told us was dug up and missing from his grave.

Glowing red eyes fixed on me, twitching. Its chest heaved with furious breathing. Signs a wild animal would display before it attacked.

It tossed Jack aside and with limbs thrashing, it ran straight at me. Behind me were stairs, so I ducked to the left, my shoulder slamming bookshelves hard. The shelves buckled. Family portraits and books fell as the creature that was once Travis crashed against the wall. I rolled out of its path. Pure survival instinct kicked in. My finger squeezed the trigger and fired once, twice, three times at the creature. It wailed, screeching, so I shoot it again — last time in the head. It fell forward, landing in a hard thud against the carpet. For a second, I was glad Logan died before he could see this. But then I remembered — his own, dead son probably killed him.

I kept my gun trained on it as I waited for any movement, even a post-mortem twitch. Nothing. Out of my periphery, Jack picked himself up.

A loud clap of thunder and an underlying hum come from the room at the end of the hallway. Blue light flashed. The creature didn't get back up. I moved closer. Its limbs appeared broken and set at odd angles, its fingers fused into hoof-like appendages that extended to overgrown nails. Its clothes were tattered and its skin looked like cauterized, blackened lacerations. Its neck was stretched, elongated, twisted. Its claws were covered in blood and other viscera. Its jaw protruded, revealing shrapnel-like teeth.

But the face… was all Travis. The same friendly and charming face in the family photographs that now lay in shattered glass on the hallway floor.

"What was that?"

"Travis Banner," Jack said, approaching me.

I glared. "No shit. What happened to him?"

"He mutated. Personification of the ugliness of his crime. My incantations didn't stop him," Jack explained as he caught his breath. "You have impeccable timing, thank fuck."

I leveled my gun at his chest. Adrenaline still coursed through my body. Reason and logic were gone. My mind was on autopilot.

Jack eyed the gun and then me. He lifted his hand in a comforting gesture, motioning downward. "You can put the gun away, Phoebe. I think we're in the clear right now."

He took a step closer. I held my stance, my firearm on him. My nostrils flared and my throat tightened.

"Phoebe, what's going on?" he asked, drawing out his words.

"I should ask you the same thing," I said. Since last night, I found out so many interesting things. What else was *he* keeping from me? My finger curled around the trigger.

"Phee," he said, his words cautious. "I'm not the enemy."

"Got a shitload of evidence that suggests you're not my friend either," I said through gritted teeth.

"Whatever that means, we'll talk about it later. Put the gun down."

"No." I grew bolder. My grip tightened on the butt of the gun. "You aren't telling me the truth."

"Yes I am," he whispered through the darkness.

"Fine. You're not telling me enough." My voice grew louder. "You're not telling me everything."

Jack's brow furrowed and he inched even closer. "You're not going to shoot me."

"Take another step and see if that logic holds up."

He took a step. I squeezed the trigger. The bullet fired out of the barrel of the gun and lodged into Jack's arm. He stumbled back, in a blur of red and dark, but didn't lose his footing.

"You shot me," he growled, both shocked and angry.

"I shot you," I echoed, dazed and staring at the wound. Blood seeped into the sleeve around the wound, running down his arm. But I watched the wound as it puckered, twitched, sealed around the bullet. I blinked.

No.

You haven't scratched the surface as far as Jack is concerned...

Victoria's words slapped me in the face. Fire replaced the cloud of confusion. I shot him. I shot Jack. What was happening? Is that why he took so long to get up when I came upstairs and the Travis-looking monster charged me? Lifting my gun at him again, I brace myself to fire.

"I shot you!" I shouted again. My mind struggled

to keep up, to make sense of Jack.

"We've covered that already," he barked. Jack dug at the wound, trying to get to whatever was inside. The bullet, I realized. He was going after the bullet.

"You said you were good with languages!" I demanded, my voice cracking. "You said you were good with languages so why are you healing?"

"For fuck's sake!" He tugged at the object embedded in his arm. "Being good with languages does not supersede everything else. Goddammit, Phoebe!"

"You don't know all of this demon and angel shit because you've been working cases across Harrow, saving some poor souls from their misery. You know all of this because you're one of them!"

Jack inhaled sharp as he pulled out the bullet from his flesh. As soon as he extracted it, his wound finished knitting itself back, removing any trace of an entry wound. He tossed the bullet aside and it clattered against the baseboards. He met my gaze. His eyes didn't waver from mine. He didn't respond. He didn't need to.

"So tell me, Jack. Which realm is it for you? Earth, wind, fire?"

"The Aether," he replied. He closed the distance between us and took my gun from my shaking hand. His admission kicked the air out of my lungs and I barely react as he disarmed me. "No more shooting for you."

I asked the question, but I wasn't expecting him to

answer me. "Aether — so, you're an angel."

Angel. The word ricocheted around in my head and my joints weakened.

"Yes." His voice remained even.

My eyes narrowed at him. "Aren't you supposed to deny something like that!?"

Maybe it was the shadows, or maybe Jack actually smirked. "Just been waiting for you to start asking the right questions."

The revelation sunk in. Angel. Angels? That was better than the alternative, right? Angels were supposed to be good. My dad was a messenger. But if Jack was here on Earth, if he left the Aether —

"You said there were two types of angels. The kind in heaven and the kind here on a mission..." As soon as the words fell out of my mouth, realization sparked in some deep recess of my brain. A third kind of angel. Of course there was. I should've known. My tongue felt heavy in my mouth. "You fell."

Defiance sparked in his dark, glassy eyes. "We flew."

Screams erupted from the other room, dissolving into begging. Blue light spilled out from underneath the door.

"Kyle," I whispered and pushed past Jack, shoving him aside.

"Phoebe, wait," he said, trying to catch hold of me but he was too late.

I barged into the room and the door slammed shut

behind me, separating me from Jack. The brightest white-blue light washed over me. It rippled like liquid against the far wall, cradled by the dark coal border. I stared into the abyss. No, the opposite of abyss.

A live Nethergate. A doorway to Hell.

Some corner of my mind knew I shouldn't be here, but when I turned, I saw the door lock on its own. A moment later, something large slammed against the door. Jack's voice was muffled on the other side.

I wrangled with the doorknob, trying to unlock it but even as I fought to escape, my resolve melted away. It was okay. My fear and anxiety ebbed. I was in the presence of the gate. The violence buzzing in my veins felt clean. Beautiful. Pure.

My forehead dropped against the door and the poison washed over me. In its immediate presence, the gate's energy was no longer nauseating. It was intoxicating. Euphoric. The power rushed through me. My heart raced, a shot of adrenaline to the darkest corners of my heart. The cold seeped from the other side of the gate.

Jack continued to beat at the door. I let go of the doorknob.

"We've been waiting for you, Phoebe Harris."

A man stood behind me. Instantly, I knew he was the one who had watched and waited as I kept Logan Banner company in his final moments. He was the one I remember. That voice. Deep and familiar. Burdened for his years. He was the hooded man.

For an instant, we were the same. It resonated in my blood. We shared the same anger. I could understand him and his purpose in a way that I couldn't understand myself.

The Keeper of Keys.

The Maker of Nethergates.

The Royal Gatekeeper.

TWENTY-FOUR

The gatekeeper and I stood in the Banners study. At least, the room used to be a study before it was ransacked and repurposed for the gatekeeper's evening. Heavy, built-in bookshelves collected shadows among the leather volumes. The furniture, pushed out of the way, was replaced with a large, chalky circle carved into the hardwood floor. Kyle Banner, tied by the wrists and ankles, was placed in the middle of the circle. The Nethergate, the light in the room, couldn't keep the darkest shadows at bay.

The gatekeeper circled around me, studying me from the bottom of my feet to the top of my hair. Why did the gatekeeper seem familiar? A hood cast a shadow over the upper half of his face.

"Who's been waiting for me? You and Kyle?" I asked, trying to regain some sense in the presence of the open gate.

"No," the gatekeeper said. "Well, yes. But also someone more important than any and all of us combined."

"Do I get a name?"

"Do you need a name?" he volleyed.

The manner in which he carried himself, the inflection of his voice all teased me with an identity that was beyond my recollection. I feel like I've spoken with him before but I couldn't remember when. "I think it's only fair to know who I kept waiting all this time," I said, facing him after he stopped on the far side of the white circle, with Kyle between us.

"She's my queen," he said. "*Our* queen."

His declaration smacks me in between the eyes and the images reemerge, flooding the forefront of my mind. Of course. Of fucking course. The fractured woman with the rivers of red hair. Shattered. Broken. Humpty Dumpty. She haunted my dreams after I touched the inactive Nethergate over in Dundee. She wasn't alone when I saw her.

That's why I recognized the gatekeeper. He was keeping vigil. How could I forget my visions of them? I always trusted my visions. But this one escaped me after I regained consciousness. Now, in the presence of both her royal attendant and a gate to her world, did the broken queen come back to me.

"I've seen her," I admitted.

The lower half of his face relaxed into a warm

smile. "You found the message she left."

When I touched the left over coal from Dundee's inactive Nethergate, the vision ignited and nearly burned my brain. "Yes, in Dundee. Why would your queen leave me a message?"

"A broadcast. A cry for help." The gatekeeper's demeanor changed. He was no longer the proud, sullen guard who kept watch, but a giddy boy scout who found out he wasn't alone in his conspiracy. He clapped his hands together in joy, rubbing them together. "You found her message!"

"So she goes about leaving visual messages in case someone picks them up?"

"Considering she's been cursed for nearly a century, she leaves her traces where she can," the gatekeeper explained, composing himself. He smiled at the open Nethergate, then at me, before looking down at Kyle. He smoothed his robes against his chest, inhaling deep. "Even broken, you must agree she is the highest form of grace and beauty."

"She's all right," I said, fixated on the Nethergate pulsing behind him. The light, like liquid, churned.

Perhaps it wasn't the smartest thing to say to the royal help. The gatekeeper fell silent, following the white line on the floor toward me. If he lashed out at me, the gate's power would absolve him of his passion. I did dismiss his Queen's awesomeness.

Instead, he laughed. Something throaty and human. He understood me.

His empathy didn't sit well in my stomach.

"What're you doing to help your queen?" I asked, keeping my voice nonchalant and shifting the focus back on him.

"I'm collecting souls, deceased or condemned. Once I have enough of them, I can begin the arduous task of recreating her body."

Souls. His explanation sunk into my mind and heart. The gravity of the room shifted. Smaller objects grazed surfaces and papers floated in the air. As the Nethergate grew stronger, the gravity in the study released its hold little by little.

"So that's what you've been up to in Harrow," I said. "Collecting souls."

"Yes."

My mind raced, calculating the number of those that committed a crime in the presence of a Nethergate. Two Henderson boys, two Lance boys. Karen Banner was found dead and I suspected Kyle might have been with her then, landing into the hands of the gatekeeper. Was Karen trying to get Kyle far away from Harrow? If so, did she end up another soul for the gatekeeper's plate?

I couldn't think about Karen now. With Travis, his mother, and the younger Henderson and Lance boys, the gatekeeper maybe had four dead souls. Condemned? The older Henderson and Lance boys who admitted to the killings. That brought the count to at least six souls.

But then there was Kyle Banner, all tied up and nowhere to go. If he was here, he must be one soul that kept slipping through the gatekeeper's fingers.

"I admit, I didn't know what I was doing with Travis and Kyle Banner. It haunted me knowing I had unfinished business," the gatekeeper explained, as if he could read the math going through my head. He gestured at the boy bound on the floor. "All my hard work would be a waste and those souls would go un-harvested. Travis was stronger than I expected. He wouldn't listen to reason. I got angry and killed him before he had a chance to prove himself."

At the mention of his brother, Kyle struggled against his binding and cried from behind the gag in his mouth. I knelt down next to him. He shrank from my touch and I couldn't blame him. What he had been through the last few years, what he had been through this *week*, all leading up to tonight — I wish I could send thoughts or anything to him to calm him down, to let him know that I was on his side. But I had to play along to keep the gatekeeper talking.

As the gatekeeper paced around the white circle, I kept him in my line of sight. My hand went for my boot. Kyle glanced but I gestured to keep his eyes on my face. I couldn't have him give away my move-ments at this critical moment. I unsheathed the knife I stole from Jack's truck and concealed it in the sleeve of my jacket.

"Even in death, Travis couldn't fulfill his role in

my work. His primitive, mortal brain remembered his last stand — unwilling to comply with the opportunity I gave him," the gatekeeper was saying when I started listening again.

Travis, mutated. Broken in a heap in the hallway outside this door. Lost his mind and possibly missing his soul. My fingers brushed hair from Kyle's panicked eyes. A shock of panic sparked against my fingertips. "You brought Travis back to kill his brother?" I asked the gatekeeper, turning to look at him from over my shoulder.

"Unorthodox, I know. It was worth a shot." His mouth stretched into a thin, smug smile as he dragged his thumb along his chin.

I pushed myself to stand, leaving Kyle's side. "I shot him a few times."

"He would've been put down at the end of this," the gatekeeper said. "Now that you're here, you can help me extract Kyle's soul."

Strangeness laced the gatekeeper's gaze and tone, like he was trying to project words into my head. My eyes slid shut and I took a deep breath. Energy laced the air but didn't seep in. I parsed it, remembering who I was and what the gatekeeper had done.

"I can't do that. I can't help you."

The gatekeeper pursed his mouth. "What?"

"I get it. You want to finish a job. I can understand how frustrating that can be," I explained. "But I won't help you."

"We are the same, Phoebe Harris. You found the queen's message." The gatekeeper looked from the Nethergate, to me, then back to the gate. His confusion turned his expression sour. "Together we can restore her."

The gatekeeper and I were the same in a way I couldn't pinpoint. The anger we shared manifested itself different within my heart. "I don't give a shit about your queen. You've taken everything from this family. I owe them everything in my blood."

The energy in the room tilted and I staggered. All semblance of humanity drained from the gatekeeper. In a split second, he discarded any sense of hospitality and dove at me. He knocked me back off my feet and I hit the floor. Momentum carried me back. I reeled my leg back and kicked at his chest. Before he could grab onto my leg, I rolled out of his way and onto my feet. I dodged his next blow and jumped as far from the circle as I could, tripping over a side table. My one thought was to get him away from Kyle.

The gatekeeper clamored after me, one large swipe revealing strong arms and hands. I maneuvered the knife, waiting for his next move and wishing Jack didn't take my gun. We circled each other, sizing each other up. When the gatekeeper moved close enough and took another lunge, I jabbed the knife forward, stabbing him somewhere in his torso under all those robes.

The backside of his large hand smacked me across

the face. My head jerked right with a sickening crack and I stumbled back. Holy shit. The strength behind that blow surprised me and knocked my senses backwards. I swiped at the air, catching his robe but nothing more. I realized, too late, that I was possibly out of my league.

The knife fell away from him, clattering on the floor. The gatekeeper came at me again. This time when he struck me, I fell back, crashing onto my side and my head thudding against the hardwood floor.

The gatekeeper kicked my shoulder, rolling me onto my back. He loomed over me. He was a tower of darkness and robes, brute force and business. My head throbbed. I was conscious enough to know I wouldn't be quick enough if I wanted to walk away from this.

He planted his feet on either side of me and straddled my waist, pinning me against the hardwood floor with his weight. His large hands wrapped firmly around my neck. He squeezed. My fingers dug for any space between his hands and my throat. I clawed at the back of his hands, trying to get him to let go. He pressed harder, pinching my airway closed. I kicked and bucked, rooting the soles of my boot on the floor. My body thrashed and twisted, trying to get him off me. The harder I struggled, the harder he pressed the life out of me against the floor.

"Phoebe Harris, you should've been dead a long time ago—"

No.

No.

"Another one of my mother's messes I have to clean up—"

The light from the Nethergate bled into my sight. At least, it better be the Nethergate because I wasn't ready to see the light at the end of the tunnel. I was suffocating, black spots mixing with white energy. The gatekeeper's hood fell back but I refused for this to be the last face I would see. I groped at his arms, trying to find any weakness in his grip but I was losing.

Get up.

Somewhere in the distance, the boy whined and twisted in the white circle. Elsewhere, gunshots fired. Wood splintered. My fingers and my arms went limp as an ancient fire was stoked deep in my mind. The gatekeeper was hauled off me. I remained limp on the floor. The black spots morphed into something I saw weeks ago. The dark sideways eyes that stared back at me in the rearview mirror of my Jeep.

Delia.

Get up.

I coughed and wheezed, air rushing back into my lungs. On the other side of the room, two men fought with each other. One of them is the gatekeeper, all violence and too much fabric.

Your window is closing, Phoebe. You need to get up now.

Swallowing hurt. Blood pounded in my head and I couldn't get air fast enough to inflate my lungs. But if Delia was speaking to me, back in that familiar space in my skull, that had to be a good thing right? That meant I was still alive.

You won't die.

I know, I thought. *You'll never let me.*

The dark spots dissipated from my vision, but Delia remained. She wasn't a reflection or a disembodied voice. Separate and in her own physical form, she leaned over me. Her face mirrored my own except hers was orange. Purple. Now, yellow. Her skin changed too quickly for me to keep up. My eyes squeezed shut. Her translucent color made me wonder if she's warping my perception again. Whatever was under her skin was unstable.

I look up at her again. Her glassy black eyes observe me, worried. She frowned and fretted.

What is it, Delia?

She pointed at Kyle. No, the base of the gate. No, past the gate. The brightness of the gate masked a fireplace that was at the center of the doorway. Next to the fireplace was a set of tools.

My window of opportunity wouldn't be the one that closed here tonight.

Delia evaporated as I scrambled to my feet and lurched toward the wall. Snatching the fire iron from the fireplace's side, I swung it around with all the strength in my shoulders. The sharp hook lodged into the wall and the coal marking cracked. I yanked the fire iron out and struck the wall again. Again. Again! The light of the Nethergate splashed, rippling from the impact of the fire iron on its threshold.

With one last strike, the Nethergate thundered and knocked me back. Everyone in the room turned to me, including the gatekeeper. A flurry of robes, he shouted profanity in a language I didn't understand. He vaulted over Kyle and dove at me. Past him, I caught sight of Jack's face before the gatekeeper slammed me against the wall. The Nethergate's light lapped at my skin. I jammed the fire iron forward, stabbing the gatekeeper in the gut, hopefully near where I cut him earlier. His mouth fell open and I dug the fire iron deeper.

"Phoebe Harris…" the gatekeeper wheezed, blood dribbling down his chin. Twisting the iron, I yanked it out of his torso before kicking him off me.

The adrenaline that had fueled me seeped out of my body as quickly as his blood and I dropped to the floor.

The Nethergate swallowed the gatekeeper, then collapsed in on its center, closing the doorway between this ground and hell. The puddle of light snapped, boomed, and then left us in darkness. Objects and furniture crashed to the floor, no longer suspended by whatever gravitational effect the Nethergate caused.

I crawled a couple paces away from the wall. Before I could lift my head, Jack was already scolding me.

"You're a fucking idiot," he accused.

It wasn't the first time I heard such a thing, and thank god, it wouldn't be the last. Jack's face came into focus. He hoisted me to my feet before I regained my sense of balance or orientation.

"You sent him back to hell!"

"Seemed reasonable," I muttered. I twisted my arm in his grip, but his fingers were a vice.

"You sent him back home!" he shouted.

"Yeah, but I gave him a hell of a flesh wound," I defended myself. "Two actually… if I count right."

Jack seethed, fueled by his anger. Did angels breathe? Could angels get angry? Part of me wanted to test that while another part of me wanted to lay down for a very long time.

"Don't you start," I said. I shoved at his chest, still trying to wrench my arm out of his grip. "He couldn't take Kyle and the gate needed closing. Two birds, et cetera."

Jack didn't get to be the angry one. Jack wasn't the one being led on. We glared at each other, tempers flared and tension palpable between us. Accusations were ready to be fired but I didn't know where to start. Twenty-four hours ago he offered to help me but after I found what he could be keeping from me, he didn't get to be my hero. I didn't want a hero. What I needed was an ally.

A bolt of lightning struck throughout the study.

Angels.

Correction — one specific angel.

Blinking rapidly, the seared crack of light in my vision faded while Beatrix materialized from nothing but light particles. This arrival wasn't as bad as Oakview, but my gut still clenched. Jack finally dropped my arm and I rolled my shoulder, erasing any sensation of him holding onto me.

Beatrix studied Kyle before turning to the two of us.

"You're late," I said. Jack stiffened beside me, but I didn't care.

"I arrive precisely when I find it necessary, Phoebe," Beatrix said.

Necessary? I bristled. "From what I understand, Harrow's your territory so where the hell were you when the gatekeeper was targeting people and taking their souls!"

"A gatekeeper," the angel echoed.

"Gatekeeper for the queen," I added. "Whatever that means for y'all."

Beatrix regarded me and then turned back to the remnants of the Nethergate. She examined the markings, touched them, maybe even read them. She twisted her body back to us.

"Jack, you know what we need to do. Prepare the house," she ordered.

His shoulders tensed and he shook his head. "Not

an option, Bea. Harrow's my city—"

"Harrow is not *your* city," she rebuked, her strong, dark features twisting in disgust. "I will do what is required to protect it."

"Harrow has been my home for longer than it has been yours. You don't get to wipe a neighborhood off the map."

Jack's accusation hung in the air. Wipe what off the map?

Beatrix narrowed her eyes and moved closer to Jack. Despite her lofty, pretentious air, the angel was dwarfed by his height. However, she didn't cower. Her voice was low and calculated. "One Nethergate is an issue. Two Nethergates is a situation. More than that… if a royal gatekeeper has entered Harrow, we need to erase any trail he has left. Demons are one thing, but neither the Nether Queen nor her gatekeeper will encroach on my ground."

"What the fuck are they? Ants?" I mocked under my breath. Both Beatrix and Jack stared at me. "Is clearing their trail really going to keep them from coming back? How about that gatekeeper was killing people! How about he tortured this family and destroyed them one by one for years! And that's not even including the other families he's targeted in Harrow. And you want to erase Ivy Heights off the grid like that will keep it from happening again? Would that even work? How about you get your priorities straight and protect the residents first?"

"Silence," Beatrix commanded me.

A strange resonance in her words took hold of my vocal chords. My voice froze and my mouth snapped shut. My throat, still sore from the gatekeeper's assault, no longer had the ability to produce sound. Startled, I touched my neck. Then I pled with Jack as hard as I could with my silent mouth and buggy eyes.

He shook his head, looking back to Beatrix. "That was unnecessary," he said.

"We don't have much time to listen to such prattling. The Nethergate has already pushed away the residents of Ivy Heights. We must strike now. This house will be ground zero. You know where the gas lines are." Passion and resolve fueled Beatrix's stance. A familiar gold flared in her eyes — the same gold that could spark in Jack's eyes.

Words pooled in my mouth, waiting to shoot out like bullets at her.

While the two angels talked about the pros and cons of obliterating the neighborhood, I scouted the room. Dropping down, I collected the knife I lost earlier in the skirmish. I crouched next to Kyle and removed the gag from his mouth, but he was too busy watching Beatrix to make a sound. Tears ran down his face, which could either be a reaction to the sight of an angel, the torture he endured, or the conversation they were having about leveling Ivy Heights. Maybe all three. I sliced through the rope at his wrists and ankles. A sideways glance at Jack assured me that he didn't see me sheathing the knife underneath my pant leg. I stood up and tuned back into their conversation.

"Say I go along with this and destroy the neighborhood," Jack hypothesized. "What about any life? You need to be positive beyond any doubt, Beatrix, that we are alone."

Her shoulders relaxed and she softened her voice. "No other life forms are in Ivy Heights, Jack. I would feel even the mice if there were any life left. We, in this house, are all who stand. A gas leak can be enough to explain why the residents evacuated their homes before an explosion."

Angels about to stage a gas explosion — I couldn't believe my ears. I wasn't sure how extensive the final damage would be in the neighborhood or if angels had some control over any of that. But the bodies of Logan Banner and his transmutated son Travis would be lost in the explosion. I braced for one of them to mention this fact in Kyle's presence but neither of them said a word.

Jack grew quiet, of his own accord, as he considered Beatrix's position. His jaw flinched and shadows casted over the gold in his irises. He reached a conclusion.

"Very well," he agreed. He turned his attention to Kyle and me. "You need to get him away from Ivy Heights. Take him as far as Oakview. I'll meet you there once our work is done."

Pointing at my mouth and jaw, I stared at Beatrix.

She sighed and waved a hand, dismissing her hold over me. "You may speak freely," she said.

Sound rushed in and I took a deep breath, feeling the oxygen sweep through my vocal chords. Having my voice removed was not something I wanted to feel again.

"You can't go along with this, Jack," I rasped, my voice still strange in my throat. "What about people's homes? What about finding justice for the Banners — for the Hendersons? For the Lances?" Destroying evidence that the Harrow-Creek police wouldn't be able to explain in human terms made sense but this was too much to lose.

Too much, too late.

The expression on Jack's face was hard and final. "I'll meet you at Oakview once our work is done."

A cold hand sought mine and curled around my fingers. Kyle Banner. Right. Well, if I couldn't reason with angels, I could get Kyle out of here.

"Close your eyes," I said, keeping my voice low.

Kyle searched my face for an explanation but I didn't give him one. He then put his trust in me anyway, his eyes sliding shut. My arm wrapped around his shoulders and I led him from the study. When we passed through the hallway, my other hand covered his eyes, reinforcing his blindness. We walked around the discarded, disjointed corpse of Kyle's older brother. Next, we tackled the stairs, moving past Kyle's eviscerated father. When we cleared the stairs, I pulled him through the living room and out the front door.

The temperature difference between the house and the outside was staggering — ice cold inside while the heat and humidity waited to ambush us outside. Kyle stopped before we reached the street. He twisted in my arms, staring up at the big house that he never lived in, the house where his parents moved after his brother's death.

My breath halted in my chest and I waited for him to burst out and react. The moonlight casted an eerie glow around his head, catching in his red locks.

"Where's my dad? My dad was inside. Where is he?" Kyle asked, a small tremble in his voice.

Wrong question to ask. Grabbing onto his wrist, I kept us moving. If Jack was getting to work destroying evidence, I didn't want us anywhere near that house before Beatrix's plan was complete.

"Where's my dad?" Kyle insisted. He dug his heels into the concrete as best as he could but I jerked his wrist harder, dragging him. He cried all the way down the street to my piece of shit rental car.

Swallowing to speak around the lump forming in my throat, I delivered the bad news once we were in the car.

"I couldn't save him."

TWENTY-FIVE

Ivy Heights disappeared from my rear view mirror. The road stretched longer than I remembered as we sped toward Oakview Memorial. Silence throbbed throughout the car cabin, palpable between Kyle and me. The young man shrank in his seat, trembling and fidgeting. The dim lights of the car and the passing street lights reflected off the fresh trails of tears down his cheeks.

I didn't blame him in any regard. I know what it was like to have your world ripped open — except most of my family, adoptive or otherwise, survived and I still had the chance to find answers. I didn't know anyone else Kyle had except his cousin. Who knew what closure waited for him, after being hunted and forced to witness the destruction of his family?

His cousin, Emily Banner, stood in the parking lot,

her face illuminated by the screen of her smart phone. I had called her after finding her phone number from Jack's call log. My shoulders slumped in relief and I was thankful she got here before we did. I didn't know what else I could do for Kyle. He needed whatever little family he had left more than anything I could provide.

Emily rushed over to the passenger side of my car before I had even parked. She opened Kyle's door and the sound that escaped Kyle echoed throughout the parking lot. He sobbed in an ugly, drowning way, pulled down by the weight of his sadness. Such sadness always left me at a loss of what to do. I was never good at consoling victims or their families — that was Charlie's strong suit. Now here I was, squirming in my seat and fumbling for the seat belt's release. The belt retracted over my shoulder and I slipped out of the car to give them their privacy.

A moment longer and I would have been crying with them.

The night air wasn't crisp enough for my lungs to feel right. I measured my inhalations, trying to regain my composure as I paced in the parking lot. Victoria's car was parked near the rear exit but there was no sign of her.

Emily finally extracted Kyle from the car, one of her arms wrapped around his shoulders. He shared some of his weight with her, leaning against her as she led him over to her Jetta a few parking spaces away. She rubbed his arm before she got him situated in the passenger seat. The delicacy she used, the patience she exhibited, sparked a little light in my heart. I hope her care could be what Kyle needed to heal.

After she closed her passenger side door, she exhaled. She turned to face me. "Thank you so much, detective. I can't even — I just — thank you," she said.

"You're welcome," I said, caution keeping me from being gracious. "You should know — we found Travis's body. And Logan's."

Emily tensed, collapsing against the side of her car. "My uncle? But Logan said that —"

"Whatever he was doing or whoever he thought he was protecting, it didn't work out."

"And then Travis… what the fuck." The words shot out of her. "What the actual fuck! It wasn't enough to take Travis, or my aunt? They gotta dig up Travis's body and kill my uncle? And mess up Kyle? Why! Why would someone do this?"

The questions were rhetorical. My answer was not. "I'm not sure yet. And I don't know if I'm the best person to get you those answers," I admitted. "You'll have to call Jack for more information. I'm sorry."

Emily puffed up, unsure what to do with her hands. A moment passed before she knew what to say. "What do we do now?"

Another question I wasn't sure if I was qualified to answer. I glanced to the Jetta. Even if Kyle returned to state custody, the gatekeeper was able to get to him before. He wouldn't be safe going back. Kyle Banner was never a killer. He was a victim several times over. The gatekeeper had pursued him to this end. I didn't want to think of what would happen if the gatekeeper could find them outside of Harrow.

I squinted at the street lamp at the far end of the parking lot and then back to the cousins. "Drive. Get away from Harrow as quick as you can. It's not safe for him here. I'm not even sure where will be safe, but it isn't here," I told her.

The cogs in her head spun. My suggestion, she could work with. My suggestion gave her action. Next steps. Objectives. I understood it — sometimes you want a task to not think about the horror.

"He's seen a lot. Be patient with him, okay?" I added, even though I probably didn't need to. Saying it made me feel more in control than I was. Saying it made me feel less horrible that I couldn't give her answers. "You can call Jack tomorrow or whenever for more information."

She stood there, trying to regain her composure. A few deep breaths later, she lifted her eyes to meet mine. "Thanks, detective," Emily said again, but this time I think she's saying it to comfort me. "Thank you for finding him."

Finding Kyle Banner was about the only good thing that came out of today, much less this mess. I nodded then moved away from her car.

"Hey," I called out to Emily before she climbed into her car. She stopped, her hand frozen on the frame of the driver's side door. "I'm sorry about your family. Tell Kyle that, too."

She tried to smile, but it faltered and tears glistened in her eyes. She nodded, and then ducked into her car. The engine reared to life. Her headlights flood me. I stepped out of the way and she peeled out of the parking lot, pausing to check for any oncoming traffic before the Jetta set out into the night.

Behind me, the sound of one person slow clapping drifted from the back door of Oakview Memorial. Even before I hear her chuckle, I knew who it was. Pivoting on my heel, I found the demon Victoria watching me.

She was dressed completely different than I last saw her — draped in thick, dark canvas coveralls and her black hair pushed out of her face with a bright polka-dot scarf. Heavy boots replaced the delicate, high heels.

"Quite the show," she announced from across the parking lot.

I crossed the parking lot with careful steps, scanning the horizon before I focused fully on the undertaker. "Thought you had plans," I said as I reached her perch, the step under the awning.

"The equivalent of watering daisies," she explained with a flourish of her hand. She glanced in the direction of the parking lot entrance and then back at me. "So I take it that you had an exciting evening?"

"Unfortunately," I admitted. I inhaled deep, collecting questions for her at the bottom of my lungs. Did she know anything about the Nethergates that Jack didn't tell me? Did she know anything about gatekeepers? Would Kyle and his cousin Emily be safe away from Harrow?

But I deflated, letting the questions escape me in a whoosh in the night air. I didn't know if I could handle any more revelations today. I had a lot of information to consider — Jack's extensive investigation of me, his role as an angel who flew, my sudden lack of paycheck, and of course, the return of Delia. There was also the gatekeeper's crimes and the fate of the Banners. But those thoughts could be shelved for the rest of the evening.

Instead, I held out my hand. Victoria's brow furrowed and she held out her hand in return. I passed her a silver flip phone. Her eyes widened as her fingers curled around the phone, turning it around in her hand and rubbing a thumb across its screen.

"This is Jack's," she said.

I nodded. "Make sure he gets that."

She unzipped part of her coveralls and slipped the phone inside her suit. She left it unzipped. "Not waiting around for your knight in shining armor?"

"Nah," I said, shaking my head. "He's busy leveling a neighborhood."

To Victoria's credit, she said nothing else. A ghost

of a smile tugged at her red lips.

I retreated, back down the stairs. Time to head home to sleep away this god awful day.

TWENTY-SIX

"A natural gas leak fueled an explosion that rocked Harrow and its Ivy Heights residents earlier this week. At approximately 9:45 PM on Tuesday night, a faulty transmission line underneath the neighborhood—"

I tugged at my shoelaces, rearranging them to accommodate my feet for a run. Nina Marquez rattled off the news while WHRW was on in the background. I got ready to leave the apartment for the first time in two days.

As sick as I was of the anchor, the news coverage, and the general press, I was also fascinated by how the story was recreated in the eyes of people who were none-the-wiser.

"Leaving a crater of nearly seventy-five feet where the heart of the Ivy Heights neighborhood once stood.

Neighbors have been advised to not return to the neighborhood until the debris cleared and gas lines have been checked."

The newscast cut to footage of the crater from above the neighborhood, taken from their helicopter. When I first saw the footage, bile had churned in my gut. With clammy palms and jittery knees, I had waited for the devastation. But no reports came in about the bodies found at the scene. Since then, I marveled at the radius of the blast. Jack — because I sure wouldn't give Beatrix credit for it — somehow managed to target a few central houses. The Banners house was ground zero. He didn't destroy the entire neighborhood. The news story should be stale and old in a few months once the houses were rebuilt. An unfortunate accident.

"The natural gas is believed to have caused residents to evacuate the area prior to the explosion. One resident reported—"

My thumb jammed a button on the remote control, shutting down the television. Deafening silence filled my apartment. The last couple days, I couldn't take the silence. I had left the television running all day and night, desperate for anything else to fill my brain that wasn't Delia, Jack, or the crazy that has been bestowed upon me.

This morning, I made myself get out of bed and back on my feet. Dishes were strewn about my living room but I wouldn't clean them up until later. Instead,

I stood by my front door, stretching for my first run since the accident a few weeks ago. I used to run regularly, every morning before I went into the office. Stress always ejected my body as my feet pummeled the concrete. I needed to get back on the wagon and regain some sense of routine. I had a lot of stress to burn.

Except I wasn't going running in Harrow. Not today, anyway.

Grabbing my car keys, I darted out the door. I locked up and raced down the steps to the ground level, crossing over to that damn rental car. Then I drove, heading westbound toward Dundee. My fingers clenched the steering wheel and I reminded myself over and over that it was okay. Relax. I was in control.

The car slowed down as I approached the site of Magnolia Plains Apartments. I scoped out the block. Construction equipment and supplies rested on the perimeter, likely waiting for the permits to clear before the company can begin demolition of the abandoned apartment complex. Turning down a random side street, I parked out of sight of the apartments.

I knew I should be happy that the damn place was coming down sooner rather than later, but the knowledge that an idle or closed Nethergate was inside didn't sit well with me. I climbed out of the car and stretched out my calves, bracing the car for support. I ran along the perimeter, checking for anyone or anything.

After a few laps and dipping into some side streets, I was confident no one was watching. I slowed my pace as I approached the gate where Jack and I entered the other day. The chain was still tossed aside, coiled on the ground where Jack had dropped it. I ducked through the chain fence and scoped the surroundings for any movement. No surveyor or construction guy would surprise me if I could help it.

Keeping a low profile, I made my way over to the building I had my sights on. The former home of Aaron Henderson, the second victim of the gatekeeper and the first time the gatekeeper got his plan right. Was Aaron happy here with his girlfriend Sandy, even if his parents didn't approve of their relationship? Was the gatekeeper the hooded guy who visited him regularly like Sandy told us?

I climbed the stairs up to Aaron's apartment two at a time. By the time I reached the right floor, my heart thudded inside my chest. No more skipping my morning run, that was for damn sure.

When I arrived at the apartment, I found the door ajar. Did Jack leave it that way? To be sure before I entered the apartment, I flattened my palm against the door. A few seconds passed, like the door wanted to keep the memory from me, but then it relented.

An image came into focus. A standoff. Beatrix blocked my view with her curls, but then she circled around the other person. As she moved, she revealed Jack, holding me in his arms. It must have been after I connected to the Nethergate.

"One more thing," Beatrix said to Jack. But in the memory, her voice sounded muffled, like it was coming through a filter. "Fire clings to her soul. It lies dormant but soon it will burn through her. Stay vigilant."

Then she was gone. Even in a vision, Beatrix's lightning rattled me. The light cleared and Jack was still holding me, cradling me close. My grudge against Jack softened as I watched him hold me. It made sense that he had to carry me — how else would he have gotten me out to his truck and back to his place? — but it was different actually seeing it. The vision cleared as Jack approached the door, dissipating before he reached where I stood.

I readjusted my hand, seeing if there was anything else. Nothing more recent from the door came to the surface. When I felt confident the apartment hadn't been visited since Jack and I visited, I stepped inside and closed the door behind me.

I unzipped my top, revealing a green sports bra. Below that, a holstered knife was strapped around my waist — the same knife I took from Jack's toolbox. Extracting it, I entered the apartment with much more caution. I didn't walk out of here last time. Jack had to carry me. But I couldn't assume the demolition crew would properly destroy the Nethergate.

The knife's handle turned in my hand as I approached the bedroom — Aaron's bedroom — where the Nethergate left its mark and reopened an old wound in my chest. I toed the door open, not wanting to touch anything other than what was on my person. I didn't need any more visions or flashes from what happened the other night. I didn't need to black out again. I needed to be able to walk away.

Standing in the middle of the room, I stared down the Nethergate where the queen left her message. I didn't know if it was meant for me or for anyone who could read it. Were there other people with my kind of abilities? Tabitha had a gift but it wasn't the same. But maybe… maybe there were other people who could read like me. Maybe the queen was casting a wide net.

The thought was a small comfort — I wouldn't be alone and the queen and her gatekeeper wouldn't single me out. Either way, I was here now. The knife in my hand vibrated. Did it do this a couple nights ago when I stalked into the Banner house? I couldn't remember. I had been preoccupied with other things at the time.

Approaching the inactive Nethergate, I raised my arm and lodged the knife into one of the markings of the gate. Blue light flashed and faded. I struck again and another pulse of blue light. Again, again, and again. I pulled the knife out of the wall and stabbed right back into the coal, into all the separate characters I can make out. If I could break the markings as much as possible, then I could feel some sense of security.

My arms drooped and the knife hung at my side after I wrecked as much of the Nethergate as I could. A sweaty sheen covered my skin and I wiped wisps of hair out of my face with the sleeve of my pullover. With a surge of emotions, a sob rose in my chest again but I swallowed it back down. No time for tears. Inhale, two, three, four. Exhale, two, three, four. Repeat.

After a moment, I lifted my head and sheathed the knife against my waist. I zipped up my top. I stared at the broken Nethergate, the cracks where the knife marred the wall. The broken queen. The broken gate. The maimed gatekeeper. It would have to do.

As soon as I was done in the apartment, I left Magnolia Plains. But I couldn't go back to my car yet. Too many emotions were coursing through my system. My feet picked up and I ran around the neighborhood for almost half an hour, trying to chase away the anxiety and thoughts that plagued me.

Returning to my car after my blood and breath felt clean, I pulled out my phone from the middle console. A voicemail from Jack waited for me. My pulse drummed in my ears as his message plays.

Hey, you might want to know – your check is ready.

Huh. Really?

That was all he has to say to me? The urge to climb out of the car and run some more laps was strong but I forced myself to stay in the driver's seat. The day after Ivy Heights, I waited — maybe even hoped — for Jack to call me and explain to me what happened. Maybe he could even sooth my suspicions about whatever secrets he was keeping from me. I could then go along with it until I regained my senses. But he hadn't called me. And if he wasn't going to call me, I wasn't calling him. My pride kept me from seeking him out, but it didn't keep me from wishing he would make the first move.

I played the voicemail a couple more times. It was so sterile and transactional. Well, he made the first contact like I wanted, but now I didn't know if I wanted to see him. I couldn't decipher anything from his tone so I dropped my phone back in the console of the rental car.

We all have to do things we don't want to do.

"Yeah, but I don't want to be part of this anymore."

But as I replied out loud to Delia, another thought occurred to me — I wouldn't get much of a paycheck anymore. Suspension without pay, pending investigation. I needed the money. I hadn't had the courage to review my financials yet, but I knew I had a couple months of expenses covered, tops. Any money I could squirrel away, including a check from Jack, would help while I figured out what to do with myself.

Take it. He owes you this. He owes you so much more.

With Delia on my side, I started the car and drove back to Harrow.

* * *

"Emily called the office. She told me they're currently in Birmingham and headed west," Jack said as he handed me an envelope after I arrived at his office. I took it, flipping it over to see my name in his handwriting. He hooked his thumbs into his jean pockets. "She said you told her to get out of town."

"I did," I said. "They have no more business here in Harrow. And if the gatekeeper isn't done, I figured being further away would help."

"I hope you're right," he said. He gestured to the envelope. "Open it."

Tearing the envelope open with my thumb, I wondered why he even bothered to seal it. Maybe he didn't expect me to come down to his office. It would serve him right. I extracted the check. When my eyes landed on the digits, I choked.

Those numbers can't be right. Too many zeroes.

Ten thousand dollars.

Ten thousand fucking dollars.

"Holy shit," I muttered, clapping my hand over my mouth.

Well, that's a start.

"It's your share of the investigation fee. Don't go spending it all in one place," he said to me, moving to the break room with his coffee mug.

I didn't know how good of a liar Jack might be. While he may be gifted at keeping secrets, I knew one thing for certain by the slight inflection of his voice — Emily Banner didn't pay a cent for his services. Left alone with that amount of money, my mind and Delia raced. The urge to not accept it wormed its way into my heart. I didn't want to be part of this, I reminded myself. But... that's five figures. But then I'd be profiting off the Banner tragedy. But ... I had helped return Kyle to his cousin. Was that worth that amount of money? Wasn't it worth so much more? I don't know if I feel right taking it.

He has more to give you than ten thousand dollars.

Squeezing my eyes shut, I stopped listening to Delia. I had to focus and as much as I appreciated her support, her bias against Jack wasn't helping me think clearly. I lowered my hand from my mouth when I trusted myself to speak again. The next words illustrated to me how thin the ice was and how I was practically tying up the laces to my skates. "Does the job always pay this well?" I asked.

Jack, returning from the break room, leaned against the doorway. He sipped on his coffee. "Sometimes, yeah. Why? You interested in making it a regular thing?"

Droning blurred at the edge of my consciousness and I recognized it as Delia. She was trying to push me past my boundaries, or hold me back. I couldn't be sure. "I don't know. Is that an official job offer?"

For the first time since I set foot in his office today, Jack grinned. I remembered how his smile almost killed me in that drunken haze the first night he sought me out.

"It'll be dangerous. Both Heaven and Hell are going to beat down your door if you invite this kind of trouble," he said, but in that way that promised adventure.

"I've already gotten into trouble enough as it is," I grumbled. "And if it pays the bills, I need it more than ever."

He narrowed his eyes at me. "What happened to your job?"

"Suspended, so I got a lot of free time on my hands for all that trouble you mentioned," I said, hoping it came off breezy in a way that I didn't feel.

I was at war with Delia, living expenses, and myself. I didn't know where I fell but I knew in what direction I was leaning. Reconciling that with the suspicions I held against Jack would take time for me to process. Jack was investigating me for whatever reason. Delia didn't trust him. A messenger angel was sent to my family in the form of my adoptive father. My adoptive mother recognized Jack's number on the phone.

Earlier this week, I had told Jack I moved to Harrow as a detective to find the answers. And in the time that I have worked with him, I not only lost my job but also stumbled upon more answers than I ever did when I was a detective. I could deny the chance to keep working with him and confront him about the information I found in his possession… but how much more could I discover if I kept my mouth shut and waited for him to betray himself? I needed to keep him within my sights.

"Before I agree to anything, I have one question," I said.

Amusement flickered across his face. He raised an eyebrow. "After everything, you only have one question?"

"You healed the other night," I started. "And I don't know, it put a lot of thoughts in my head. So you're this angel that's not exactly a messenger or regular or whatever…" I rattled off the different classifications he had explained earlier, generalizing a bit.

He squared his shoulders, as if preparing for it. "What's your one question, Phoebe?"

"You're this angel and you heal." I searched his face, preparing for my strike. "So what's with the scar?"

The flecks in his hazel eyes — the remaining embers of whatever gold flashed in Beatrix's — went black. My question wasn't the one he was expecting. His brow furrowed and he reflexively touched the scar underneath his right eyebrow. Any humor or lightness was gone from his face and his body tensed. I hit a nerve. I hit a big nerve.

The scar was one of those things I noticed the night he approached me in Lethe as I drank away my sorrows. Its existence didn't strike me until I was standing in his office right the moment, knowing now that he could heal.

What compelled me to ask that question, I didn't know — did I want Jack to know that I noticed the unnoticeable? Was it a warning to him that I was watching him?

You see things others don't. You find things people can't.

Jack's hand dropped to his side. He set his coffee mug down. "Phoebe..." his voice trailed off, leaving my name hanging in the air between us. Hurt weighed down his voice. No one has said my name like that. Part of me was tempted to pluck it from his mouth and replace the hurt with something not so heavy. Another part of me wished I could walk away. However, the answers I could find by working with him were worth everything. I didn't want to ruin this chance up by letting a little attraction get in the way of me using him to find more information. Though, maybe I could use it to my advantage later...

He has much to repay you.

Making sure I had the check in my back pocket, I backed away and left him standing in the doorway of the break room. He didn't stop me.

On my way out, I paused in the doorway. "Call me if anything comes up," I said.

He pursed his lips in confusion. Before he could say anything to make my stomach do somersaults and make me regret saying anything, I explained.

"Oh, yeah. I skipped the part of the conversation where I agreed to the job. I'll see you Monday."

HARROW

Seven Souls
Six Wives
Category Five
[and more to come!]

Thank you for reading *Seven Souls*, the first in the Harrow series. I hope you enjoyed reading!

Want to help other readers find this book? Please consider leaving a review! I adore reviews – whether positive, negative, or somewhere in between.

Acknowledgements

First, to Annabel, Tiffany, Tasha, Pam, Melisa, Melissa, Leslie, Elaine, and Janine: Y'all have supported me in more ways than the creation of this first book. Without your camaraderie, general shenanigans, and support, Harrow may have never seen the light of day.

A flurry of thanks to the following: Louis, Lesley, and Elena, who explore concepts, characters, and stories with me as if no time has passed between us; Nat, who adds sparkle to our writing adventures; and Sean, who claims he's my worst critic, but really, he's the best.

And lastly, to my mother who is a perfect example that it's okay to stay up reading past your bedtime.

About Kate

Kate Newburg attended Agnes Scott College in Decatur, GA, where she got her degree in Religious Studies and Classical Civilization. She currently lives in Atlanta, GA.

You can find her online:

Website: www.katenewburg.com
Facebook: facebook.com/katenewburg
Twitter: @katenewburg